DAUGHTER
of the
KING

KERRY CHAPUT

Black Rose Writing | Texas

ISBN: 978-1-68433-837-5
PUBLISHED BY BLACK ROSE WRITING
www.blackrosewriting.com

Printed in the United States of America
Suggested Retail Price (SRP) $18.95

Daughter of the King is printed in Abhaya Libre

*As a planet-friendly publisher, Black Rose Writing does its best to eliminate
unnecessary waste to reduce paper usage and energy costs, while never
compromising the reading experience. As a result, the final word count vs. page count
may not meet common expectations.

Cover design Asya Blue http://asyablue.com/

DAUGHTER

of the

KING

THE HEART OF A HUGUENOT

My fingernails claw at the grainy brick to loosen it from the others, shifting and grinding against mortar until free. The dark hole in the fireplace beneath the wooden mantel hides in the shadows, protecting our fragile truth. My hands no longer tremble with the secret I carry through La Rochelle. The town's eyes always searching for the next heretic to torture. It is this pure act of defiance that keeps me breathing day in and day out. Without it, I might as well die a slow death in hiding, like my mother.

Our Geneva Bible, worn with time, glows in the firelight once again. Its soft edges against my fingertips sharpen my resolve, cutting through the doubt and fear that rests just below the surface. Only Huguenot women know what our woolen skirts hide, a pocket the size of our Bible sewn into the lining of our underskirt. My hands secure it in place, but my mind focuses on the safest path through town.

"You'll end up like the rest of them," Maman says. "What will your torture be? Hands wrapped in oil-soaked bandages and set on fire? Boiling water poured down your throat?"

"Maman, stop."

"You think you'll be the only one to survive. The only one smart and brave enough to escape the Catholics."

"No, but I seem to be the only one who wants to try." I carry on, securing my linen cap. In the firelight, my chestnut curls flicker red just as they do in daylight. I tuck them under my coiffe like jewels hidden in the sand.

"They wrapped Etienne in a blanket and bounced him against the stones until the old man's arms shattered like glass. Did you know that?"

"I live every day with fear and fight in equal measure. You need not remind me."

"If you stay with me—"

"If I stay in this house I will die anyway. I'm nineteen. I belong out there. Where the light shines and people live."

She grabs my arm with her bony fingers. "Isabelle, they see you as an enemy."

"They could torture me. Send me to the galleys with my neck chained to an oar until I die. I know that. But I long to breathe free, out of the shadows."

"It isn't possible." Her fingers slip from my arm.

Her pleading eyes still hold the power to chain me to this house, to her. Shaped like almonds the color of sunlit forest moss, her eyes are just like mine. While hers see a world where suffering is our destiny, mine see possibility.

I turn from her and fill her goblet with wine. "If I don't help them, the baby will die. I can't bear it."

She lowers to the rocking chair, goblet in hand, staring at the fire as if it has answers. The chair creaks against the wood with the tap of her toes. "Go on, then. Leave me alone to pray."

My hand finds its way to my left wrist. The skin is hot, the raised webbed flesh throbbing and aching. She sees me scratch at my scar. I yank my hand away, straightening my sleeve. "Grand-mère would want me to fight."

She sips her wine and waves the words away with her hand. She refuses to discuss Grand-mère, my father, my sisters. Every tragedy strengthens her fear of the outside world.

"This is the last of our wine," she says.

The metal ring on the door creaks as I lift it. "I'll fetch more."

"Isabelle, God chose us. I dream that one day you'll stop resisting. That you'll know peace."

"I won't find that in this house with you." I tap my finger to my heart. "I will find that in here."

She retreats into prayer while I step into the light of day.

.   .   .

Like a cat pouncing between shadows, my worn boots hit the ground with precision, my path set in my mind. The men holler and the boats creak and moan. The scent of oil and wood and rope bring me back to my childhood, when we owned ships and my father was powerful. The ocean wind snaps against my cheeks and whirs in my ears.

Faces crowd the tiny windows of Saint Nicholas Tower. Prisoners beg for air. Their cries paralyze me. My legs shake, my eyes grow blurry. Every day I hear their screams. They have become the background to La Rochelle, a thundering rumble of Protestant suffering. Like a heartbeat.

A rush of blood thumping in my ears drowns all other sounds, my feet moving to the rhythm. The raucous sounds of the port quiet. The ground changes from hard stone to wet earth. Through the medieval wall, under the arch of the belfry. I slide in behind a carriage for protection.

Catholics greet each other with laughter. They walk in the bright light of the early autumn sun, their sleek clothes billowing in waves around them. My shoes splash through animal waste and bloody water sprinkled with chicken feathers.

The narrow streets filter the light. Lifting my chin to feel the warmth on my face, life takes shape around me. Lavish stone house, arched arcades. Limestone buildings that shine a golden yellow in the morning sun. Decorative gargoyles divert water from the rooftops. Marble staircases. Women draped in embroidered robes. Their hair in bouncing curls, their cheeks rosy.

Distracted, something throws me to the stones. My chest tightens, like claws around my ribs. I scurry to the dark recess of the arcade and draw my knees to my chest. Sharp tingles run up my neck. Pounding again in my ears. The clicking of heels claps toward me, yet I keep my gaze on the stones. Blinking to focus, a hand-stitched pointed shoe takes shape in front of me.

Antoinette LaMarche, daughter of the most powerful shipowner in La Rochelle, brushes her arm where it had touched me. She fiddles with the layers of gilded taffeta, puffing her sleeves.

"Careful, Antoinette, you don't want to get her filth all over your gorgeous robe," her friend says.

Antoinette lowers her eyes. "Look at this sad barn animal. With matted brown hair the color of dirt. It belongs in the mud with the rest of the swine." When she turns her nose to the air, her golden locks catch the light. She flings her robe with the flick of her wrist. The sunlight dances on the brocade of violet flowers.

I lower my head. "Pardon me, Mademoiselle."

"You should be more careful, Mademoiselle Colette," Antoinette says.

"You know this peasant?" the other woman says.

"I used to," she says.

She once set my hair on fire. I was able to jump off the dock into the ocean, smothering the smoking hair before it reached my scalp. Another time, she threw me in pig manure.

She stares at me, hesitating. "Come, girls. It's time for afternoon Mass. I don't want to keep my soldier waiting."

Dusting off my skirt, my heart settles. The claws lighten on my chest. I gather my skirt and march on.

Near the market, stifling smells fill the air. Meat hangs, rotting in the sun. Flies collect in fluttering droves around the brown flesh. The fisherman clean sea bass carcasses, the castoff scales reflecting color from the ground like a mirror to a rainbow. Hanging pottery clangs together in the wind.

The half-timbered house is in sight, but a man grabs at my robe. His mangled feet stick out in front of me like knotted limbs cut from their tree. I remember him. They burned his feet and broke his knees. His crime? Handing stale bread to a Huguenot child.

"Mademoiselle, please help." His voice is raspy and feeble.

"Monsieur don't speak to me. They'll kill you."

"My family is starving. I'm desperate."

"I cannot help."

His trembling hands fall to the ground. They are dirty and dark from days splayed out in the sun. He shuts his eyes, brow furrowed and tight.

I walk on to the house, knock at the door and glance over my shoulder. A dragoon in military dress walks past the beggar and kicks his feet. The man's howl echoes through the narrow street, bouncing against the tall houses and up into the sky. I close my eyes and shake my head. I have no time to help him. Not today.

A round pale face appears in the creaked open door. "Isabelle. Come in." Clémentine's skin is translucent in the light, like lean milk.

"We must hurry," I say.

She paces, tears in her eyes. Her full cheeks blush with the slightest pale pink. "No, I can't go outside. Not after what happened to Etienne." She balls her hands at her stomach and bends forward to catch her breath. "I'm not as brave as you."

"Clémentine, we're depending on you." She looks past me, beginning to shake. "I know you're scared. I'm always scared."

"You are?" Her eyes meet mine.

"Every day of my life. But we must protect each other. No one else will."

Her mother leads her to sit. "Darling, this is your choice." A tear escapes through her tightened eyelids and streams down one cheek, which her mother wipes away. "Staying here won't help you grieve. Helping the Campagnes might."

She looks at me. "What if we don't make it? What if they attack us?"

"There's always risk, but I'll stay with you. We'll do it together." I hold her hand. "They broke Etienne's arms to teach us a lesson. But what did he teach us?"

"Faith. Community."

I nod.

We hug the edges of the busy streets, my arm wrapped around Clémentine's elbow. Her arm trembles. We lower our heads when two men near. Their wide-brimmed feather hats shield their eyes, but their voices ring clear.

"He wants to keep us close, wasting time with food and drink at Versailles while he strips our power," one says.

"Quiet," the other man says. "You don't want word to find its way to Monsieur LaMarche that you disagree with the King."

"LaMarche. That evil bastard hates anyone he can't control."

I long to hear their discussion, but Clémentine tugs at my arm.

A commotion across the street catches our attention, where a Huguenot attempts to buy wine from a street merchant. His clothing betrays him. Simple wool, no adornments, no jewelry. We fight the Catholic Church in our clothing as well as our faith. The merchant begins to beat him with an iron rod to his knees.

Clémentine gasps, hand to her mouth.

"Don't look. Keep walking." I march her forward.

At last, we arrive at the farm just outside of town, the baby's cries high-pitched and angry. Clémentine throws open the door and rushes to hold the baby. She cradles him in her arms, lowering to the rocking chair by the fire. She unties her bodice, pulling back the front of her shift. The baby thrashes his head side to side searching for the milk leaking from her breast.

"Shhh, shhh," Clémentine whispers calmly. The baby latches. The cries turn to whimpers, and the whimpers turn to rhythmic breathing and swallowing. My stomach releases its tension, and everyone sighs. Through puffy eyes, she smiles and rests the back of her head against the chair.

The baby's mother rushes out to their small garden, gasping for breath.

I step outside and place my hand on her back. "Madame, it's all right now. Clémentine is here."

"What if she didn't come? What would have happened?"

"We mustn't think of that now. Everything will be fine."

"I begged the dragoons to leave one goat. It's the only way we can feed him." Her face twists and sobs, then she wipes her eyes. "I nursed my older children without difficulty. I failed him."

"You are not just saving your baby. You are saving Clémentine," I say.

An unknown soldier raped Clémentine a little less than a year ago. Onlookers ignored her screams. The man dragged her down to the bowels of a ship where he took her in a puddle of moldy wine. I found her trembling behind cargo, blood dripping from her nose. I helped her home, where she has spent the last seven months. Her baby lived for three days, enough time to grow her breasts full of milk.

When I arrived at this farm yesterday, I found a desperate family and a screaming baby.

Once Madame's emotions settle, I help her stuff linen with straw. Madame frequently stops to glance upon her sleeping baby, milk dripping from the side of his mouth. We place the mattress in the kitchen near the fire, and next to the cradle. Clémentine's new bed.

Clémentine smiles at Madame, whose eyes fill with grateful tears. Etienne's spirit fills the room.

"Goodnight." I slip out the front door.

"Isabelle, wait." Madame follows me, and hands me a jug of wine and a small round of cheese wrapped in cloth.

"Thank you, Madame. Clémentine will stay as long as you need her."

She looks around then whispers to me, "Midnight. The forest east of the barricades. You'll be there?"

"Yes. We'll be there."

Retracing my path, my arm aches from carrying Maman's jug of wine. Near Clémentine's home, I approach the beggar whose hand covers his face. Moving past him, I drop the cheese in his lap and keep walking. The faint sound of "Merci" settles my nerves, washing over me in a warm embrace.

Suddenly, a hand on my arm. I yank it back but then exhale. It's just my friend Henri. His wild black hair flies in the wind, and his bright red cravat shines against his dark gray clothes.

"Hurry," he says.

We run behind a dark corner of the barricade and crouch in its shadows.

"Isabelle, what were you thinking, walking at the port by yourself? You are a careless girl."

"What are you doing here? Looking for trouble?"

"Waiting for the cargo to be unattended. The salt barrels look heavy." He flashes his usual devious smile.

"You steal salt now?"

He leans forward, one elbow on his propped knee, "They steal from us every day. I take back what I need."

"You leave your father alone with his silverwork while you go to the port and steal salt?"

"I can't be held in that room all day, making fine silverware for Catholics that treat us like rats." He tosses his hair out of his eyes. "If they refuse to give us our due, I will take it."

"You'll find yourself chained to the walls of the tower."

"I won't be in danger for much longer," he says.

"What are you talking about?"

"The Americas. The British colony is full of opportunity. There we can just be Protestants and people, no longer spit on. My parents won't leave. They still believe we should stay here and suffer endless torment."

Leave France? His words have sliced open a cavern I hadn't known was inside me. One where a crack of light shines through the darkness. "If they catch you fleeing the country, they'll send you to the galleys. Why would you risk that?"

"Because living here is just as awful. The beatings, the torture. I can't live the same life our parents force on us." He sees me rub my forearm and scratches at his leg, looking away. "Opportunity is out there, Isabelle. We just have to be strong enough to fight for it."

There is no safety in our world. They punish us for grasping for it. Henri is brave enough to fight for what we have never known.

The sun begins to lower in the sky. "It's time."

"Yes. Do you have the Bible?"

My hand pats the skirt over my hidden pocket.

"Good." He glances at the port, eyeing our path back through town. "Etienne is not well. The poor man is suffering. He needs our prayers."

A deep ache settles in my chest. "I'm ready."

Past a crowd of shipyard workers, behind a stack of wood crates, we slip back under the arch into town. It always exhilarates me. Taking part in the living, breathing world, danger at my fingertips. We find our quiet resistance any way we can.

Henri and I split when the street quiets. Two young Huguenots are ripe for harassment. Separated, our presence is smaller. The shadows flicker past me through the arches of the arcades. The sun casts its orange glow approaching twilight.

Ahead, women of the nobility. I turn my body, leading with my shoulder to move sideways past them. Their perfume fills the air with lilac and the long feathers of their hats tickle the top of my head as I duck past.

Henri returns to my side, his shoulder touching mine like a boat at the dock, bouncing against its stable home before setting off to the wild sea. At Etienne's door are two dragoons. My chest seizes, a small gasp escaping my lips. Henri yanks my arm. In a dark alley next to the house, we crouch behind a barrel.

"What are they doing here?" I say.

"I don't know." Henri's face has softened into worry.

A scream breaks the afternoon quiet, catching my breath with it. I grab Henri's arm. We know.

They're here to force him to take the sacrament.

My forehead throbs in time to my heartbeat. "He'll never do it."

"No, but they'll torture him. The bastards think if they crush our bones and slash our skin that we'll break."

"Don't they understand that we don't have a choice?"

A deep, howling cry grips me again. I shut my eyes and curl my knees into my chest. We could run, but neither of us want to. We need to be with Etienne as he dies. I need to know he's not alone.

"Converting on one's deathbed after a life of Protestantism. How does that solve anything?" Henri says.

"It doesn't. It shows the rest of us what our future will be."

A scream so deep, so aching, sets the birds flying from the rooftops. I resist the urge to cover my ears. "Etienne is like a father to me," I whisper.

"He's a father to us all."

Etienne's tortured screams send shocks through me.

He throws all his strength into one sentence. "You may take my body, but my mind remains free!" As if he knows we are here, listening. Watching.

His scream is snapped off, turning to a gurgle. I recoil, face in my hands. Henri wraps his arm around me. My vision black. In it, images of Etienne, his tongue sliced from his mouth, his ears ripped open. Tortured so barbarically he is unable to scream as he heaves toward death.

Whimpers. Animalistic grunts with pauses of silence between them. Wet, hot beads drip down my neck. Stabs pierce my stomach and the ground shifts under me. Then, silence.

Worse than the screams of a tortured man, is the moment that they stop. Thump, thump in my ears, my vision shakes with the beat. I gasp for breath. Henri's head lowers, a tear rolls down his cheek then drips off his chin.

"Bring him out," a man says.

We lean against the wall, under the shadow from the roof. The priest steps out of Etienne's home, in a liturgical vestment and gold-stitched robe. The giant cross around his neck glitters in the lowering sun, its glare forcing my eyes to squint.

A dragoon steps into the light and catches our eyes. I back into Henri, my hands and feet prickling. We turn to run down the alley, but a force yanks me back. The dragoon catches us by the backs of our clothes. My feet scrape the dirt. My body tightens, my hand pressed against the Bible in my skirt.

He presents us to the priest. "What do you want me to do with them?"

The priest runs his eyes over my hair, my body. "Leave them here," he snarls. "Let them watch what happens when you disobey the King."

His mangled, yellow teeth drip with spit, as if he's salivating from anticipation. The dragoon shoves us against the house, taking my breath for a moment when my ribs hit the wall. Panic sets in. Then, like a shock, my chest opens.

The soldiers step out of the house. They lean forward, ropes over their shoulders. They pull and yank, forward then stop. Forward then stop. The clawing ache returns to my chest.

"What did they do to him?" I whisper in Henri's ear. He shuts his eyes and shakes his head.

The dragoon grabs Henri's arm. "Watch."

They drag a naked Etienne over the doorstep that smells of piss where the soldiers relieved themselves. He is bound by the ankles and wrists, his head clunking over the step and into the dirty streets. They lay him at our feet so we may see his damaged face.

"You may avoid this punishment if you convert," the priest says.

He steps close, so close I can smell his stale, rotting breath.

"There is one God and one church. All else is heresy. By order of the King, you will denounce Protestantism. Or I will have you all beheaded. The choice is yours."

A wave of bile rises in my throat. I swallow the stinging acid and shut my eyes. His breath fades from the skin of my ear. I can't stop myself. I steal one last glance at Etienne. His mouth is open to a black hole, filled with curdled blood.

The dragoons begin their parade through the town, dragging the body behind them. A trail of blood follows where his ashen skin rips against the cobblestones' jagged edges.

The priest stays behind. He holds out his rosary to me, dangling from his bony finger. "Your torture awaits." He nods to one of the soldiers. The dragoon throws Etienne's bloody tongue at my feet.

I stumble back, catch myself on the wall.

In the sky, the birds soar above the wicked happenings on the dirty ground below. A lone black swan flies from the marsh near town, beating its wings in a loud thump, disturbing the stillness around me.

We step to the middle of the empty street, gaze down at the trail of dark blood that begins to clot in the sand. Deep in the town's belly, Etienne meets his fate. Dusk settles over us, the only sounds, far off screams and the close whistle of Henri's deep heaving.

I pull back my sleeve to the hard, raised flesh on my arm, throbbing with heat. My fist tightens, pulling the skin taut. Jagged edges and webbed tendrils. The blood coursing through it beats with the rhythm of my quickened heart. An H. A terrified eight-year-old branded by a drunken dragoon.

This life means sacrifice and pain. Etienne knew this would be his end, yet he chose it anyway. To believe in something so powerfully that you would die for it, that is the commitment this life demands. Henri grabs my hand, pulling it down to my side. We stand united.

Etienne, Henri, and I share a predestined fate. Suffering is our badge of pride. This is what my future holds unless I fight to change it. This is the expectation and the heart of a Huguenot.

.   .   .

There was a time Maman was part of the world, but killings and beatings have caused her to recoil like a snail in her fragile shell. Tonight, she steps outside for the first time in months.

Careful to avoid the soldiers wandering the streets, we move east. Through the crumbled areas of the old barricade, into the woods. The glow from the moon lights our way, reflecting off the trees in a silver glimmer.

A few others move across the dirt, shrouded in black, to the clearing we know so well. This patch of earth is where Protestants secretly share life's moments. Moments that are punishable by death. Marriages, prayer, and baptisms bring considerable risk, yet we carry on.

Through the trees, quiet faces welcome us with a bow of their heads. Catholics spit the name Huguenot, to mean a banished people praying in shuttered homes. We have adopted it, unashamed of our secret prayers. A white mist hovers in the crisp autumn air.

Henri nudges me. We smile at each other, surrounded by the only church we know. Our pastor steps to the middle. Unlike the Catholics, our leaders walk among us.

As we settle into the silence, the late summer evening stillness pulls me into focus, my hands grow steadier with every breath of wet, cool air. The pastor speaks in a low calming voice.

"Let our presence here remind us that God has chosen us. Do not allow the fear they drive into our hearts to remain for longer than it must. Our purpose is bigger than ourselves. It is to carry on our faith against all manner of intimidation. The true church is not in a hierarchy of corruption and excess. It is here, in the society of the faithful."

He gestures to the smiling parents, who present their baby boy wrapped in velvet and white lace. Clémentine smiles, her eyes focused on the baby.

"This child's life of purity will allow restoration of the primitive innocence of Christianity. Our truest faith lies in patience and humility," he says.

We are born into this impossible life. Without agreement, without knowledge. We grow in a secret church reserved for the unwanted before we understand what it means. I pray life will be different for this little boy than it has been for me.

The pastor raises a cup of water and dabs several drops on the baby's forehead, concluding our forbidden ceremony amongst the foggy trees. The smiles of my fellow worshipers light the night sky in a rare moment of peace. We do not find faith in a church, but in the quiet of the trees and under the light of the stars. We begin to sing.

The whisper of the Psalms of David fills the air, enveloping us in the warm familiarity of song in our native tongue. We worship in French. No Latin to be heard. The rolling French is close enough to reach and soft enough to pull me in.

They call us heretics. Because God rules us. Not man, not kings. Because we don't need priests or saints. Because we can read. Because we cannot be controlled.

The voices drift off to silence as they hold hands in gratitude. I slip away to the edge of the clearing to take in the glow of night. The flickering fires light up our town of chaos. Henri steps next to me, and we peer through the hazy white cloud around us. My heart aches with the sharp realization that outside the forest's protective arms lies an empire that wishes us dead.

A SMALL FIRE BEGINS TO BURN

The door latches shut. The dark of the morning flutters away to gray before the sun rises. I walk the streets with empty hands. No weapons, no arms. Only risk. Goods handed between houses so we may survive. Wool stockings, a jug of ale, a loaf of bread, candles.

These mornings remind me of Grand-mère. One day, I asked why she risked danger to trade herbs and wine.

"We don't hide from our faith. There's no shame in being a Protestant," she told me. "So, we live, and we serve."

"But Maman tells me not to leave the house. That they'll hurt me again."

She knelt and rubbed my fat cheeks. "Your mother arrived in this world during a war on the soul."

The Great Siege is webbed into our lives. The few who survived the King's attack carry the burden heavy on their hearts. He walled the city in for fifteen months. Once they devoured all the rats and vinegar-soaked leather, our families died by the thousands.

"I often wonder why we survived," Grand-mère said. "I choose to believe it was for you. You will do great things, dear girl. I knew when I saw those glowing green eyes that you had a fighting spirit that poor Angelique could never find. Your mother will never recover from her losses, but you can still start a fire where there has been nothing but darkness."

"I will be strong for Maman," I told her. "And for you."

Gone a year now, her words come to me at times when I need her wisdom. I want to start a fire, yet I have no one to show me the way out of the dark.

The figure of a young man appears. Broad shoulders and wavy copper hair. His hand rests on his hip, relaxed. Smooth. My stomach flickers with excitement. Ducking behind a wall, I peer one eye out at him. Watching a royal soldier feels like staring down a lion. Yet, my mouth parts slightly, trying to breathe in the slightest hint of him.

Leaning for a closer view, I see his companion. Antoinette. Her coiffed hair seemingly spun from gold, dazzles against her gown of lace and maroon taffeta. She laughs, light and easy. Stepping back into the shadows, my strength wilts into dust. A fool swept away in a moment of fantasy.

The dark corner behind the door of the apothecary shields me from Antoinette's view. On the other side, the tremulous voice of a young girl. I peek through the opening between the door hinges. Her rosy cheeks and wispy eyelashes reveal her innocence, but her eyes are wide with terror. She whimpers as she pulls back from the man who holds a grip on her arm.

"Please, Monsieur, let me free." Her big eyes dart in all directions, her hands trembling.

"Come, girl, it's just a kiss. My wife is a dull woman, and I need affection." His foot stumbles on a rope, then recovers while he wipes his mouth with his ruffled shirt sleeve. "You're out walking alone. It's obvious what you're looking for." He snarls as his gaze lowers to her narrow hips.

He yanks her arm, and they disappear around the corner of the alley. My chest tightens. Breathe. Settle. Focus. Weakened knees and a racing heart don't stop me from venturing down the darkened path.

He has her pressed against the wall, her eyes wide and urgent. The man grips her wrist and forces her to rub between his legs. His stance is wide, his other arm braced against the wall, so his drunken legs don't falter. As she rubs him, his eyes roll back, and his hips thrust toward her.

Tears break the twisted fear on her face as she stares at me. "Help." The faint child-like voice shatters me. My forearm scar throbs hot and angry.

A pile of ropes entangles the man's feet. Rapture has taken him away and he has not noticed me. Without a thought, my hands grab the rope and yank it back, pulling it tight against his feet. In the blink of an eye, his face smacks the ground through a puddle of filthy water.

I gesture for her to run. As she passes me, our eyes meet. She cracks a hesitant smile. We are not a Catholic and a Protestant or a noble and a peasant. Just one scared woman helping another.

"Filthy bitch!" he says.

I turn to run, my gaze still on the man as he stumbles to his knees. My chest hits something. I flinch, stepping back with my head down. My arms ready to fight, my legs tingling. My gaze climbs the figure of Antoinette's soldier. His silver-blue eyes meet mine and a hint of a smile creeps onto his face. A smattering of brown freckles dusts his cheeks. We stand dangerously close for a long moment. Then, through wavering breath, I say, "Pardon, Monsieur."

The drunken man stands and stumbles toward us. I slip past the soldier, a thrill rippling through me when my shoulder brushes his.

Boots thump the ground, increasing speed, until the soldier jumps in front of me. His arm juts out, preventing me from slipping past. "Wait, are you all right, Mademoiselle?" His voice drips like honey over me.

He scans my features the way I did his.

"Monsieur Beaumont! Do not run away from me." Antoinette lowers her chin when she sees me, narrowing her eyes like a snake hissing. "What are you doing here, peasant? Go back to your barn at once." She slides her hand around the soldier's elbow.

"It's all right, Mademoiselle." His voice calm, like taming a wild horse. "She did nothing wrong." He breaks a smile in my direction.

"Wherever this heretic is, trouble follows," she says.

The soldier peels Antoinette's hand from him, uncurling her fingers and flicking them off him. When he steps toward me, my stomach tightens.

"What is your name?" he says.

Antoinette's shoulders lift, her hands ball into fists.

"I must go," I say.

My feet rush over the uneven stones, his freckles still on my mind. Tall houses and arcades filled with merchants fly past me in a cloudy rush. Slipping behind crowds and dropping into quiet streets, my foolishness stings my memory. At my door, I stop to catch my breath.

"Wait!"

I grab fistfuls of skirt, crouched and ready to run.

"It's all right, Mademoiselle," he says through heavy breaths. "My, you certainly move swiftly."

My legs tingle and my vision blurs. "What do you want?"

"I saw what you did." He steps closer to me.

"No, Monsieur, I did nothing."

"You're a Huguenot?" He softens his stance.

I nod my head, yes, looking in every direction.

He lowers his voice to a whisper. "What's your name?"

I bite my lip and hesitate. "Isabelle Colette."

"Isabelle, a heretic who risks herself to save a rebellious Catholic."

"She's just a girl."

"She's a foolish girl. I know because she's my sister."

My skirt drops from my grip.

"Your courage is inspiring," he says. His vivid blue eyes scan my face. "Be wary of bravery getting you into trouble. The next man may not be so understanding."

"I'm painfully aware of the challenges I face." I turn toward my door, preparing to open it, but my hand stops at the handle.

"I'm sure you are, Mademoiselle Colette, girl who makes dangerous choices." He strides away from me.

My hand still rests on the handle, my eyes on the door. "Dangerous choices are all I ever make."

His footsteps halt. The dirt crushes as he spins on his heels. He walks up behind me, his body near mine.

"The man stumbled drunk from the apothecary, tripping over ropes and crashing to the ground from inebriation. No man would dare contradict a royal soldier."

Turning my cheek to my shoulder, I catch a glimpse of him from the corner of my eye.

"My name is James Beaumont. It's a pleasure to meet you, beautiful and courageous, Isabelle."

I turn to watch him walk away, smiling as he disappears around the corner. I stop for one breathless moment, the danger seeming to float on my tongue. Inside the house, my mother slams the door behind me.

"Isabelle, what are you doing speaking with that man?" She pulls me away from the window as if I am more protected on the other side of the room.

"Maman, calm yourself. We were just talking."

"It's a perilous game you're playing, child." She grabs a loaf of bread and slices, the knife trembling in her hand.

"I am not a child."

"Then stop acting like one!" She pauses to regain composure. "It is time to stop this dangerous running around and settle down."

"I don't need an arranged marriage, Maman."

"Don't be foolish. Marriage will protect you. It will protect us both."

"None of us are protected. They will always attack us. Torment us. A husband won't be able to stop that. The last thing I want is to bring children into this horrid life."

The knife thuds on the table, Maman's mouth agape. "You *will* have children."

"No. I won't."

"You are the last Colette. Our bloodline will die with you. Are you that selfish?" she says.

"I am that practical. No child should endure searing hot metal burned into her flesh."

She flips her head to the side, closing her eyes. It's as if my words attack her and she fights them by disappearing.

"Monsieur LaMarche is planning something terrible," I say, coaxing her to look at me.

"Did your soldier tell you that?"

"No. I overheard it."

"Whatever Monsieur LaMarche is planning, I assure you that soldier allows it. Encourages it. What sort of friend would force you into their beliefs?" she says with a brittle voice.

"I don't know. What sort of mother would?"

She blinks to steady her vision. We stand motionless, my words still ringing in my ears. She collapses into her chair with a loud sigh. "Isabelle, you are a Protestant. God chose you."

She holds me like a prisoner, like a bird in a steel cage desperate to fly. She only unlocks the cage when the wine runs dry. I try to pray, but all I see is James and his bright smile, calling me beautiful and courageous.

Maman is right, this is a dangerous game. A game that has no winner.

· · ·

Maman did not try to stop me from leaving today. She didn't even look at me.

The morning sun has yet to rise. The steam from freshly dropped horse waste rises into the cold air. The men at the port gather around small fires to warm their hands, waiting for their next load of cargo.

In the silver light of daybreak, the red cloth catches my eye, something only I would see. I slide behind the crates where my friend snacks on dried meat.

"Where did you get that?" I ask.

Henri splits it and hands me half. "Never mind that."

Our backs lean against the cold wall. The waves grow in speed, indicating a ship's arrival.

"What did your parents say about Etienne?"

"That suffering is part of our life. Etienne could do nothing. As I should do nothing."

"Why are we the only ones to question? Our fate doesn't need to follow that of our ancestors," I say.

"Etienne questioned. Your grandmother questioned. Things can be different for us." He sighs and leans his head against the wall.

"Not if France continues to force its will. Monsieur LaMarche is planning something. I heard the nobles talking."

"Things are growing more dangerous. I don't doubt LaMarche is behind it. He is wicked. Just like his daughter."

"Antoinette used to be kind. When we were children."

"We aren't children anymore."

I blurt out, "Maman wants me to marry."

He snorts with a small laugh. "I love you, Isabelle, but I cannot imagine you married."

"Nor can I. I prefer to stalk these streets and do the work Etienne taught us to do. What husband would allow me that?"

He takes my hands. "Promise me you'll always fight. We are not destined for suffering." He looks straight into my eyes. "Do not believe them. Our future can change. If we demand it."

My always hopeful friend keeps the fire inside me burning. "I will never stop fighting. I promise you."

In the distance, metal shackles clank in step with prisoner's feet. We peer over the top of the crates. As the sunlight warms the air and lights the world, misery descends upon our shores.

Rows of men. Dark men. Black as night. Their raven skin glistens in the sun, like tar dripping from their bodies. Tight curls of hair recoil against their heads. Bound at their ankles, they step in unison. Stripped to nothing with a vacancy in their eyes. Their captors look on, whips resting at their feet.

Henri's hands grip the wooden crates. I swallow my tears. The metal clinks rhythmically against the wood dock. Clink, jingle. Clink, jingle. The shackles ring like bells then lilt to a scrape as they drag across the wood.

A man resists. A swift whip against his legs brings him to his knees. The deep howl of pain grips me. My hand covers my mouth to stifle a gasp.

"Slaves," Henri whispers. "They bring them from Africa to trade with the Americas."

"They trade them. Like wine or salt? They're people."

"Our King is hungry for power. War. Famine. Death. It means nothing to them. Those who don't serve the Catholic Church aren't people. Not to them."

A man looks back, desperate for someone to rescue them. I long to tear their chains off and let them dive into the ocean and swim home to freedom. I do the only thing I can — say a prayer for the terrified men experiencing hell on earth.

"Come," Henri says. "I can't look at this for one more second."

We enter town, without our usual lithe bouncing from shadow to shadow. We lurk, hesitant. Despondent.

Our feet drag us into the recesses of the alley across from Etienne's house. The door is boarded, the windows shuttered.

"Should we break in?" I ask.

Before he can answer, a voice. "Mademoiselle Collette."

It's the young Beaumont girl. James's sister. Henri jumps, hands out.

"It's all right, Henri," I say.

"She knows your name." His voice is tense.

"My brother asked me about you. He told me your name," she says.

"Leave us be, Mademoiselle. You'll have us all killed." Henri peers out to the street.

"I saw you in town. I followed you because I want to say thank you," she says to me.

"You're welcome. Now, you really should leave."

She looks at Etienne's house. "Was he a friend?"

Henri urges me not to speak.

"Yes," I say.

"It's awful. What they do to your people."

Footsteps around the corner. We step back under the shadow of the roof.

"They've gifted the home to a young Catholic couple," she says.

"It belongs to us. It is a Huguenot home," I say.

"My father says they shouldn't own property. He says it's dangerous. That you are all dangerous."

"And you and your brother, do you believe that?"

Henri shifts and fidgets. "Why does it matter what they think of us?"

I scowl at him.

"I'm not afraid of either of you. My brother has a kind heart. But he allows my father to control him. There's no telling what he truly believes."

"He needs his approval?" I ask.

"Yes. And my father will do whatever the King asks of him. James will never be strong enough to stand up to him."

"Isabelle, let's go. No more of this nonsense." Henri pulls my arm.

"I pray for your safety, Mademoiselle," she says.

I yank my arm from Henri and lean toward her. "Why were you alone with that man?"

"It was foolish. I like to walk through town, listening. Watching. My home is stifling. They don't let me speak. And when I do, they don't listen."

"You didn't scream for your brother."

"I wanted to handle it myself. James wishes me to stay alone in my room all day, staring out the window. Like fine porcelain only brought out at dinner parties to be admired and then forgotten again. I want to be like you. Wild. Free."

"Wild, maybe. But free I am not."

She has the same big blue eyes as James. The same dusting of freckles.

Henri and I traverse the hidden alleys, hugging the curves of the medieval wall.

"Isabelle, what were you thinking?"

"I just helped a girl. Nothing more."

"And her brother, what of that?" he says.

"He was kind to me. Thankful I saved his sister."

"You're blushing."

I speed up, turning my face away from him.

"James Beaumont, royal soldier and Antoinette's betrothed? You are either brave or foolish." He grabs my arm, turning me to face him. "You know how dangerous this is."

"Of course, I do."

"Then why?" he says.

"Why do you want to escape to the colony? Because believing there is nothing but evil in the world is too great a burden to bear."

"Be careful. Evil may not be everywhere. But it often rests in those promising to do good."

His hands slide down my arms and we back away from each other, disappearing into the danger of La Rochelle.

BETRAYAL OF FAITH

Maman's nerves are very unwell lately. Today's expectation is to refill our wine barrels. Once I have, I'm free to wander the hills.

The last of the chestnuts will have fallen from the trees. I trek into the forest to fill my basket with the spiny husks. My feet slide down large stones and through the crumbling wall to the fields behind La Rochelle. The quiet whispers of the hills deepen my shallow breaths, which turn into a cloud of mist in the autumn breeze.

There's peace among the wavering trees, calmness in the brisk air. My shoulders soften. Deep in the hills, I stumble across a sweet chestnut tree. Dirt collects under my fingernails as I dig for fallen fruit. I drop them in my basket like little gems.

Sticks crack in time to footsteps. Reaching under the cloth in my basket, I grab my forbidden blade and spin, jutting out the steel. Shallow breaths.

James.

"Alone in the trees with a knife. Aren't you a clever girl?"

"What are you doing here?" My fingers tighten around the handle of the blade.

"I followed you."

"Why would you follow me?"

"Most of your people hide and cower. You do not." He tilts his head to the side. "You fascinate me."

I drop the knife in the basket and straighten my shoulders.

"Come, I'll walk with you," he says. "I just want to talk."

"Talking with me is dangerous."

"I thought you liked danger?" He winks.

He saunters away, looking back with a smile. Against my will, my feet begin to walk as if independent from my mind. He strolls with his hands clasped behind his back.

"Your sister should be more careful," I say.

He stops and faces me. "Your bravery. It saved my foolish sister."

"What makes her foolish?"

"She's a reckless child who doesn't appreciate how we protect her," he says.

"Maybe she feels stifled by how you protect her."

"Until she's old enough to marry, she requires supervision."

"I don't have a husband. Do I require supervision?" My neck flushes with heat.

"You are clearly capable of handling yourself. When I ran to find out who saved my sister, I found a peasant Huguenot girl. Emerald eyes, flecked with gold and filled with determination."

"It's called survival." My fingers tighten over the basket handle.

"I know the look of survival. Yours is something different."

"What do you know about survival? You're a Catholic soldier in the Royal Army. You're free to terrorize people without recourse."

He waits to catch my eyes. "I have no intention of doing that."

"You may think you're noble because you don't swing the blade. But your army has my people's blood on your hands." My eyes sting holding back tears.

"We work for the King because we must." His voice deepens. "I was born in Normandy. Into a family of Huguenots."

The tension in my body softens. A hot prickling patters up my arms.

"My parents tried to protect me, but they never could. They marked our door with pig's blood and threatened to kill my sister. She was six months old."

"Which explains your protectiveness of her."

"We stood in the town square, condemned our error in judgment, and accepted the sacrament. Papa made a deal with a childhood friend, securing a position at the Royal Court. He's been loyal to the King ever since, virtually erasing any memory of our heretic past."

"You were once just like me," I mutter.

"I barely remember it. I was five." He lowers to an old oak and leans his head against its rough bark. "My father never wants to look back. He expects my full loyalty."

I sit next to him, setting my basket to the side. "My mother treats me the same."

"Maybe we have more in common than at first glance," he says with a slight lean toward me.

"I was taught that you are all evil." I pull back from him.

"We are all capable of evil. But we're capable of goodness, too," he says as his blue eyes flicker with light.

"There is no good or evil in my world. Only impossible choices."

His fingers brush against mine. My neck tightens, my breaths shallow and tight. "Someday, you might change your mind."

"But today, I am nobody. A helpless girl."

"You don't believe that," he says.

"It doesn't matter what I believe. That is what the world sees when they look at me." I pull my knees into my chest, shifting away from him again, leaving an aching in my belly.

"That's not what I see."

"What do you see when you look at Mademoiselle LaMarche?"

He sinks back into the tree trunk. "I see the future my family wants. Power. Loyalty."

"Her family has been the cause of so much suffering." Memories of my father bite at my heart.

"She cares only for power. I could never love her."

"Does anyone ever marry for love?" I ask.

"I would like to think so."

His stare is deep and focused, and it rattles my resolve. I break the tension and force myself to stand. "I should leave. This is dangerous for us both. What would your parents think if they saw you with a Huguenot?"

He stands, dusting the dirt off his hands. "The same thing your mother would think of you with a Catholic soldier."

"So, it's decided. We won't speak again."

His dashing smile returns. "I'm not willing to accept that."

The sky darkens and thunder grows in the distance. His scent soft and smoky. My heart thumps loud and fast as he extends his arms around me. He grabs the sides of my hood and places it gently over my head.

"It's time to get you back," he says before looking up at the stormy sky.

We hurry back toward town, sneaking glances at each other. It begins to rain. Close to the stone wall, there's movement. James pushes me against a tree, placing his arm above my head to shelter my face from the men that walk by. Without thinking, I adjust my hood and bury my face in his chest.

He nods to acknowledge the men who snicker and leave him to his conquest. The wool jacket is rough against my skin, his scent intoxicating. My face buried into his neck, the silkiness of his cravat against my cold cheek. He doesn't move his body but turns to look down at me. The rain drips down his temples, loosening his curly bronzed hair.

His chest touches mine. We breath in unison, rising and falling together. His breath is sweet and brushes my lips like a warm wind. His hand slides down the tree, running his fingers near my cheek, barely touching my arm.

He leads me through the broken wall and down the narrow streets. His hand finds its way to the curve of my back. I arch to pull away, but my heart still flutters. Near my door, James stops in front of me, chest heaving.

"I will see you again. I'll make sure of it," he says.

He turns to walk away, my heart still racing. James is a Catholic, but also a Protestant, somewhere inside. God came to me in the forest once again. I take a deep breath and suppress my smile before stepping inside the house.

"Isabelle! What is wrong with you? Letting yourself freeze in wet clothes. You will catch a cough." The agitation in her voice matches her fierce eyes. She rips off my skirt and bodice, making sure I feel her disappointment. "Warm yourself by the fire, and I will fetch some dry clothes."

As she brings a clean shift, she finds me spinning, unable to contain my smile. She crosses her hands in front of her. "Isabelle, we must talk."

"What is it?"

"That man. He's one of them. You must never speak to him again."

"Maman!"

"He's an agent of the King." She leans in toward me. "He cannot be trusted."

"He's kind."

She steadies herself on the table. "He is nothing of the sort. You will stop seeing him. Immediately."

"Why, because he's Catholic?"

"Because every time you're close to one of them, you're in danger." She rubs her forehead. "He knows that, too."

"We're always in danger. I'm growing tired of being afraid every day." My voice sharpens.

"I forbid it." Her eyes close, shutting me out. "Now, fetch my wine."

I am to live the dangerous life of a fully grown woman while still treated as a helpless girl. I fear my restless heart can't take much more.

.   .   .

Every day since, I wait until Maman finishes her wine, creeping out of our darkened house to meet James in the bustling streets. We sneak away to the hills or hidden alleys or the broken remains of the ramparts outside of town. We talk about his father, how he has changed from the man James remembers as a boy. I tell him of my mother and how tragedy changed her as well. So many things about us are the same, and yet, our differences keep space between us.

Yesterday I told James about my father, a proud man, who fought to regain his ships after Monsieur LaMarche seized them. As I spoke, he reached for my hand. Father was backlit from the light of the morning sun, smiling as he left the house. Etienne arrived later that day to tell us that he was gone, killed by a drunken sailor. I sometimes wonder if my father preferred death to being unable to provide for his family.

Today, Maman nods off as I read her scripture. When she peacefully slips away, a pang of guilt grips me for allowing her steady flow of wine. I escape toward the town square. My eyes now scan the buildings, searching for a glimpse of my secret soldier.

"Hello, beautiful."

I turn towards the familiar voice. "Monsieur Beaumont."

"Come, we'll find a quiet street." Evading the prying eyes of the market, he leads me to a darkened alley.

"My father questioned me this morning," he says.

"What about?"

"My future. He wants me to set a wedding date with Antoinette."

"Oh." Every muscle in my body tightens.

He places his fingers gently below my chin. "Father suspects something. I can tell."

"How?"

"I'm not sure. He would be furious if he knew how attached I've become to a Huguenot."

"How are we to keep seeing each other under these circumstances?" I pull away from his touch.

"I'm not sure. Maybe we only meet in the hills? We can claim the chestnut tree for our own."

My heart begins to race. "I've spent my life in hiding."

"If anyone sees us, it would be too dangerous," he says.

"Maybe this is a mistake." My hands rub together, coming to rest at my lips.

"I will find a way."

"Why?" I ask.

"I can't explain it. I need you close to me."

I shake my head no. "Maybe it is wrong."

He steps close enough that my knees weaken. "Maybe there's a way."

"We live in two very different worlds, and you left mine long ago," I say.

"I admit, this feels like an impossible challenge." He backs away and begins pacing. "You question your faith, I know you do."

"You know nothing of my beliefs."

"I know you want more than what your mother demands of you."

"What use is it to hope? I can't change my station, my life."

"You can be whatever you want to be," he says.

"I don't understand." I shake my head.

"Isabelle, when my family converted, we found a way to thrive. The beatings, the intimidation, it all stopped."

I scan his freckles again. "What are you saying?"

"You have a choice. I know you want more from life. I see it when you look at me."

"You don't know me, Monsieur Beaumont. And you should not presume to understand my struggles." My heart thumps in my throat.

"Convert. You and your mother will be safe. It seems you only need someone who has been through it to tell you that you can demand a better life."

"A better life? One of betrayal and lies. How dare you suggest that to me?" I push past him and look back with disbelief. "Your family made a choice. And we've made ours."

"We made it out of that life and are better for it. Just do what they ask. God does not care what Bible you pray to."

"I care!" The pressure builds behind my eyes.

He pulls me to face him. "You may still be a Protestant in secret. But in the eyes of society, you would be a loyal subject of France. Wouldn't you like to walk through life without fear?"

He whispers the word Protestant and his shame grips me with an overwhelming sadness.

"We can be together," he says.

"A long as I become what you need me to be." I yank his hands from me. "If I turn on my faith, everything my people have fought for would be lost."

"And what if you never get the chance to breathe free? The dragoons are out of control. They send men to the galleys and women to jail. Chain them to walls. I want you to stay with me." He rests his hand on my face. "Ask yourself, is this the life God wishes for you?"

"It is the life God gave me." I exhale and try not to cry. "I should never have trusted you."

"Isabelle, wait, I don't want to hurt you."

Tears fill my hazy vision. "I am afraid you already have." I slide his hand from my cheek. I step back, stumbling away into the dark alley.

Around the corner, Antoinette stands against a half-timber house, eyes cold as stone. We say nothing. I stare into her vengeful eyes, knowing she has been watching us the entire time.

· · ·

It has been three days since I left the house. I've joined Maman in her misery. We spend hours in silence, sipping wine, praying. My wild heart has run away on a dream and I cannot return to the girl I was before I met him. My restlessness suffocates me, begging for fresh air.

My fingers crawl along the remnants of the medieval wall, where moss spills from the dark, black stones. The late autumn sky darkens, the air filled with billowing smoke from the communal outdoor ovens. The smell of wet earth calls to me near the edge of town, through the barricades.

My steps halt, a bright red strip of linen crumpled at my feet. Around the corner, Henri lies on his back on the ground, a dragoon's boot perched on his chest. His nose swollen and bloody, his hands claw at the dirt. I jump behind the cover of the wall, the bright cravat in my fist.

"I told you not to ignore me, filthy Bastard," the man says.

Henri looks up at him, face motionless.

"When you make me a poor-quality item, I expect you to apologize and offer me something for my inconvenience. You should grovel for my forgiveness."

"Your silverware is superb. I took a great deal of time to engrave your requested cross on every piece." Henri speaks, yet his body remains flat and still.

"Not only will I not pay you, but you'll make a special gift. For my troubles."

"No, Monsieur. I will not," Henri says.

My eyes grow wide, and my stomach tightens. I watch through a crack in the wall, the cold stone like ice against my cheek. The dragoon's sword bounces off his hip as he waves his arms.

"What did you say to me?" The dragoon picks up his foot, slams it into the fleshy part of Henri's abdomen. Henri responds with a loud grunt, pulling his knees and hands toward his belly. My eyes tighten shut, my mind in silent prayer.

"You will do what I say. You are nothing."

Henri writhes in pain. The soldier's feet straddle him, releasing a mouthful of spit that lands directly in Henri's eyes. Stunned, he blinks and wipes his eyes to clear them.

Henri could never walk away from such a despicable action. He's too proud. Too volatile. *Please, Henri. Don't.*

The dragoon lifts his foot, but not before muttering, "Worthless peasant."

The pressure of this life is too great. It's in his eyes. He is about to crumble under its weight.

As the dragoon walks away, Henri jumps up, wiping his face with his sleeve. For a moment, he stops, leaving me hopeful. Then he turns to the wall. He grabs a large stone and marches toward the dragoon, increasing speed as he nears. He lifts his arm and brings the stone crashing down on his head. Everything slows, my body floating somewhere between imagination and reality. Henri pulls a dagger from his boot and slashes through the soldier's shoulder, again and again, his chest heaving.

Time crashes down on me. My feet jump over the wall and run toward him. I reach him just in time to grab his arm as it recoils back for another stab. He jumps to face me and holds up his blade.

"It's me! Henri, it's me!" My hands shield my face, still hearing his heavy breaths. I pull my hands down. He stares at me, as if he might weep. He looks at his blade and drops it in the mud next to the soldier. His head begins to shake so softly, like a leaf in the breeze.

A trickle of rose tinged water runs past my boots.

"What have I done?" he says.

The dragoon isn't moving. Face down in the crimson mud. I pick up the blade, the wet dirt dripping off the tip, blood spatters on its handle.

"Henri, you're in danger. We all are."

NIGHT OF DESPERATION

Word of the attacked dragoon has spread through the town. The darkened walls of our timber house grow smaller, the air tighter. If Maman knew Henri was involved she would never let me out of the house again.

"I fetched wine." She pauses. "Since you have not been out to trade for it lately."

I turn my back. "Sorry, Maman. It isn't safe." Our neighbors were close to my father. They live only a few steps from us and allow Maman to take from their barrels.

"There is news of the dragoon," she says.

"Oh?" *Steady.* "Did they discover who murdered him?"

"He's alive," Maman says.

My stomach turns rigid, my stare frozen on the fire. I swallow and steady my breathing.

"I wish he were dead," she says.

"Maman!"

"It would be one less monster to torment us."

I should have let Henri kill him. Now he's facing arrest. Torture. Death. Why do I do good and cause more suffering? The idea squeezes at my heart. Slowly, like a trickle, envy seeps into me. Envy for those that believe in confession. In our world, God alone determines forgiveness. Free will can't change that.

Maman hands me a glass of wine. "They will seek one of us to blame. You can be sure of that."

The large gulp of wine burns my throat, and another and another numbs my questioning thoughts. The firelight casts shadows on Maman. Her goblet trembles against her lips.

The ghosts of our past rise from the depths of my memory. A house once filled with prayer and love. When faith was easy and my purpose clear. We had ships, food. We had each other. When Maman smiled and her emerald eyes shined. My arms held reasons to stay, and my belly didn't burn with anger. I hadn't yet felt regret. Sorrow. The naïve world of my childhood long ago faded, replaced with the knowledge that freedom might only come when we trade in this world for the next.

"Maman, If I agree to marry, what will happen to you?"

"I'll stay here and live as I always have."

She rests her hand on mine, forcing a smile. The sadness in Maman's eyes reveals something I had not seen before. All the years she was protecting me from danger, she was also holding me captive for herself.

．　．　．

Three torturous days later, we receive word that the authorities suspect another soldier of the attack. A drunken brawl or a scuffle between low-ranking officers. The tightness in my throat begs to be set free, desperate for the fresh air of the hills.

The barrel of wine has run dry, and Maman's hands tremble, her skin damp and pale. I used to be fearful of this. Now I understand that I merely need to fill her goblet again.

"Maman, I'm leaving the house. You need more wine."

"No, Isabelle! I am fine." Her teeth chatter and her shoulders curve towards her knees.

"You are not fine."

She shakes her head and begins to whimper. "No, it's not safe."

I pull out a handwoven bit of lace to trade for a bottle of eau-de-vie. My hand rests softly on Maman's shoulder. "God will be with me." Her cold cheek rests against the back of my hand. She looks like a lost child. In need of something I can't give her.

My shoulder brushes against the wall under the arcades, hidden in the comfort of shadows. Several houses have refused a trade, urging me to return home. Today feels different. Hushed voices. Heavy faces. The injured soldier... when will he talk? What will he say? Nervousness climbs my legs and burrows into my gut.

Through an alley, movement. The delicate lace trembles in my hands. My back against the wall, images of Henri, a knife, bloody water. Maman shaking and writhing in pain. Deep breaths course through my chest, the fire in me stomps out the whispers of doubt. I creep down the alley and peer around the corner. A soldier leads a girl into the tavern by a tightened grip. She's one of us. Needles prickle at my hands and feet. More stumble through the door, shoved over the threshold when they resist.

Antoinette looks on as the girls cry and stumble, begging to return home. And then, Clémentine. Weak, frozen. The dragoons pull her, one on each arm as she screams "No, no, no." The door to the tavern closes behind them. My face flushes hot, my jaw tightens.

Marching toward her, the needles settle, leaving a pounding anger whistling in my ears. "What have you done?"

"You, again. Filthy peasant. You should slink back to your barn and never show your face again. Don't you understand that your time with Monsieur Beaumont has consequences?"

Her skin is radiant. Her eyes glow the color of a summer sky. Her beauty is a stark contrast to her blackened soul.

"Did you think a girl such as yourself could ever be with a Catholic soldier?" She sneers. "A filthy heretic with one of the King's agents."

"There is goodness in you somewhere, Antoinette. Please don't do this."

She turns her head, flicks her eyes to the sky with a deep breath. "Without Monsieur Beaumont I have no future."

"Take him. He was never mine."

"He wants you."

My chest tightens. "What is happening in the tavern?"

Her gaze back at me, she pauses. Shakes her head and smooths her skirt. "Why don't you go inside and see for yourself?" She gestures to the door. "Those are your little swine friends. I know you want to save them."

I turn toward the door, my promise to Clémentine eating away at me. She won't survive another attack.

Faith. Community. A fire in the dark.

"Well, go on then," she says.

My hand rattles the handle as the door creaks open. The dark room is silent. Black. Antoinette shoves me inside. My legs stumble and the light closes with the door.

My eyes struggle to adjust. Then, a voice. "There's another one."

The shadows take shape. A line of girls shrouded in fear. Clémentine comes into focus. The dark fades and the lines sharpen. Her bottom lip trembles, her pale skin almost translucent.

A towering man grabs me by the arm and throws me to the back of the room. I join the others. All Protestant girls. All terrified. A rowdy group of dragoons sips on ale, watching us. Some grin. Some salivate. Others stare on, disgusted or excited. Clémentine's eyes meet mine.

The tall man brings one forward and asks her to dance for the soldiers. She shakes her head no, tears streaming down her face.

He cracks a baton across her back, sending her to her knees. Her wail turns to a weep. He stares at her, tightens his grip. My forearm burns hot, pulsing and throbbing. Another girl steps forward. She squints her eyes and says, "No."

Shadows pass the warped yellow windows as people walk by. No one will help us. The next girl and the next, the same outcome. They all say no. Another whack from the baton. Each hit sends a jolt through me.

The tall man stands before Clémentine. A small circle of milk soaks the cloth over her breasts. She closes her eyes, her voice trembling. "No."

He leans back and urgency courses through me.

"I will dance for you, Monsieur."

The whimpering girls look to each other, eyes wide. The expectation for our moment of torture is that we will stand in strength. Suffer. Pride. The dragoons know this.

"Let them go, and I will dance for you," I say.

The man steps back and sits, leaning with an easy tilt of his head. "Dance, whore."

The rest of the men grab the girls by the arms, shoving them out the door into the mud and filth, kicking them after they collapse. As the door shuts, the light of morning disappears, and darkness falls upon me.

Up and down, twirling slowly, I dance. My face blank with submission, but inside fire spits and stings. Heart throbbing. Anger boiling. Every step I grow farther from my people and my purpose. Then I remember the other girls tucked safely in their beds, and I carry on.

Minutes turn to hours, and daylight turns to night. When I stop, he yells at me, so I dance. I dance through the stabbing in my feet and the aching in my back. The blackened sky has turned the musty tavern into a dungeon. Oil lamps cast their shadows over dark corners. Drifting across the floor, my legs weaken and my ankles throb.

The men drink and sing and yell. As the ale sets in, they grow louder. Belligerent. The tall one doesn't drink. He watches. One man comes up and grabs my waist to dance with me. The sickness rises in my throat. Another in his drunken state throws his beer on us, yelling for the other to sit down.

"More hips," his filthy mouth says. "I want to see your curves." With moldy smelling ale dripping from my curls, I wipe my face and dance again. With more movement of my hips this time.

All night. I dance all night. The hours bleed together. I close my eyes and pretend I'm in water, swimming with my sisters in the ocean.

When the sun shines its way through the tiny, yellowed window, my vision grows cloudy. I blink again and again but can't focus. My knees give way, the ground pulling me in.

A sudden thundering whack burns into the back of my thighs. I scream out in pain, tightening my hands against the wet wood.

"Get up," the tall man says.

My legs shake, wetness seeps from my mouth. I force myself to my knees, but my legs won't bend. The pain is too intense. My palms slide across the sticky wood as I crawl to a chair, My face rests in my arms on the seat.

"I said, get up."

My arms struggle to pull my body upright. Exhausted, I stare at the room of drunken men with only one left awake. He stands in front of me, baton in hand.

My feet sink into the ground, heavy as stone. I stumble sideways as my shoes squeeze my aching toes. I rub my eyes, my vision starting to darken. As the sounds fade, I again fall to my knees. I wait for the beating.

My shoulder hits the floor, my vision obscured. My head follows, my body releasing all the tension. Brightness floods through the open tavern door in a blinding white light. Figures of two men yell at each other, then something lifts me up. I float away from the wet and stale ground, helpless. The scent of James brings my focus back, and the pain lessens.

My eyes begin to focus. The dragoon lies on the ground with blood dripping from his mouth. He spits on the ground and says, "Until next time, pretty one."

The smell of old ale and wine wafts away. The bright autumn sun pierces my sore eyes, my hand attempts to shield them, palm to the light. A small shape comes to focus on the ground. The lace I dropped, covered in mud, crumpled and torn.

"No one can see you with me," I whisper into the soft fold of his neck.

"Shh. It's barely daybreak."

The memory of his betrayal seems far away. His skin warms my cheek, my weak arms cradle his shoulders.

He kicks open the door to my empty house. Lowering me to the bed, he softly lays my head on the pillow.

"Where is your mother?" he asks.

"We were out of wine. When desperate, she drinks from our neighbor's barrels, where they let her sleep by the fire until she can walk home."

He wets a rag and rubs it over my face and hair with a gentleness that makes my rigid body soften. He lifts a jug to my lips, helping me sip the cool water inside. He begins to step away, but I grasp his hand. "You saved me."

He lowers to the chair at my bedside. "Your friend Henri found me early this morning. Told me you were in trouble."

"How did he know?"

"A girl named Clémentine. She walked across town during the night to find him."

Clémentine faced her fears to save me. The thought floods me with warmth.

"Antoinette," he says with a shake of his head.

My mind begins to sharpen. "How did you know it was her?"

"The dragoon told me. Antoinette brings them entertainment. In turn, the man with the baton makes sure the LaMarche ships get an extra load of cargo."

"She follows you. She'll have me sent to the galleys if she sees you with me."

"Let me worry about her."

He unlaces my boots, undeterred by their frayed edges. My hand stops him. "I'll do it."

My swollen feet slither from the leather shoes. My stockings seep red and brown, stained with dried blood. I cringe as I pull them from the weeping blisters. My bruised toes wiggle, the fat purple stubs grateful to breathe free.

James watches me, not saying a word. I should feel embarrassed, but I don't. This is the reality of my world, and I will not hide from it.

The tender skin on the back of my legs burns fire hot. I run my hands along a raised line from the lashing. Again, I wince. James breathes deeply to stop the tears cresting his eyes.

"Isabelle." He reaches for my face.

"Mother wishes me to marry," I say.

His chest drops as if I've stolen his air and left him with an empty, bleeding chest. "I will not allow you to suffer like this any longer."

I turn from him, so his soulful eyes don't break my will.

"The Catholics, the dragoons, they all see themselves as warriors, carrying out the wishes of the King," he says. "They won't stop until everyone has converted. And everyone else, they'll kill."

"Then leave me to my destiny."

"This is not your destiny," he says.

My head shakes no, eyes closed.

"I know I'm special to you too. I can feel it. I see it when you look at me. Become Catholic. Be mine."

"It's not possible, James."

He takes my hand in his, runs his fingers along my wrist. They find their way to the inside of my arm, grazing the outline of my scar. I pull away and tuck my arm in my sleeve.

"What is this?" He pulls back the loosened fabric, examining the ugliest part of myself. The crudely outlined letter H, raised and thick, stares at me.

"I was eight. Mother and I were walking back from prayer at Etienne's house." My neck tingles with the memory. "Dragoons prowled the streets, seeking out the people who lived in secret. They grabbed the children. The men held down the mothers with knives to their throats, while others seared us with a branding iron." The thumping in my head grows. "An H. Huguenot or heretic. I was never quite sure."

I lift my arm, examining the tendrils of webbed flesh, and I remember the screaming. My own. The other children. The mothers rocking and covering their eyes. "My arm. Henri's calf. We carry the ugly memory on our bodies. Our skin smoked, turned black, and settled into the scars that now bond us closer than we already were."

The large bump on his throat slides up as he swallows. His chest rises in a deep inhale.

"When I feel powerless it burns hot in memory of that day. The day I learned that we would never be free. Look closely, James. The girl you long for is a symbol for all that society hates."

"It doesn't have to be that way. Let me protect you."

"From what, the world?" I say.

"Yes, if that is what it takes."

"The Catholics killed my father after stealing his ships. My grandfather, uncles, and aunts all died in a siege where the King starved them for fifteen months. I watched a man I cared for dragged naked and lifeless by a rope, and the dragoons gifted me this." I lift my scar. "You want me to turn on all of them? What will I have then?"

"You would have me."

"It would devastate my mother."

Still holding my hand, he says, "What do you want?"

"Why must you make it so difficult to see the world clearly?" I say.

"I see it more clearly than I ever have before."

His smile almost breaks me. "But my community. They're part of me."

"I'm sure they're good people. But the premise that suffering is one's destiny? I can't believe that."

He holds my wrist in his hand. Lifting it, he gingerly touches his mouth to my forearm. His lips land softly on my scar. My eyes close and I grow dizzy from the thrill of his touch. He leans closer, his breath in my ear.

"I wish you to be free."

My eyelids flutter open. James's face is nearly touching mine. I whisper, "I hope to feel that someday. But if I leave Protestantism, it will be of my own choice, not to feel the touch of a man."

My branded arm still in his grasp, he lifts my palm to his face. The bristling roughness of his skin shifts under my hand as he smiles. "I will wait for you then."

The ground has disappeared, hovering somewhere over my head. I now stand precariously on the sky as the world surely has been turned upside down.

FIRE IN THE DARKNESS

Maman bursts through the door with darkened, wild eyes. "Isabelle! What happened to you?" She rushes to my side. "I've been sick with worry. Are you all right?"

The stale smell of her breath tells me that Maman found a flowing jug of wine to ease her worry, fighting the reality that waited for her when she awoke.

"I'm fine, Maman."

"No, you are not."

Raising to sit, I wince, causing her to whimper.

She throws the blanket off me and sees the swollen ankles and the torn flesh of my feet. She stares at me, motionless, mouth open. She drops to her knees and flings her head onto my hand. Through sobs, she says, "What has he done to you?"

"He? Who is he?"

"That Monsieur Beaumont." She curls her lip and shakes her head. "I knew he would only cause us pain."

"Maman, stop! This was the dragoons. They made me dance for them all night in the tavern. Henri found James, who saved me."

"No, no…" Her head shakes wildly to push out the notion that James was anything more than a devil in soldier's clothing. "You will marry. I can arrange for it immediately." She begins pacing the room, stopping to clutch her stomach.

"Maman, no. I'm not ready." I struggle to the chair, my head foggy and pounding.

"They live outside the walls of the city. They have a farm, and food. We'll be safer there." She speaks to herself in the reflection of the window. She turns to see my fallen expression.

"We won't be any safer in the country. They've set fire to farms and beaten families. The Catholics steal animals and burn crops. It's the same fight out there as it is in here!"

Maman clasps her hands in prayer. "Please, God, save my child from the wicked Catholics and bring her back to faith. Let her find truth."

"Maman, I never left."

"This is where it starts. You fall for a Catholic soldier. He makes you believe you're special when you are nothing but a conquest for him. He tells you what you believe is wrong. And finally, he takes you from me."

"Nothing is taking me from you!"

"He already has." Tears crest her reddened eyes. "You think about it. I see it on your face."

"Think about what?"

"Turning from your faith. Betraying your people. Leaving me to die."

"Enough. I would never leave you." A twisting pain tightens deep in my stomach.

"He's seduced you to believe that life will be better if you come to his side, hasn't he? He's no better than a dragoon."

My eyes lower to my knees.

"Don't be a fool. You'll always be one of us. They will never accept you." She squints her eyes. "Believe me when I tell you, James Beaumont does not love you. He wants to control you."

"I don't believe God wishes us to suffer. You and I could live a peaceful life and still practice our faith in secret, like we always have." Desperation drips from my voice.

"And you could marry the soldier? Carry on as a Catholic and spit in the face of your family?"

"No," I say, tears leaking from the corners of my eyes. "To save us."

"Listen to me, child." She grabs my arm. "The man is dangerous."

"What would you have me do? Fade away alone in this house drinking wine until I feel no pain, watching everyone I love die?" Regret stings my mouth, tinged by my hateful words.

"You walk these streets every day, risking an attack, and every day I fear that you will never again open that door. You're all I have left. The thought that you've been hurt by one of..." Her voice shakes as she turns her eyes to my bruised feet. "Those monsters. I cannot bear it."

"I don't wish to be Catholic. But..." A long breath settles my nerves. "Imagine, no more suffering. No more torture."

Her face turns gray. Her fingers clutch her chest as if to keep her heart beating.

"It could save us both. No more hiding in the prison of our home, no more threats from the dragoons. We would be free."

She turns from ash to fire red, swiftly whipping her hand across my face. I gasp, my cheek stings and tears spring to my eyes.

"Shut your mouth, child! Do not betray your commitment to God for the promises of a selfish liar." She stumbles to her goblet, knocking it over with her trembling hands, pouring out the last drops of wine from our jug.

"James was a Huguenot! He understands our pain." I rub my stinging cheek.

She halts. "He what?"

"His family converted when he was a child. He was one of us."

"And what is he now? A traitor who helps them kill our people." She shuffles toward me, looks me in the eyes, and says, "What would Etienne think of you now?"

My stomach drops. "I'm confused." My shoulders collapse into a deep cry. She stands over me, watching me sob. I force myself to stand against the searing pain of my feet. "I want to make you proud. I want to make Grand-mère and Etienne proud and live a good life. But I don't want to suffer any longer." I hang my head. "They will kill us all."

"Then that will be our fate."

Maman is like spider silk. Thin and spindly and yet a strong wind cannot budge her.

"I want more for us, and I 'm not afraid to risk our lives to get it," I say.

"Neither am I, Isabelle. Neither am I."

I collapse on the bed, crushed. Mother is right about one thing — I am certainly no longer a child.

.   .   .

I've spent days in bed while my feet heal. Maman tends to my skin, cleaning and wrapping my feet with little spoken between us. I've been quietly questioning if I'm meant to follow my mother's wishes and accept the challenge of this life or find the fire amid the darkness Grand-mère always spoke of. The confusion is only made worse by my longing for James. My mind keeps wandering to Maman's words. Is James not as he seems?

I wrap my toes in cloth and squeeze them into my well-worn boots.

"What are you doing?" Maman asks.

"I need rose oil to rub on my feet. I can't stand to be in this room any longer."

"Fine, then I will go with you." She stands and wraps herself in a cloak.

"Maman?"

She raises her hand. "I will no longer let you risk your safety, and I can't trust you to stay away from dangerous people. So, we go together."

The darkened clouds hover over us. Maman has not seen these streets in years. Her eyes dart from side to side, wary of all that move past her. The only thing she's more committed to than her faith is me. We approach the home, but something rumbles in the distance.

"Isabelle, what is that?"

"I don't know." My feet move toward the sound. The rumble forms into chants and screams that cause my fingers to tremble.

"Isabelle." Maman pulls at my cape. "Let's go home."

I ignore her, pulled to the belly of our town square, calling me to witness something. What, I'm not sure.

Maman presses against my back, clutching the sides of my cape. We arrive at a crowd of townsfolk filling the space between the tall buildings. Onlookers peer out their opened windows, screaming and pumping their fists in the air. The thumping of riotous voices surrounds us. We hover at the edge of the crowd, silent. A tingle crawls up my neck. My swollen feet prickle as if my shoes are full of needles.

"No man is above the law!" A booming voice rises from the center of the square. The Catholics cheer in triumph, while the others lower their eyes. Maman begs me to turn back, but I can't walk away.

"Lawlessness, and heresy. That is what we have here today, my friends!" The crowd erupts while Maman tightens her fingers on my arm. "Our soldier identified his attacker as the silversmith. He has confessed, and today he will pay for his sins!"

My knees buckle. A stifling fear grips my chest. "Henri. No," I cry. Tears pool in my scratchy eyes.

"What?" Maman says.

I make my way to the front of the crowd, pushing through the mass of people rich with body odor. Tears stream down my cheeks, my body aching. My mother follows closely behind, the yelling thunders in my ears. My hands pull two women apart. Then, I see him. Henri's father Louis tied to stakes suspended over branches and leaves.

Maman holds my arm tight as she whimpers, "Louis."

I scan the crowd and see Henri, standing in full view of his father's execution. He tries to pull away, but a guard holds him by a fistful of hair. They force the family to watch. A warning for what happens when heretics rebel. Louis keeps his head tall, eyes focused on his only son. His face reveals no fear, but his hands ball into fists.

My head grows light, my legs ready to collapse. The only thing stopping me from wilting to the ground is Maman, crying into my shoulder. I scan the other side of the crowd and find James. He takes a step toward me. I raise my hand, gesturing for him to stop. He steps back, his eyes steady.

"This is why we must fight against heresy, for the church is our only defense against evil. Those who fight the Catholic church will face the full vengeance of the Sun King!" Cheers erupt from the angry crowd.

Henri screams, "It was me! It was me! Let him go."

Henri's father roars, "I sliced his flesh with my knife and shattered his bones with my bare hands. I did it."

The villagers erupt. Henri drops to his knees, sobbing. He rocks back and forth, until the guard pulls his head upright. Tears stream down Henri's face. The sight hammers into my soul like nails.

The soldier preaches of lawlessness and loyalty to the Crown, the evils of Protestantism, and the mighty Sun King. Louis closes his eyes, muttering a prayer to himself. My insides churn. The thumping in my ears drowns out the ringing of screams that surround me.

Another man pours oil over him, his dark hair dripping down his face. His shirt shines, reflecting the light of the torch. The flame comes into my view, forcing out a gasp, my eyes wide. Desperate for goodness to prevail, knowing there is none.

The Catholic raises the torch high in the air, screaming, "Long live the Sun King! Those that attack us will perish under his mighty fury. This heretic has refused the sacrament before death, and for that, he will live eternity in the hell he has chosen."

The man with the torch lights the fire, smoke billowing up all sides of Louis. He coughs and thrashes against his bound arms and legs. Amid his torturous fear, he turns his head for one last glimpse of his son. The heat catches the oil, and the flames of red, orange, and blue overtake his figure.

My breath gone, my chest frozen.

Henri, helpless and crying, watches his father's last moments. Louis's head begins to glow white. He releases a horrid scream that pierces the air. I bury my face in my mother's arms as I sob. She places her hand over the back of my head, forcing me to look away.

Her stomach jerks, trying not to retch as she covers her mouth. The screams of Louis and the crowd disappear, leaving only the crackling fire and unmistakable bitter odor of seared flesh turning to ash. Louis took the punishment for his child's sins. Nothing is stronger than the love of family. Mother drags me back home. I turn to look back at James, who watches Mother pull me away, the divide between us growing wider.

. . .

We sit in stunned silence for hours, the quiet of the day broken only by occasional bouts of crying and sniffling. I stare at the blackened fireplace, still smelling the burnt hair in my nose. If odors bear pain, this is one that shall suffocate me with its emotional scent until the day that I die.

She pours glasses of wine, setting one in front of each of us.

I turn from her. "I'm not thirsty."

"This is not for you. It's for Louis." She hands me the glass.

I reluctantly grab it, my arms weak.

"He is with God now. Let us raise a glass to him and remember his kind soul, and may his family find solace in the words of prayer." She sips the wine ever so slowly.

I can't bring myself to drink, so I let the wine touch my lips in honor of Louis. I place the glass down and wilt onto my bed. The air is heavy. I feel it on my skin. My mother prays, but her words bring me no comfort, for I know that my life will only bring more suffering. More pain. I have no choice but to lie enveloped in agonizing sorrow until the night swallows me.

. . .

The events of last week hang over us. Not just mother and me, but every Huguenot in town. As though the world shrinks around us, getting so small that our bodies barely fit in the space they take up.

It's a cold October evening, and the sky is black with impending winter. In our clearing, protected by trees and darkness, we share the only church we know — nature in secret.

"We must leave immediately," one whispers.

"They would burn us all at the stake! We aren't permitted to flee," another says in a hushed tone.

"Where would we go? It's happening all over France. Is there anywhere we can be safe?" a worried mother asks.

Our pastor puts his hands up to quiet us. "Friends, these are trying times. This struggle has always been difficult, and never more so than when one of our own meets a painful end."

Everyone listens, as if he has answers from God.

Henri stands alone in the darkened shadows at the edge of the crowd. Stepping away, I reach for his hand, his eyes not leaving the blackness in front of him.

"What have I done?" he says. "How do I continue to live, knowing what he did for me?"

Tightness grabs at my throat. "I'm so sorry."

He hangs his head. "What is it all for?"

"I don't know, Henri." I hug him, leaning my cheek on his shoulder.

"You should have let me kill the dragoon."

"Yes." Tears prickle my eyes. "Your father's death will sit heavy on my heart forever."

"I can't stay here. I have nothing left. We all have nothing left," he says. He pulls away from my arms.

"We have each other." I gesture to those in prayer.

"And we shall all perish together. Is that what you want?"

"I don't know what I want."

"Yes, you do. You want freedom. Come with me," he says.

"Leave La Rochelle?"

"Yes. We can escape this hatred. This senseless suffering. Maybe start a new Protestant community, far away from here."

"Oh, Henri. I can't leave." I lower my eyes. "Our people need me."

He grabs my arms and shakes me to attention. "Isabelle, our people will all die. Including you. Your soldier can't save you. You must save yourself. Do you understand?"

I nod, too afraid to reason with him.

"I would rather die reaching for freedom than allow them my surrender. You and I, we have questioned this life when no one else would. You know there's more to our faith than this, don't you?"

"I hope so." My heart sinks again. Bubbling inside are the words that are always with me, *find a fire in the darkness.*

"I'm going to escape tonight. Please pray for me. I can't look at this place for one more minute. It's too painful."

"How will you get to America?"

"I'll hire a shipowner to take me or pretend to be Catholic or insane. I'll find a way." He shakes his head and closes his eyes.

I squeeze his hand tight. What is right or wrong, good or bad? Who knows anymore.

"They killed my father," he says in a broken voice.

I throw my arms around him, my body shaking with his as he weeps. I move his black curls aside and tighten his scarlet cravat. "Please be safe, Henri. I wish I could convince you to stay with us."

"Someday, Isabelle, we will see each other again. I promise you that." He flashes his wild smile, still hopeful after all that he has lost. He disappears into the night.

The aching in my chest softens as I imagine him starting over in a faraway land. Free.

I place my hand on my mother's arm, "We should head back, we've been out here too long already."

"Yes, soon." She joins the rest in a tight circle.

Walking through the trees, I turn to watch the circle of figures in black, standing in silence, enveloped in prayer. They form a ring with intertwined hands. Through touch, they speak to each other in understanding without a sound moving between them.

Drawn to the edge of the clearing, I pull back bare branches with the dwindling leaves of fall. Lights flicker from the lanterns in town. My entire life has felt like standing in a dark forest outside the world of other people, looking in at what might be.

EXILE

The wet November morning carries a heaviness, the air saturated with something thick. I wake with the weight of it on my chest, restlessness stirring inside me. I walk to the window, inspecting the dark clouds that block out the sun.

"What are you looking at?" Maman asks as she lights the candles from the fire.

"I'm not sure," I say, my eyes scanning the sky.

"Well, stop daydreaming. It's time for morning prayers.

I ignore her. "Is it something in the sky? Or in the air?"

"I might faint if you tell me you're going outside today. The wind is screaming, and the sky looks ready to burst."

"No, I don't think I will." The room bounces with shadows, the darkness bathed in yellow candlelight. "Do you hear something?"

Maman, worried by the smallest of sounds, looks to the ceiling and rubs her palms on her thighs.

"Is it thunder?" A candlestick resting on the rough-hewn table shakes ever so subtly.

Maman's fingers crawl over each other, twitching.

A faint rumble begins far in the distance, the sounds of a disturbance. My hand slides to my belly, feeling the hard pulse of distress deep in my stomach. Working to calm my breath, I listen as the rumble begins to carry high pitched wails.

The shadows flicker as our neighbors run past the window in a frenzy. My trembling hand opens the door. "What is it?" Maman asks, her hands clasped in front of her mouth.

Stepping into the wet air, the rush of frightened families whirls around me like a windstorm. Tears fall from their eyes, clutching items of worth against their rounded chests, shoulders at their ears.

My breathing swooshes through my ears. I grab a woman's arm. "What is happening?"

"The Catholics are driving us from the city. You must leave right away."

She tries to flee my grasp, but I pull her back. "I don't understand."

She yells over the loud drum of thunder rolling, "They're tearing Huguenots from their homes and beating them. Killing them. Get out of the city walls as fast as you can!" She snaps her arm from me and joins the rush of people.

Maman leans against the wall, praying. "Not now!" I pull her toward me, grabbing her shoulders and shaking her. "You must hold yourself together."

She blinks, nodding to indicate she has heard me. I don my cape as Maman fills a small pouch with the few coins we possess. "We must be smart. Don't leave my side and do not run. The Port is too dangerous, it will block us in. We must cut through town."

As we leave our darkened house, I hold back tears and focus on Maman, who pulls back from me.

"Wait." She runs to the mantel, loosening the stone. She tucks our Bible in the hidden pocket of her skirt, the bag of coins in her tightened fist. Our Bible bears more value to her than the money we will need to survive.

I pull her against the wall, away from the thumping feet. I look over my shoulder to watch our house drift away. Droves of peasants crawl the streets and alleys, yelling for their families. The rain pours down over us. Around the corner, a man and woman huddle over their children, as angry Catholics beat them with sticks. A mother cries, clutching her baby, her husband dying at her feet.

Maman crumbles. Holding her keeps me from falling to my knees. Around me, screams roll out in waves. Torturous, terrified screams.

The next street, a man fights for his home, struck with the blunt end of a sword, then with the soldier's fist. My legs wobble on the uneven cobblestones.

All the years I've traversed these streets. I know how to do this.

I pull Maman into an alley, behind a barrel. Men storm past with purpose. "They aren't just dragoons. The nobility too. The regular townsfolk. They're all turning on us."

Maman closes her eyes and rocks. "We'll never make it."

My hands tighten around her shoulders, shaking her to look at me. "The staircase to the town hall. There's an alcove hidden from view just behind it. We do this one street at a time. Understand?"

Her head shakes yes. Her pale face is damp, her hands clammy. Stepping sideways, our hands glide across the wall. We move left at the butcher, right at the curve of the turret.

Under the arches, we rush through the arcade, under the elaborate, beautiful carvings where the screams echo and magnify. Into the courtyard. No time to think. Maman pulls back, but I yank her forward. Behind two men ripping a basket of clothing from an old woman, then kicking her in the ankles. I won't let the image settle in my mind. If I accept the awful things I see as real, I will wilt to the ground with Maman. Into the darkened corner, we hug the wall, the cold air enveloping us.

Outside, the patter of feet. Two little girls sneak between arches, holding hands and searching for their parents. My face grows hot. My aching heart forces my feet to move. With a swift grab of one arm, "Come," I tell the older one. She grabs her sister's hand.

I motion to Maman, who presses her cheek to the wall, weeping. My arm linked through hers, I drag her out. We make it to the end of the side street, but we're still held in by the towering wall.

"Stay close."

Back toward the center of town. Swords fly. Water runs past our feet, bright red. Blood splashed on the walls seeps down with the rain. Blood and screams everywhere.

"North from the Mayor's house, a broken area of wall takes us to the woods. No screaming. And don't look closely at anything. Understand?"

The girls nod, their trusting eyes watch my every move. The sky rumbles. A deep breath cleanses my fear.

One arm around Maman's waist, the other around the tiny hand of a terrified child. We enter the belly of chaos.

Past a dragoon beating a man protecting his family. The soldier's baton cracks against the man's face, his blood splatters onto me. I wipe my forehead with my sleeve and carry on.

A twelve-year-old boy, dead. Crumpled and blue in a puddle of blood. A grandmother, dead. Our pastor, dead. Bodies scattered like they were dropped from the sky with the rain. I yank at Maman, ignoring her cries.

My fear turns to anger. Rage. Hot pokers light up my feet and send fire up my legs. We slide against the walls, waiting for the men to attack those crying. We slip past while they meet their fate. We might all perish, but I will not give them the satisfaction of my fear.

A dragoon steps over the body of a woman in a muddy puddle, marching toward us. I stand firm, shoving the girls to the side. "Go now." They stare at me, lips trembling. "Now!"

My stare unflinching on the soldier, his baton in hand. He approaches, his face red. I shove Maman away and ready my stance. Exhale. My moment is here.

He raises his baton, landing it on my ribs. A sharp, fiery stab steals my breath, claws at my chest and stomach, leaving nothing. No air. No sound. Only the hard cold stones hitting my shoulder. My body coils, seizing. A thud to my chest pulls me back to earth, air filling my body. Searing pain sends my side into a hot, tight spasm. My wet hair hangs in my eyes, obscuring my vision. Everything is foggy. Sounds float somewhere outside of myself. Time slows to a halt. My hand clutches my side, the cloud out my mouth ensures I am once again breathing.

Why hasn't he hit me again? My head begins to throb. I wait for another blow, focusing my eyes and wiping my curls from my face. Maman.

She's crouched, hands over her face. Her skirt pulled back to her knees. The soldier hovers over her, our Bible in his hand. My limbs tingle. He opens the Bible and releases a ball of spit, which slowly drips down his chin onto the pages. He throws it to the side, cast into a pile of filth from emptied chamber pots.

My back won't straighten, so I crawl. Shaking hands in the bloody water claw my way toward Maman. He slaps her. Hard. Maman is on her side, not moving.

His fist balls up the front of her dress. His baton sits on the ground behind him. Heaving, I pull my skirt from my knees and stumble, crawling closer. I drag it from the ground and swing at his legs. The sound whips through the air as the iron lands on the fleshy backs of his knees. They buckle. He catches himself at the ground with a scream. Maman crawls to me. I should run, but something takes over. My legs find their strength and both my hands grip the baton. My feet wobble but my arms find the swing against the stabbing pain in my side. The baton lands across his back, the snap of a cracking bone. The man howls in pain.

Something heavy and thick drips into my eye. I wipe it with the back of my hand and shake it off. The blood spatters on our Bible, already spoiled by a Catholic's spit. Maman reaches for it. I stop her. "No."

We stammer away from the writhing dragoon. My arm around Maman, I drag her, weak as a baby, past the Mayor's house. At the foot of the stairs, James. He throws a dragoon to the ground and kicks him with the tip of his shoe.

He sees us, and my legs begin to falter. He swoops us in his arms, tucking us into the curve of the staircase.

Maman falls to the ground. James wipes more blood from my brow. I wince, hand on my ribs.

"Isabelle."

"I'm fine." I choke back tears, the images worming their way into my mind.

"You weren't at your house. I couldn't find you."

"What is happening, James?"

"Monsieur LaMarche convinced the leaders to seize property from Huguenots. By any means necessary."

"Why?" I grab at his arms, growing weak.

"To prove loyalty to the King. My father is one of them. He's too weak. Too afraid our past will return."

"They killed them. Children. Babies." The wind snaps at my cheeks. "They killed them."

He pulls me into his embrace, caressing my hair. "I came here to convince the mayor to retreat. It appears it's too late."

I pull back from him. "Did you know about this?"

"I heard grumblings. I thought it was merely chatter. We must get you out of here. They're thirsty for blood."

"You're one of them, James." I step back from him.

"No. You know me. I'm not the same as them. I'm just trying to survive. Let me prove it to you."

He lifts Maman and wraps his fingers through mine. He leads us down one more street, nearing the edge of town. Past the wealthy and powerful houses where they watch the horror from their terraces and windows. As if it were theater. Entertainment.

The pain grows in my side, my temples pulse, but my legs now march with force. We pass the LaMarche home. The giant, stately, ornate home of the most wicked man alive. My fingers uncurl from James's grasp. In the second-floor window, Antoinette stands still, watching me.

Anger thunders inside me. She lowers her gaze, partly hidden behind a curtain. James wraps his arm around my waist, pulling me closer. My gaze doesn't waver from hers. The shame in her dissipates like the ocean tide. Her shoulders grow tall. She purses her lips and throws the curtain shut.

"No!" Maman screams.

A man yanks the coin bag from her hand. She tried to hold on, but he shoves her to the ground.

James lifts Maman, hand out to the man who sneers with blackened teeth.

"I got all I need. On your way," the man says.

We climb over the remnants of the ramparts, built by Protestants that came before me. They destroyed our temples during the futile resistance to build this protective wall. All these sacred stones that once housed prayers and wishes and hope for a better future now lie silent and decrepit, reminding us of our failures. Nothing can protect us from the evil that rests in man's hearts.

The rain falls faster and louder as we climb into the hills. My mother falls to her knees, hands trembling. My hands are thick with wet earth and blood. Wiping them on my dress leaves finger streaks along my hips.

James grabs my shoulders, his face doused in rainwater. His amber curls rustled, one stray lock tumbles over his right eye.

"Isabelle, go to our chestnut tree. Stay there until I can come back for you."

"Where are you going?"

"We'll need supplies. A horse. Food," he says.

"You will come back for me?"

He pulls me into him, his soft lips pressing against mine. My shoulders relax into his hands, the strength in his grip melting to a softened embrace. He pulls back and looks in my eyes. "I will always come for you."

He runs down the hill, back to town. The kiss floats like a cloud in front of me. Then, as the dreamy haze dissipates, I'm left with the reality of exile.

The sadness rolls out of town in waves, each one bleaker than the last. The desperate faces fill me with aching sadness as they cry and shake. The rain washes over me, blending with the tears streaming down my face. All the pain I've seen in my young life, and I'm always powerless. My fist tightens, my scar pulsing. I run my fingers along the raised outline. All my questions suddenly fall away, and all I feel is determination. The letter H burns with symbolic fire, feeding my soul with the courage to fight.

I pick up Maman, deep in prayer, and lead her to the chestnut tree. We sit in the dirt, backs against the broad trunk. There's no way to escape that our life is gone. Taken from us. So, we huddle, and we pray.

.   .   .

We spend the night leaning on each other's shoulders, arms around each other for warmth. I sleep some but spend most of the night watching my breath dance away from my mouth and form shapes in the air. The sounds still haunt my mind. Bloody families, Dead bodies. Shrill screams. Maman manages some sleep, trying to escape the overwhelming fear.

I wake to tightened cheeks and a dripping nose, hands tucked inside my cape between my knees. The sound of footsteps jolts me awake.

I jump, seeing only my warmed breath again meet the frost. My hands shake, facing the empty morning as my eyes dart back and forth. Then comes the image of James leading a dappled grey Percheron up the hill.

"Maman, wake up." I jostle her shoulder. "James is back." Her sleepy eyes try to focus.

"Isabelle." He wraps his arms around me, cradling my head in his steady hand. My cheek against his chest feels like my only hope in the world.

He helps my mother to stand. "I was able to find a horse, and here." He points to a bag draped over its side. "There's food and money."

"I don't understand." My mother looks to me for reassurance. "Can't we go home now?"

After a pause and a glance at the ground, he says, "No."

"What do you mean, no? They can't take our home. It is *ours*," she says.

"A Catholic family has already taken over your house." My knees buckle and James catches me. "Gifted to them by Monsieur LaMarche at the urging of his daughter."

"Antoinette." My legs stumble for their footing, turning me east to the hills to hide my eyes welling with tears. "We have nowhere to go. Without our house, we have nothing." My voice trails off with the wind.

Silence settles. James helps my mother to the horse, onto the saddle for an unknown journey. His hand reaches for mine, softly grabbing my fingers and turning me toward him.

"My sweet Isabelle, I'm so sorry it's come to this." He shakes his head.

"Won't you come with us?" I say, like a child. I hope for the words I want to hear but know what words will come. He shakes his head, no.

"I can't leave. My father has threatened to arrest you both. He will hunt you down and chain you to the tower wall if I don't return. I need you to get far away from La Rochelle, and I'll find a way back to you."

"Where will we go?" I ask.

"Follow the post roads to Rouen. There's a priest there, he's kind. His name is Father Hyacinth. He helped me once. I believe he will help you as well."

"You want me to walk around a strange town asking for a Catholic priest?"

"It's the only place you have a chance at safety," he says.

"And you?"

He looks over his shoulder, then back at me. "I'm not welcome in Rouen. They remember who I used to be."

"So, we must lie about who we are."

Maman says, "We will not do it."

"Thank you for helping us," I say, my voice trembling. The hopes of yesterday now a fading memory.

He reaches into his pocket. He places in my hand a delicate gold chain with a Catholic cross pendant. "If you find trouble, put this on. Tell them you're Catholics traveling from La Rochelle to visit family."

Maman gasps. The necklace shines in my hand, feeling as if it might burn my palm. Looking deep into James's eyes, my stomach drops, and my heart splinters.

Tears cascade down my cheeks. The choices I once had are now gone. My only option is to trust James and journey to Rouen without him.

He places his hand on my cheek. His voice firm but tender. "I need you to stay safe."

"That might be impossible now."

He takes my face in his hands and pulls me in to kiss him. Feeling his lips on mine, and the protection of his arms, I long to return home.

"Merci, Monsieur Beaumont." Maman looks away as the words leave her mouth. "Say your goodbyes, Isabelle."

The hard line of his cheekbones and the softness of his broad smile will be the image I hold onto through our long journey. The tears fall once again. "Will I ever see you again?"

"I'll make certain you do. Promise you won't forget me." He pulls me into him, and I bury my face in his chest, feeling the last moments of his touch.

When he looks in my eyes, the pain of it all fades, only for a moment. I breathe in the quiet of it, never wanting this feeling to leave me.

Rope in one hand, James's fading touch in the other, I take my first steps as a new woman, one without a home, a community, or the resolve of her faith. All I have now is hope.

As we set off northeast into the rolling hills, La Rochelle becomes a fading vision, remnants of a home that has shown me little outside of disappointment and loss. The family I once had now gone, left to scatter the countryside alone.

I pull back my shoulders and look ahead, saying goodbye to the hills I've tiptoed through in the dark for secret church and forested berries in the summer sun. Saying goodbye to the horrors of our past, I welcome a chance at a new life. I begin the arduous unknown path before us, armed with the trust of a young man and the strength of a woman who has nothing left to lose.

THE LONG ROAD TO ROUEN

My feet ache like they did the night I danced for the dragoons. We stop for our horse to sip water, my weary legs grateful for the rest. We eat small bites of bread and cheese and sleep once again under the November sky. The farther we travel from the coast, the colder the air. Filled with mist, it blankets the countryside in an ethereal haze. If not for the protection of its secrecy, I'd be cursing its icy temperatures as my legs feel like creaking steel.

"We won't lie. We will find another way." Maman's voice breaks the long hours of silence.

"Yes, Maman." My fingers tighten around the reigns.

"We stay true to who we are. Always."

Riding the horse with her, her hair catches my attention. Once thick brown that flickered red in the sunlight, the strands have now thinned to silver. Spending all those years in the dark prevented me from seeing who she had become. I still remembered her as the woman I saw through a child's eyes. Only now do I see how broken she is.

"I threw the necklace away. You need not worry."

"Good," she says.

We settle under an oak tree, our trusty horse by our side. The ground is cold and hard. Our coiffes over our heads, followed by our capes and hoods, we curl together for warmth. My mind floats to my bed back in La Rochelle, fire roaring, belly warmed by food and wine. I've spent much of the last few years fighting my mother, and now, I lay on the frozen ground with only her embrace to keep me warm.

Her arm around me sends me into a deep and painful memory that hides in the far corners of my mind. One that is better to remain forgotten.

We never speak of my sisters, it's too painful. The only sounds are a howling wind, Maman's breath on the back of my head, and my thoughts. Elisabeth and Anne were one and three when sickness ripped through the town. I was eight and stronger than my little sisters. My father died when Elisabeth was still in my mother's belly, and that night she had only the support of my grandmother to help care for her sick children.

Our skin had turned rough like scratchy wool, covered in rouge spots. We were pink from the heat inside our bodies, with searing pain in our throats. Grand-mère placed wet linen over our foreheads and rubbed oil on our sore bodies.

We teetered in and out of sleep. On my side, their little bodies curled into mine as Mother fetched water. My arm wrapped around them, the heat from their bodies felt like fire drifting into the air. The bucket full of stench filled the room with a suffocating foulness even after Grand-mère emptied it. The retching had passed, and we lay ever so still. Their breathing slowed, and their limbs stopped shaking. They were calm, and so was I. I drifted to sleep listening to the wheezing of their breath in and out.

The next day was a blur of confusion, as the heat in my body sent my mind into a trance. Maman and Grand-mère were crying but I was unable to focus my eyes. I would wake briefly for one of them to force me to sip water, wondering why I didn't feel little Anne and Elisabeth next to me. Hours later, I woke wet with a clear focus to find that they were gone; their tiny bodies wrapped in white linen, Maman weeping and praying over them.

She never forgave herself for leaving. By the time she returned, Elisabeth was gone, and Anne drew her last breath a few hours later. I'm grateful I was able to wrap them in my arms during their last day on earth. I've slept alone every night since only now feeling my mother's arm around me like I did for them many years ago.

Maman sleeps soundly, and tears stream down my cheeks. I pull her arm around my shoulders and welcome the iciness of the earth.

. . .

We continue our trek along the post road towards St. Maixent. The air warms as we head along Sèvre Niortaise, a river that meanders like a serpent. We stop midday for the horse to rest, letting him graze on patches of grass as we find them. We sit beside each other, eating the last of the dried meat and savoring the break from the cold. Maman is stoic and quiet as ever.

"I'm so sorry. For everything." I burst into tears.

"Isabelle, what could you be sorry about?"

The memories that washed over me last night sit heavy on my heart. "I'm sorry for being so difficult. I've been a selfish child. Focusing on the wrong things when I should have committed to my family. We've lost so much."

"Child, you could never disappoint me." Her arms tighten around me. Resting her quivering hand under my chin, she turns my face toward her. "Your spirit is why you have survived. It's how I can stay strong when all seems to be falling apart." She turns her head to cough.

"But you are so much stronger, Maman. Your faith is resolute and unwavering. I find myself questioning what God wishes for me."

"Isabelle, I've lost most everything." She smooths my hair at its part and flashes a warm smile. "I never question my faith because, without it, all of this would have been for nothing. I cannot believe that would be the end of our already tragic story." Her arm rests across her belly, trying to hide a wince.

"I'm tired of all the loss. Is it ever possible to feel free?" I ask.

The worry stretches across her thin face. I lean my head on her shoulder, her damp cheek resting on my head.

"We always have freedom in our choices," she says. "It's consequences we cannot escape."

. . .

We travel into the country of Northwest France in this foggy December. Our words are few, leaving the sounds of the hills to reverberate in my ears. My body sinks into the horse, straining to hold up Maman's weight against me. It's becoming harder to ignore the cough she tries to hide. Her ribs rattle against one another, as her lungs gurgle, full and wet.

I sit tall, so she doesn't feel me weaken. My skin tingles with anticipation. Change is coming.

Late in the afternoon, she begins to moan. I move closer to listen to her words and notice her pale face. "Stop the horse, I need to lie down," she says. Her voice is small and breathy. The bones on her back are sharp and protruding. She falls limp against the horse's mane. I jump to the ground just as she slips off the side and I catch her fragile, wasted body.

I had ignored her slow demise, beginning long before we set out on this journey. Now I have no choice. I help her to the ground, as fragile as glass.

"I can find you some wine, that will make it better," I say. Of course, knowing that nothing will make her better.

"It's too late," she whimpers. "I cannot do this." Her cough rattles again, doing little to dampen the gurgling that rises in her chest.

"Yes, you can, Maman."

"I have no place outside of La Rochelle. My family lost their lives there. I don't belong in Rouen, asking a priest to shelter us." Her head turns as she looks out at the hills. Her voice is scratchy and quiet as her body withers from sickness, or heartache. Maybe both.

We tremble with the rush of icy wind that blows through the holes in our clothes. I must face the grim truth. Soon, only one Colette will be left to face the burden of this life, for the other will finally rest free.

My hands shake with the cold that breaches my skin. Resting on my knees, I rub Maman's hair. Our breath meets in the air and swirls like a ballet before the dancer retires for eternity.

"Are you scared?"

"No darling," she mutters between a coughing fit that forces her to her side. "I'm only afraid of leaving you."

I bury my head in my palms then collapse next to her. The struggle of my mother's breathing softens as night approaches, announcing its arrival through a champagne sky beckoning in raven clouds. Beside her lies a fern, wet with dew. As the wind bounces the leaves about, one drop lies still, unmoving on the rustling greenery.

Over the next few hours, her face moves farther away. Darkness coaxes her into a deep slumber. I curl up to her, to comfort us both. Hours of a rattling cough shake her body next to mine. I pull her closer to feel the last of my family here in my arms before she slips away to my memories. My arm rests over her in a deep embrace, as she did for me our first night without a home.

And then she rouses, calling out, "Isabelle? Are you there?"

"I'm here, Maman." Desperate to soften her pain, but I lie empty in the dark of night.

"Soon, you'll be on your own, dear girl, and I need you to know something."

Swallowing against the burning in my throat, I say, "What is it?"

"You've always been on a path toward something magnificent. Your eyes glowed with promise, even as a tiny baby."

"Maman, you're dreaming. Please rest." I roll her to her back and cushion her head in my hand. The bony parts of her skull protrude through her thinned hair.

"I've always known it, and I am sorry I held you too tightly. I was afraid." Her eyes close. "Afraid of losing you to something bigger than me. Your wit and your fire will take you places I could never dream." The rattling has quieted. Her voice is clear.

I squeeze her hand, hoping to hold her to earth.

"It's fitting that I take my final breaths as those before me have. Cold and alone," she says.

"I'm here."

"You left me long ago, Isabelle."

My tears drip from my chin. I wipe them with the back of my frozen hand. My cries echo into the black sky. I want time to stop, but that will only prolong her suffering.

"I'll make you proud, Maman."

She surrenders her final breath. Her lids close over her cloudy green eyes, and her hands slip off her stomach, sweeping her away as they fall. The worry lines between her eyebrows are gone. Her bony fingers stop twitching. Her mouth rests open. Her body at peace.

Her hollow eyes no longer see the fear of the world that trapped her. Her soul called to another place by Etienne, her mother, her husband, and her lost children. Her touch is now a memory. The sharpness of the biting cold lifts from my skin.

Her frail hands lie motionless in the dirt. The hand I still hold is limp and cold, my fingers not strong enough to keep life in them. A tiny spider makes its way up the pallid skin of her neck. I don't swat it away. She belongs to the earth now, not to me.

I sleep, only awakening with a hint of sunlight. My wet tears have turned to ice and my skin crackles in the early morning frost. My mother's once full cheeks have now sunk into hollow craters, showing the outline of her teeth through feathered skin. I cannot bear to see the hint of green peeking out, so I rest my fingers softly on her lids, lowering them closed.

The strong little dewdrop on the fern begins to slide with the sun's glow. It drips to the ground, absorbed by the dirt, where it disappears.

As day breaks, I sit alone atop a hill watching the sun cast its light over Blois. It shines on the River Loire and illuminates the rooftops of the city's palaces and terraced gardens. Another day will course through these streets, ignoring the life lost above last night. My fingers scrape the ground, uselessly trying to dig a grave. The ground is too hard, and my hands are too weak. I lay two sticks on my mother's chest like a cross and kneel next to her, whispering a Protestant prayer.

The warmth of the sun softens me. My breaths are deep, and open. The expanse of my chest feels untethered. I pull the Catholic cross necklace from my pocket and hold it up to the sun. It flickers in the beams of morning light. I place it back in my pocket and watch the sunshine fill the world with warmth and an amber glow.

On this hilltop, I say goodbye to the life of La Rochelle, and goodbye to the family I've lost. They hover behind me with my mother's spirit, waiting until I'm ready to take my first steps. My hands open to the sky, feeling the air of a new day. With clear eyes I scan the rolling hills that will carry me to a new home. On this hilltop, I say goodbye to my childhood.

AN UNEXPECTED FRIENDSHIP

Each day bleeds into the next, the sounds of winter whistle in my ears. My breath in the mist. The silver firs wave in the wind. Every day the same, every night sleeping alone. The hollow sounds of my worn shoes hitting the earth let me know my body carries on.

I arrive in Rouen, feet numb, and vision cloudy. I leave my horse in a barn outside of town, with a bucket of river water and piles of old hay and oats. The city is sprawling and majestic, with colorful stick homes and lively streets. How strange to waft through this town, so alive and thriving. I begin asking where I might find Father Hyacinth. Everyone passes by me as if I'm invisible.

The wind begins to whip through the narrow paths between the tall houses. My fingers poke through the holes of my cape, the pale skin glowing through the tips of the worn gloves. My legs falter with every step.

A pull on my arm. It's a boy. Dirt covers his face, and his tattered clothes flap in the wind. "What are you doing, boy? You can't go around grabbing at women." My voice sounds hollow. My ears ring.

"I'm sorry, Mademoiselle. I'm hungry and looking for money." His voice echoes like we're in a cave.

"You won't find any here. I've nothing to offer you." My heart aches. I am no different than this beggar child.

"I like the color of your dress," he says.

His young face looks so familiar.

"It was much nicer before my journey. Now, can you tell me where I would find Father Hyacinth?"

"No. I've not heard of him."

Flurries begin to fall, and snowflakes gather in my palm. The flutters of cold touch my skin where the wool is thin and frayed. "Do you have parents?" I ask him.

"Yes, a mother. She's so sad since they killed my father."

He can't be more than twelve, and yet he has a look of determination in his young eyes. He looks exactly as Henri did at that age. He has the same devilish smile and mischievous spirit.

"There's a storm coming in. You must get to shelter before nightfall. You'll die if you stay out here," the boy says.

My lip quivers. "But I don't have anywhere to go. If I can't find this priest, I must endure another freezing night in the streets." We both look up to the falling snow.

"I'm sorry, Mademoiselle, but you can't stay with me. I have no home."

The wind swirls. The boy throws a dusty red covering around his neck. "Good luck, Mademoiselle." He turns to run as the crowds of people scatter to the warm shelter of their homes. People hurry around me while my feet remain frozen.

In the distance, little Henri stops and turns back. He stares at me through the blinding white. He runs back through the haze of snow, now blanketing the streets in pillowy clouds. Its beauty will rob my body of heat and blood, leaving me as I left my mother, in an eternal slumber alone in the cold.

"Isabelle, come." The evening now dusk, settles on us in an eerie stillness.

"Did I tell you my name?" I stare at my feet, my boots swallowed up by frozen air and piles of white.

"Come now, Isabelle Colette." He grabs my arm and leads me down the empty streets, hushed by the snow. It swallows all sounds other than the whistling wind in my aching ears.

We float through the streets as my eyes blink to focus. Little Henri still pulls me by the hand, but I start to sink to the ground, desperate to fall asleep on the clouds of snow. Brought to my knees, I'm at the steps of a grand cathedral.

The arches and spires climb tall, the falling snow collecting on my eyelashes. Little Henri drags me up the stairs and leans me against the cold stone wall.

"You saved me?"

"Yes, Mademoiselle. It's too late for me, but I can still help you. I never did make it to the Americas. Freedom is not for heretics, it seems."

"Henri? Is that you?" The storm of white closes around me.

My eyes shut and I drift into the numbing slumber of wintertime. He bangs on the door and yells for help, but I'm lost in a daze and see only white all around me. The massive door creaks open and a woman gasps.

"Please, Sister, take her in. She's weak and needs your help."

"Oh, heavens, poor girl." She calls for assistance, and I float into the air. A man appears, with deep brown eyes and a glow of yellow light reflecting off a large cross around his neck. The priest smiles, and I succumb to the slumber that has been calling me for days.

.   .   .

I wake warm, covered in layers of heavy blankets. The glimmer of the fire reflects off the paned window. A faint memory of last night hovers in my mind, the smiling man's face amid the blurred visions of snowfall. My toes tingle when I wiggle them. My ankles pop when I flex them against the weight of the blanket. My mouth is dry as sand.

I blink and flutter my eyes to focus my vision. My fingers are bright red and prickle like my toes when I move them. Pulling back the layers of satin and wool, I sit at the bedside, my arms locked to hold me up. My head spins and aches. Clean white stockings cover my feet and a white shift far too large for me hangs to my ankles. I reach for the wine on the side table and take a sip. It drenches my parched lips, traveling down my throat in a glorious wave.

The fire cracks and pops as I stand to swollen feet and wobbly knees. Sitting back down on the bed, I bend my knees and ankles to loosen them. Standing again, I lean against the wall. My fat feet slide toward the door. Still struggling to sharpen my mind to the odd feeling of waking up in the echo of an empty chapel room, I open the door dressed only in my nightshirt.

The thick slab of wood creaks open, and I drag myself into the center of a breathtaking stillness. I've always lived on the outside. Only glimpsing a church through my imagination. All around me, the structure grows taller and expansive, the rows of columns unfolding in waves of limestone carved to resemble intricate lace.

Cavernous arches surround me, reaching their curves to the heavens. Jeweled stained glass circles crown the columns, letting in a flood of rainbow hues that bounce across the stone. The colored glass bathes the room in light, the color flickers over my hands as I twirl them. My feet slide closer to the altar. The glass windows above shine a cobalt blue on the gold panels.

Here stands a lonely Huguenot in her stocking feet and cotton nightdress under the majestic nave of a Catholic church. The air hisses outside as the storm unleashes on the town and I stand in the quiet. In a place intended for priests and monks and those upon whom God bestows grace. The sound of only my small body moving across the marble floor breaks the silence of the hollow stone church, facing the altar where countless people have taken communion.

It seems it would only take a few steps and word of commitment to wash away everything I am. With nothing left, perhaps a change of heart could change my fate.

The echo of footsteps grows from deep within the halls. "Oh, dear!" A nun hurries up to me, holding out a wool blanket. "We can't have you out here in nothing but your shift!" She wraps the blanket around my shoulders.

She stops to admire the altar with me. She has a round, weathered face, framed with a white linen wimple and black wool veil. "Beautiful, isn't it?"

"Yes, Sister."

"How I wish the original sculptures were still here to admire."

"What happened to them?" I ask.

"Protestants." She says with a sigh. "The wars of religion. They damaged much of the cathedral, including the stained glass, furniture, and even some of our sacred tombs."

I swallow to clear the lump in my throat. My only thought is, *we used to fight back.*

She turns to me and smiles, the corners of her eyelids drooping over her dark brown eyes. "I pray we will all someday know peace." She places her arm around me and leads me to the room where I slept.

She sits me down by the fire, pulling my chin up to examine my face. "I will get you some oil for those blisters. Here, drink some wine."

It warms the cold hollow of my stomach.

"You poor girl. We had to feed you small sips of broth as you were delirious with cold and thirst."

"Thank you for taking me in." The red wine evaporates as soon as I swallow, leaving me again with a dry mouth and a thick tongue.

"It so happens that the friars are on a visit to one of the neighboring monasteries to help repair a damaged roof. Father Hyacinth and I are stuck here during the storm. I stepped out to determine if the snow needed removing, and to my surprise, there lay a freezing girl, barely alive." She shakes her head and gives thanks to God.

"What happened to the boy that was with me?"

"Boy?" she says.

"There was a young man, about twelve. He took me here and called for you. He wore a red cravat."

"There was no boy, Mademoiselle, just you."

She carries on, stoking the fire and tending to my lips. Had I dreamt it? The deep connection with my Huguenot family came to me in a dream and guided me to safety. Henri held my hands, who it seems, never did make it to the Americas.

"Come, darling, drink some more wine. You need your rest."

Another cup of the earthy wine heated by the fire sends me into a sleepy daze. She tucks me in as my mother used to do, and the soft sheets drift me to a restful trance, one that I have dreamed of every night since leaving La Rochelle.

. . .

The morning finds me clear-headed as I emerge from my room dressed in the gray and brown clothing Sister Marie left for me.

"Come, dear!" Marie beckons to me from the far end of the cathedral.

She leads me to the kitchen. A smile from the friendly face that welcomed me in from the cold. He stands to greet me. Portly and red-faced, his resting expression is a smile curled up at both ends. His olive skin is reddened at the cheeks as if he has just come in from the whipping wind. He teeters side to side to accommodate his rotund belly, his smile widening as he approaches.

"Good evening, Mademoiselle." He rests his hand on his chest and bows his head. "You gave us quite a fright last night. Glad to see you looking well today.

He is unlike any priest I've met before.

"I am Father Hyacinth. Please sit. Sister Marie prepared supper. She makes a delicious potage."

As she presents the bowl to me, the scent of rosemary floats through the air with the steam, causing a deep craving in my belly. I must restrain myself from diving deep into the warm hearty stew.

After a quick prayer, Father Hyacinth gestures for me to begin, and Marie hands me a large slice of dark bread slathered with butter. I might faint with gratitude.

"Tell me, child, where are you headed?"

I consider telling him that James sent me but think the better of it. "I'm not sure," I say.

"How did you end up alone in this snowstorm?"

"I traveled from La Rochelle." My eyes shut like a trap to halt the tears.

"Where is your family?" Marie says.

Father Hyacinth's eyes are welcoming and soft. The weight of all that has come to pass tumbles out of me. I mutter that we had lost our home and my mother had died on the journey to Rouen.

"Oh, dear, it's all right," Marie whispers as she places her arm around me. She rocks me as a mother would, and Father pours more wine. An exiled orphan finding solace in the company of her oppressors.

"Isabelle," Father says, "one of the families of our congregation requires a house servant. It pays little but gives you shelter and food. Master Dupre is a stern but fair man. I can arrange for it if you like."

I certainly am not above being a servant. But the idea makes my stomach drop. A few weeks ago, I was beginning to see a future with James, and today my only choice for survival is a life of servitude.

"That is so kind of you, Father. But I've never been a servant."

"Sometimes God gives us opportunities that we do not yet understand."

I finish two bowls of soup and Sister Marie helps me to my room. "Mademoiselle, while Master Dupre is as Father Hyacinth describes him, that house is dangerous."

"Why is that?"

"The children have some...well, troubling behavior. I've witnessed their son Jacques injuring animals for amusement." She looks around to ensure no one hears her.

"That is troubling."

"Endless prayer might not be enough to change that boy's ways."

"Thank you for your honesty, Sister Marie. I'm afraid I have no other choice."

"Once the storm lifts, the friars will return. They won't look kindly on us taking in an orphan, I'm afraid."

I'm an orphan.

"Father Hyacinth has a kind soul. He lives the teachings of goodness and love. The others have different worship philosophies," she says.

She hands me my tattered clothes, cleaned and folded with the gold Catholic cross necklace resting on top. "I shall see you at our Mass very soon."

I nod, forcing a smile until she leaves the room. They all presume me to be one of them. I hold the necklace dangling in front of me. The cross flickers in the sunlight. *It's just a symbol, nothing more*, I tell myself.

My reflection in the window, I hold the ends of the chain, lowering it over my head and allow the cloak of lies to cover me. I don't know what it will feel like to take on this deception, but it's a risk I must take.

With a deep breath to cleanse my fears, Grand-mère's voice rings, reminding me that somehow, I must find a new path of courage.

It's heavy on my neck, the cross hot where it touches my skin.

HIDING BEHIND LIES

It has been two years since I first walked through the Dupres home. Two years silent and obedient as a chambermaid for Madame. Jewels and pearls line the long, elegant lines of her elaborate robes. Feathers or rosettes pin back the long braids of dark hair flecked with silver. The elaborate layers cover a woman barely visible. She floats in and out of her bedchamber, snapping orders with closed eyes. She spends her days sleeping or dressing for family meals. Her children are burdens, and her husband is utterly disinterested in her.

Monsieur Dupre is focused, leaving little time for his family. There are no exchanges of affection between the family members, and their stately suppers are filled with silence until the silver hits the fine china.

The daughter is sixteen, a rotund girl lacking in both beauty and grace. They tighten her corsets to create a figure, which forces the mass of fat up through the top like dough rising in the heat. Her red face beads with sweat. The family looks on as she piles her plate with extra helpings of everything. While children starve in the streets outside their stately home, she soothes her unhappiness with piles of roasted hen and oysters, shellfish soup, creamed peas, and butter cake with honeyed figs, all served on silver-gilt porcelain.

Young Jacques is not so young anymore, now a young man of seventeen, eager to prove himself worthy to his distracted father. Sister Marie was right to worry about him. He's a monster.

The older valet has finally warmed to me. Monsieur Clement is humble and soft-spoken. He appreciates my quiet nature. He tells me that few girls have been able to withstand the pressure of this demanding household.

Another constant in the revolving world of Dupre servants is the maid, Jeanne Belanger. Focused on her routine, she rarely speaks. Who knows what hides behind her stoic look.

It hasn't been so difficult, working as a servant. I've spent a lifetime learning how to stay out of trouble, being invisible.

I quietly go about my work, emptying chamber pots and keeping Madame's bedchamber spotless. It suits me, blending in with the background of the damask drapes. But circumstances keep me moving, as they always do.

Madame accuses her lady's maid of stealing. She promotes me. Although this might seem a favorable position, I prefer emptying buckets of waste to carrying on a pretense of caring for this cold, unfeeling woman. My pay is equivalent, but I have a room in the attic rather than a cot behind the stairs. I stay at Madame's side, catering to her every need. The long periods of silence break when she orders me to fetch something, only to place it down unused. She likes to remind her staff that we are no more significant than a spot of mud on her shoe.

Tonight, Jacques is particularly disruptive, dropping forks on the floor for servants to replace, even holding one of their skirts below the table as he salivates over her décolleté. Her face flushes as she returns to the wall next to me, holding back tears. He turns to her, licking his lips, causing the tears to flow down her cheeks. His behavior is unnoticed, or ignored, by his family but we see every moment.

As Madame retires to bed, I begin the nightly routine of preparing her bed warmer, tending to the fire, unpinning her elaborate hairstyles, and disrobing her. Without so much as a word, she collapses onto her satin bed sheets. There isn't a stitch of linen in this household. Only the finest fabrics in vibrant colors.

Back at my room, Jacques waits by my bed, spinning a diamond-encrusted chain attached to a pocket watch. My stomach drops. My feet spin, rushing for the door. He pounces behind me to swiftly shut the door, his arm extended next to my face. His hot breath moistens my neck, which tightens as I pull away from him.

"No need to run off." He takes a deep inhale to take in the scent my hair.

My arms press into my sides when his other hand reaches around me, his arms locked in place against the door. He thrusts his stomach against my rigid back. The sickness rises in my throat, and I close my eyes.

"You're a lovely treat. I want to take a bite out of you." His words drip like oil, thick and greasy.

My hair grazes my neck as he moves it over my shoulder. I flinch away, which causes him to laugh, low and controlled.

The edges of his curled mustache brush against my ear. "I will have you, Mademoiselle. I always get what I want." His breath smells of hot, spoiled wine. I wonder what I will do the day he finds the strength to take everything he wants.

My toes curl into the ground, the top of my feet aching against my shoes. My ribs bind tighter, and I shut my eyes as his breath cycles in and out against my ear.

One. Two. Three. I count the seconds, staring at the black from my shut eyelids.

It's always the same. Always over my clothes, from behind. Always three hundred seconds.

Will today be the day he decides to lift my skirt? I have my own room now. More private than the stairway close to the rush of servants.

Twenty.

The tip of his tongue caresses my earlobe, wet and bumpy like a cat's. His hips push into me harder, and I keep counting, *thirty-one, thirty-two...* never seeing anything but black. His breath shakes as he groans. His hips rock up then down, forward then back.

Sixty, sixty-one.

My stomach churns when his licks turn to a bite, soft and precise on the flesh of my ear. *One hundred.*

He trembles into my back, his lips rest on my hairline, heaving hot air onto my neck.

One hundred and fifty.

His leg wraps around the front of my thigh.

Two hundred.

A final thrust leaves his mouth open against my neck, his body jerking in rhythm to loud grunts. His chest heaves into my rigid back.

Three hundred.

His arms drop from around me. My throat stings from holding back screams. He opens the door, stopping to smile at me as he adjusts his wet pants. He takes one full grab between his legs, kissing at me in the air.

Jacques slithers down the hall. Jeanne peers out disapprovingly from behind her door. Without a word, I close the door to my room, my hand shaking against the knob.

My back slides down the wall of my dark room. I rub my neck, scratching wildly at the skin where Jacques's lips and tongue touched me. In these dark lonely nights, Madame Chambord is not here to protect me. Instead, her son finds his way behind me, pawing at me like a lion. When I resist, it angers him; his attempts at intimacy turn threatening, and his paws turn to scratches. So, I close my eyes, and I count to three hundred until the door closes on another evening.

Removing the lie I wear around my neck, I hold it to the moonlight. I remember James and our goodbye kiss to lighten the stifling air in my tiny attic.

. . .

She snaps her fingers to get my attention.

"Yes, Madame."

"Leave me now," she says.

I close the damask curtains as Madame covers her eyes with a silk cloth. I suspect this turn of melancholy relates to Monsieur's rumored evenings with his young mistresses.

"When I wake, I will expect lavender tea to soothe my headache." She adjusts her eye cover.

"Yes, Madame."

She flicks her wrist in my direction as if swatting a fly from her face.

My feet glide down the creaking stairs as I slip out the glass doors to the garden. The sun warms my face, and a light breeze carries me into the fresh air of this spring afternoon. My fingertips dance across the greenery that lines the rock pathway, relishing in the sweet perfume of white lilacs. The red roses climb the side of the house, framing the entrance to the kitchen. I pick a handful of lavender, bringing the purple tips to my nose for a deep inhale of their woodsy scent.

I stretch my arms and let the fresh air fill my lungs. Despite everything, I still find moments of magical sweetness in the clear air. On occasion, I let my mind wander, pretending James will appear behind the green of a topiary, finally returning to save me from this life.

I come across Jeanne who sits silently on a stone bench behind the tapered bushes.

"Pardon, Madame." I bow my head and continue walking.

"You're a bright girl," she says.

"Thank you."

"He's dangerous. You know that, yes?"

"I know it all too well, Madame."

"You do not wish to be in his company?"

"I wish only to serve Madame Chambord." I pause, knowing what she must think of me. "I have no say in how Master Dupre treats me. If I did, I would spend my nights alone."

She stands to meet me. "Young Jacques likes the strong ones. He takes pleasure in breaking them."

"Why are you telling me this?"

"You shouldn't be away from Madame Dupre. Jacques is up to something." She lifts her black skirt from the dusty ground and hurries back inside.

Back in the kitchen, I hand the lavender to the chef with a smile. "For Madame's tea, please."

"Madame is resting?" she asks. "Here you are, then." She pours wine into a glass goblet, demoted from the dining set for its chipped edge, and sets it down next to the lavender.

The rhythm of stomping boots accelerates towards us. My eyes dart between the workers. Through the door, Jacques emerges, a string of pearls dangling from his pointy fingers.

"Mademoiselle, would you like to explain this?" he asks me.

"Are those Madame's pearls?"

"Shouldn't I be asking you that?" He holds the strand of shining beads to my face.

"I don't understand, Monsieur."

"Leave us be," he speaks to the kitchen staff. They look at each other in hesitation. "Now!" His voice bellows through the still room.

They glance back at me before shifting their eyes to their feet and rushing to leave me alone with Jacques.

Monsieur Clement rushes through the door, presumably alerted by the chef. "What is the problem, Master Jacques?"

"I'm glad you're here, Monsieur Clement. Our dear Isabelle has been stealing from us."

"No, Monsieur, you are mistaken." I step forward. "I've never stolen from anyone. Those pearls were in Madame's dressing chamber this morning."

"You've stolen from us." He whips the necklace into his palm, then into his pocket. "And now you must be punished."

"I will speak with Master Dupre about it at once when he returns home," Clement says as he steps in front of me.

"No, no. That won't do." Jacques circles us, his hands clasped behind his back. "We must deal with this right now."

"Please, Master Dupre, I don't want to lose my position." I turn as he moves, never leaving my back to him.

"I'll keep you here as I am magnanimous and forgiving. But you must be punished. Yes?" He gestures to Clement.

"We shall withhold her pay. One month," Clement says.

"Again, it's not enough. The punishment must be strong enough to deter her from stealing again." He reaches for a long skinny dowel used to roll dough, slapping it in his palm and moving toward me with a perverse smile.

"Monsieur, you do not intend to…" Clement asks.

"What, rightly discipline my staff? Why yes, Clement, I do."

"Please, Monsieur, your mother will need me soon. I'll return to her bedchamber." I move toward the door where Jacques steps in front of me.

"Master Jacques, I really must object. This is highly unusual. Master Dupre has never disciplined his staff this way," Clement says.

"Well, I say a Master Dupre is standing right in front of you, ordering you to obey. Certainly, you would not object to that, would you Clement?" Another loud whack slaps down on Jacques's palm. "That would be a grave mistake, seeing as how your feeble body and elder years would make alternate employment impossible?"

Clement's face drops as he replies, "Yes, Master Dupre."

"Now then, let's get on with it."

Jacques slams my cheek into the rough wood, keeping pressure at my back with his left hand. His fingers rub against the wood stick in his other. Clement's bottom lip begins trembling. He closes his eyes and turns from me.

"Pick up her skirt, Clement."

"Master Jacques, I simply cannot." A fast whip of the stick on Clement's aging knuckles sends a flash of pain across his face. I pull from the wood slab, only to be shoved back down harder, my cheek stinging.

"Go on." Jacques waves the dowel at him.

Clement's eyes redden as he whispers, "I am so very sorry."

Turning his head, Clement holds my skirt at my waist. The first whack hits my backside. The sting bites at my skin like I have sat on a hive of angry bees. I bite my lip, too afraid to cry.

A long pause.

My feet slide across the floor as my legs tremble. A second whack fires lightning through my body, and I grab Clement's sleeve. The rough wool smells of the horsehide brush he uses to shine Monsieur's shoes.

Five lashes later, tears flow. My face is buried in my arm, muffling my cries into the bend of my elbow. My skin is fire hot, and each pause between lashings grows longer.

The goblet of wine sits next to the lavender. Each thrashing sends the liquid trembling, barely coming to still before the next wave. The purple wisps of lavender wait, fresh and fragrant.

"Please, Master," Clement begs with a shaking voice. That is quite enough."

"I say when it is enough!" His pressure lifts from my back.

My neck yanks back sharply, my hair in his tightened grip. A pause. A grunt. A flash of searing pain lights up my skin when the stick hits my raw backside.

I release a full wallowing cry as my knees give way, the blood dripping down the back of my legs. I stop screaming, retreating to blackness until it stops. Four more lashings.

The dowel drops to the stone floor with a high-pitched bounce. Clement rushes to cover me and holds me in his arms. Jacques wipes the beads of sweat from his lip, looking down on me as the useless peasant that I am. He gulps down the wine, slamming the glass to the table. He picks up the lavender, crushing it in his fingers and waving it under his nose, then dropping it to the ground. He stomps out of the room.

The old man embraces me and cradles my head as I shake and cry.

Clement hands me off to Jeanne, who quickly orders another servant to fetch her water, linen, and boiled vinegar. She lifts me up the stairs, my legs dragging like there are no bones.

"Wait, Madame's tea. She requested lavender tea," I whimper.

"I will send another servant." She nods at the girl who brought the boiled vinegar.

Jeanne acts as a mother would, removing my ripped and bleeding stockings, soaking them in water to soften the tearing of skin. She lifts my robe and provides me with a clean shift. She sees my branding scar, pausing to examine it. My hand rushes to cover it, and I turn my body from her. She carries on without a word.

The whole process is slow and painful. Bracing myself against the window, I lock my knees to stand as she tends to me.

The sun sets through a splash of pink across the amber sky, as I hold my nightdress to expose my backside. I flinch every time the cloth touches my exposed flesh. The tears run in quiet streams down my cheeks.

"All right now, that's all done. Come lie in bed." Jeanne assists me to my side, where I lie, subdued. The fight I once had now tamed, my fire gone.

She sighs and kneels at my bedside to caress my hair.

"Madame, why did this happen?" I ask, my fingers tucked up to my mouth.

"He's never come into the servant's quarters. Not until you arrived."

My eyes fill with tears. "Madame, I never wanted any of it."

"I dismissed you as an eager girl participating in dangerous behavior with her Mistress's son." She rests her hand on mine. "I misjudged you, and I'm so very sorry."

"None of that matters now, I suppose."

"I wanted to believe he would outgrow his atrocious behavior." She adjusts the blanket over me. "I didn't know it would become this awful."

"He was testing his power. Building himself up by rubbing me and scaring me. I let him. I had no choice." The tightness grips my throat. "What have I become?" The tears stream down my face.

Jeanne sits softly on my bed, hands crossed in her lap.

"Many years ago, my husband left me with our baby in the middle of winter. We had nothing left. I fought to keep her fed, but I was not even keeping her warm." She looks away as her voice quivers. "My priest knew a young couple that was desperate for a child. They offered to take her in, to their home in Paris. They would give her everything and be kind to her, as long as I promised to never come for her."

The throbbing pain in the back of my legs softens.

"She would be just about your age now. I think of her living a comfortable life in Paris, and I must still remind myself that I did something unforgivable to save the one that I love."

"I'm so sorry, Jeanne."

"I fall asleep every night smiling, remembering her tiny hands and thick raven hair. I would trace my finger along a purple mark on her upper arm shaped like a little heart and kiss her forehead as I rocked her. I hold on to those memories because if I don't, the reality will devour me with grief."

I prop on my elbow, looking into her aging eyes. "That is why you're so quiet."

"Pain is part of living, my dear. We all find ways to move on. I did, and you will too."

I hold her hand. The skin is rough from years of work, but her touch is soft as velvet.

"Remember what I said. Stay close to Madame Dupre."

After a smile and a soft caress of my cheek, she shuts the door, and I am alone. I remove the blanket and lift my shift, the edges of blisters stare at me, swollen and red. The moon shines on the soft, pristine front of my legs. I twist to see the mangled and bloody back of my thighs. I cover myself and rest my head on the pillow, staring into the dark and tiny attic.

Maman had hopes for my life. James and my grandmother, they saw a fire in me. How could they have been so wrong? They presumed me to be more than a helpless girl. My fight is gone, and I'm not sure I'll ever find it again.

ENLIGHTENMENT

Over the past two weeks, my wounds have turned to thick yellow blisters and purple bruises down the back of my legs. My body aches, but my fear receives an unexpected gift.

Jacques left for Paris to discuss his future at Court, representing the houses of Normandy with his father. The house breathes with relief, the servants humming with ease as they go about their duties. Madame Chambord has few expectations, only that I accompany her anywhere she wishes.

"Girl!" She snaps to get my attention.

"Yes, Madame." I rush in from her dressing room.

"Which robe shall I wear today?"

"The sapphire taffeta with brocade leaves?" I present the robe for her approval, head down.

"Yes. That will do."

I set to work fastening her whalebone corset through her exasperated sighs. I position her petticoat, lower her satin bodice that slides through my fingers like soft sand, and pin back the layers of overskirt. I ensure each crystal is set in place to shine and be noticed.

My hands ache as I ensure every stray hair has a place, her swept back curls neatly pinned with pearls and blue crystals to match her gown. Then, a long strand of pearls worn crossbody. My legs ache, but I never flinch.

"Why must they travel?" She sighs.

I glance to acknowledge her concern but do not dare answer.

"My dizzy spells carry on." Madame's hand rests on her forehead. "Stay close to me, girl."

"Yes, Madame."

"There will be music at tonight's salon. This lonely house is more than I can bear."

I fluff the bottom of her trailing overskirt as she stands and positions her matching parasol. I walk behind Madame, nodding to a fellow servant carrying trays of food from the daughter's room. If only my employment could always be like this.

We meander through Rouen, delighting in the long days of the unfolding summer. She sometimes speaks. The only words I utter are, "Yes, Madame." The warm breeze calms my restlessness, just as it has always done.

We've observed theaters from the balcony, watched artists paint in the gardens of Rouen, and my favorite activity, attended numerous salons.

Standing in the background, I'm a voyeur to provoking thoughts and intellectual awakenings. No one notices me as I'm invisible, dismissed as illiterate, and incapable of learning such advanced ideas. Little do they know that Protestants expose their children to theology, philosophy, and reading.

Intellectuals discuss topics that would be unthinkable in usual social circles. Men and women together discuss politics, government, the working class, and poverty. I long to hear every word, while Madame Chambord simply smiles and wishes to be left alone with her champagne. She prefers the musical displays, as she can shut her eyes and drift away to nothingness.

Tonight's salon greets a hot August evening. The men with flushed faces gather in the elegant drawing room of another grand home. I fan Madame as she sips apple cider from a hand-blown glass goblet, blush, as delicate as her temperament.

The Madame of the house takes command of the room, offering tonight's topic of debate, the colony of New France. She speaks with authority and directs the discussion. A widowed woman, still vibrant and relevant, who advances theories of enlightenment? Under my humble servant demeanor, my insides light up with the notion of it.

"Immigrants and frontiersmen are writing the rules of our new society, starting fresh where France has failed them," one man says.

"We're losing our most skilled laborers to the New World. It could be disastrous for our economy. Religious persecution forces people to flee our country in staggering numbers," another one says.

I flutter the fan quicker, in beat with my racing heart.

"One might argue, those that wish to conquer new territory and fight untamed land represent the best of us. Our Frenchmen are brave. We should encourage them to discover new possibilities," a younger fresh-faced Norman says as he points his glass of ale at the other two.

With words like untamed and possibility, my face warms and I try to contain a smile. Henri was right. There is hope, we just must be strong enough to reach out and take it.

With a roll of his eyes, the older man says, "Although it is incredibly naive, our young friend does make a good observation. The colonies are an opportunity for people to break the chains of poverty that shackle them here in France."

I continue fanning Madame, moving to her other side, so I may lean closer to the action. They carry on, "If one can change their mind, they might be able to change their circumstances. Possibility is a life-altering experience."

"You suggest poverty is a choice, and I dare argue," the spirited young man continues, "that it is merely a symptom of a poorly regulated society where the wealthy and powerful deem all others unworthy."

The other two look about the room, rubbing their beards and scowling.

"We're born into a world that is not of our choosing. What might happen if we make our own choices, and start anew in freedom?"

"Then life can finally begin," I absentmindedly mutter. The younger man hears my words and turns, mouth open, eyebrows raised in piqued curiosity. My lips tightly purse, and I turn to Madame, who is half asleep and sees none of my foolishness.

The lady of the house interrupts the festivities, sensing the arguments growing heated. "I'm delighted to offer you spiced cognac, candied oranges, and a magnificent musical display." She gestures to the grand hall. An older gentleman presents his hand to Madame. They walk arm in arm through the hand carved wooden doors.

As the group floats to the next room, the opened-minded scholar jumps in front of me, a grin cast across his youthful face.

"I've not seen you before. You work for Madame Dupre?"

"Yes, Monsieur." My cheeks flush warm as I lower into a curtsy.

"You seem like a spirited girl," he pauses with a subtle snicker, "with a rather large mouth."

"My humblest apologies, Monsieur. Your words moved me. I should keep my ideas to myself." My eyes shoot to the floor.

"I hope you don't think me angry, Mademoiselle. On the contrary, I find you quite refreshing."

"Pardon?"

"We stand with nobles dressed in fine linens, as we drink expensive wine, ostensibly changing the world with our ideas. I often wonder what the elite would learn if we could listen to the people who serve us. I believe you've answered that question. We could learn quite a bit."

"I'm sure you're right, Monsieur. I really must return to Madame now."

"Mademoiselle, might I see you at another salon?"

"Perhaps." I curtsy again. "Madame does love the lively discussions."

"The only thing your Madame enjoys is the champagne." His cheeks flush crimson with a half-smile.

"If I may be so bold, Monsieur?" He nods encouragingly, and I continue, "What servants do not say might change your view of France forever."

"Possibly, then, I shall begin listening more. I hope you find the opportunity to make your own choices — so life may finally begin." His hand on his chest, he bows. "Enchanté, Mademoiselle." He clicks his heels, smiles, and carries on to the grand hall.

I stand alone in the drawing-room, the light of possibility around me. The music has started. The quivering notes rest on my ears, calling me toward them. In the gilded hall shining with mirrors and crystal chandeliers, a single violin begins. The sounds fill the air like a swan gracefully gliding through water. The music surrounds me in waves like silk that quiver in the wind. It turns from a dance to a whisper, floating away to silence. The crowd stand still, mesmerized, and enchanted. The room erupts in cheers, and my eyes line with tears.

Servants carry silver platters of candied figs and oranges, brie and Roquefort, chocolate tarts, and chestnuts. Madame yawns from her chair, sleepy-eyed from the cognac. I linger, smelling the sweets, the violin still on my mind. I savor every minute, for the lies I live cannot remain hidden. This simple protected life will come to an end soon enough. It always does.

. . .

The summer has found me exposed to a world of gilded taffeta and champagne and learning about life in the colonies. This great enlightenment will end when Jacques returns from Paris. Madame only attends the salons to soothe her loneliness when the men of the house are gone.

I attend Mass with Madame, assisting her to the front of the church. I take my place standing in the back with the other servants and companions. Madame so frequently requires us to leave early or not attend at all because of her headaches. I walk beside Catholics every day without becoming one. My Protestant life is far in my past, now living without much faith at all.

My skin bristles. I fidget with my dress, my weight shifting from one foot to another. A fellow lady's maid jabs her elbow into me when the arrival of the Dupre men pull every eye to them. Jacques's elaborate fabrics are more ridiculous than ever.

"It appears Versailles has taken effect on Master Dupre," a servant whispers under her breath.

Father Hyacinth presides over mass, which is, as usual, long and nauseating. Stifling incense fills the air. Jacques yawns and stretches his arms, smiling at the young women all around him. Hours of the parishioners standing and sitting leave my legs exhausted. No more secret church in the forest after nightfall. I stand in this chapel, yet remain the girl in the darkened forest, watching from afar.

Madame's carriage will now carry Master Dupre, and I am to walk home with another servant of a neighboring house. Master Dupre notes that the step on the carriage appears wobbly, sending me to fetch the groundskeeper of the church. "After our generous donation, I should say the church owes us a favor," he says.

My fellow servant tells me he is likely in the shop at the back of the church. I wave her on, as her Madame is known for impatience.

"Hello?" I holler into the workshop. My voice echoes. The room is a mess of tools and storage for broken pottery and furniture. It's dark, except for the fading light that trickles in from a high window, illuminating the floating dust particles in the air.

I rub the sides of my legs to dry my wet palms. The air seems to speak to me, nudging me back toward the light. A cold tingling crawls up my arms.

In the doorway, the outline of a wide-brimmed hat with tall feathers backlit by the morning sun. Tightness clutches my chest.

He saunters toward me. Slow. Deliberate. For every one of his steps forward, I step back. His face emerges from the shadows. Jacques grins, eyes flickering with excitement.

"Bonjour, Isabelle." He removes his hat, slowly strumming the feathers before placing it on the table. "I've missed you."

I shift back, watching him. My vision clouded and my hands shaking, I trip over a broom. My heart jumps and then stings as he prowls toward me.

"Now, now, Isabelle, it's time we get to know each other better. Haven't you missed our secret encounters?"

"You know I have not." Broken down scaffolding, dented pots. Piles of gravel. Nowhere to run. My chest pokes with a thousand needles, my eyes squinting from the darkness. He forces me into a dark corner. Something thready catches on my hair. A cobweb, sticky on my hands as I wipe it away.

No servants in the next room. No Madame to attend to. This time will be different. He sneers, his dark eyes dancing. Sliding to the back wall, I topple a shelf of pots. He easily maneuvers over them, crushing the pottery shards under his boots.

"You're wasting your energy, Mademoiselle. In this scenario, I will do as I please, as you are, well, nothing." I pull back, but his hand finds its way to my face, slapping my cheek and forcing the flesh of my lip into the sharp edges of my teeth. I try to run, but he grabs me by the waist. Throws me over a filthy table covered in oil.

I scream and wrestle. My body is too small. He pulls up my skirt, and I frantically pull it back down.

No. Not this.

I begin to sob, begging him to stop. His familiar mustache pokes my ear. "I've wanted you for so long."

Visions of my mother and James and Henri and Clement and Jeanne all gather in my mind. He crushes me, my body trapped under his back, the table edge pushing into my belly.

He drops his breeches, fumbling and grunting in frustration. I pull away, but he pushes me back down. His other arm shakes as he speaks to himself. "You are powerful, Jacques. Take her. Yes. Yes."

My stomach thumps. A hue of red mist covers my eyes. Again, he pushes me down. He grunts, rubbing against me like he always does. This time, his skin touches mine. The fleshy mass poking into my leg grows hard.

I can't count my way through this.

My fists ache as they grip the wool of my skirt, yanking it down. His body behind me hot and giant. I writhe and whimper like a caged animal.

Jacques grabs my arm, pulling it over my shoulder, shoving my palm onto his cheek. He rubs my hand on his face, pushing his hips into me once again.

"You want me," he says.

I pull forward. His arm wraps around my waist and thrusts me back into him.

No. No.

Heaving, he turns his face into my hand, then down to my wrist, which he begins to lick.

My hand beside my face, I turn to see the H.

"What is this?" His voice drips with disgust. The pressure on my back lifts. Then nothing.

Is he done? Maybe he doesn't want to touch a dirty Huguenot girl.

He grabs both my wrists, slamming them to the table. He rubs his hips on me, rough and angry. His wet bare skin slaps against my legs and backside.

The voices of those who cared for me begin to whisper. And then they begin to scream. The force of every Colette that died before me grows like a fire raging. Years of cruelty and torment for trying to exist, trying to live. The anger becomes a hum. Louder. Louder.

"Not only will I taste you, then I will have you hanged." He releases his grip. He pushes the flesh near me but begins yelling again as it turns flaccid.

Breathe.

My hands brace the table. My neck flexes forward. A long, slow exhale breathes out my doubts, my fear. As swift as a horse's hoof, I slam the back of my head into his face. His nose cracks, and his weight finally lifts. I wrap my hands around a broken beam and turn toward him. I blink to maintain control against the throbbing pain in my head.

His hands cover his bloody face, and with stunned eyes, he smears the blood to his cheek. He opens his mouth to discolored teeth and ruby-stained saliva. He spits on the floor, wiping the dripping blood from his swollen nose. My eyes widen, my breath steadies. My only option now is to fight.

"I will end you," he says through gritted teeth.

He rises to his knees, his breeches still around his ankles. He reaches across his body and wipes the drops from his nose.

Do it now.

My hands tighten against the thick beam. My feet widen. He launches at me, grabbing my skirt, pulling me toward him. I kick his chest, forcing him to the ground. Again, he rises.

Retightening my grasp, the fire grows in me. No options left. I take a deep breath and I swing. Every memory, every hope, every betrayal rests on the tip of that wooden beam. The massive block of wood cracks onto the outside of his knee, throwing him to the ground, screaming in pain. The beam is heavier than I thought.

Higher this time.

My dress bathed in black oil, cobwebs in my hair, my arms pull back over my shoulder. Rapid, shallow breaths. I retighten my hands.

"Will you let me free?" I yell. The words sound far away as if from someone else's lips.

His eyes meet mine. "You miserable waste. I should have killed you right in front of Clement and made him watch."

The weight of the beam pulls me back, my torso rotating. I ground my feet into the stone and swing. It explodes out of me. The beam flies and crashes down against his cheek, blood sputtering from his mouth. He wilts to the ground.

The only sound a high-pitched crack as my hands release the beam to its bounce on the stone floor. My breath echoes loudly in my ears. The blood gathers in a pool around his face. His naked lower half crumpled under him.

A muffled sound flutters in the distance. I blink my eyes.

"Isabelle?" Time comes back from whirling confusion. Sister Marie stands in the doorway.

I begin shaking.

"Oh, dear, what have you done?" She circles Jacques. His left eye bulges and blood drips from his ear. She looks at my torn dress. My desperate eyes. "Come, we must get you out of here right away."

She leads me away as her eyes settle on the body of Jacques Dupre. She found a murderer in place of the pious servant they all presumed me to be.

REBORN

Sister Marie sends word to the Chambord house that I'm ill, and the nuns will look after me. A rickety carriage takes us to the abbey. I stare out the window, counting my breaths. Sister Marie prays and wrings her hands together.

She enlists the help of another nun she trusts. They hold me in a storage house next to the abbey. She brings me clean clothing and a bowl for washing. Hours pass. Every sound sets my heart thumping. Flashes come to me. Rubbing. Grabbing. Blood.

The door creaks open.

"Oh, Jeanne." I embrace her and weep, like a daughter in her mother's protective arms.

"When I heard you were with the nuns, and that Master Dupre is missing, I knew something horrible had happened. Sister Marie told me the details. Are you all right?"

"Yes." I hold back tears. "Just terrified."

"It's a dangerous thing you did yesterday. It was also brave," she says as she holds my hands.

"I was just trying to save myself."

"But you did it at great cost. You will lose everything."

"I never really had anything to lose."

The door creaks open. It's Sister Marie with Father Hyacinth.

"Father. I'm so sorry for all I've done. You must be so disappointed." My voice wavers.

He crosses his hands at his hips. "Child, it is I who is ashamed."

"Pardon?"

"I placed you in that home. I put you in danger when God presented you to us in need of help. I hoped that young Jacques would grow out of his behavior. He has only grown more connected with the ways of the devil, and I am to blame for your pain."

I lower my head and exhale. It is I who spilled Jacques's blood, and it is my soul that must pay.

"I called for the doctor, who is caring for his wounds at the church," he says.

"He's not dead?"

"No. The injury to his head prevents him from speaking. He's strong and will most likely recover. And when he does, you'll be in grave danger."

"I hope you know, Father, that I had no choice. I was protecting myself."

"Yes, I do believe that." He glances back at Sister Marie, who folds her hands and lowers her gaze.

"What is it?" I ask.

"Isabelle, you must repent and ask forgiveness. You must confess your sins, so your soul may be absolved of evil."

"Yes, Father. I understand."

"That is a problem, Mademoiselle, seeing as how you are not Catholic."

My darkest secret. Jeanne's eyes widen. How will she react to my betrayal? My legs begin to tremble.

"How did you know?" I ask.

"I wrote to the La Rochelle Archbishop. I was trying to reach family who might assist you. You were so lonely and weak. He returned my request with information that he did not know of any Isabelle Colette from the church. He did, however, know of Isabelle Colette, Huguenot exiled in November of 1661."

I hang my head. "You've all been so kind to me, I'm sorry I lied to you."

"Do you still wish to be Protestant?"

"Must I choose? I prefer to find God in the flowers of the gardens and the wind of a warm summer evening."

He holds my hands. "I too find myself closer to the almighty in the quiet sounds of nature. But we live in a world where religion and politics are not separated." He sighs. "You must first agree to baptism. Without your commitment to the Church of France, I'm powerless to help you."

It is upon me. The moment I've been fighting since the day I watched Etienne killed. The ground gives way, and Jeanne rushes to help me sit.

"We must act quickly, Mademoiselle." Father gestures to Sister Marie, and they step outside.

The walls begin to close in. "Jeanne, are you disappointed?"

"Oh dear, I'm nothing of the sort. I gave up my faith long ago."

"I've been hiding my past. But in truth, I've long held questions of my beliefs. I've wondered if being Catholic might be an easier life, but the thought of betraying my family is too great a burden to bear."

"This life will hand us all pain, regardless of which bible we pray to."

I collapse on Jeanne's lap, curled like a child desperate for comfort. The stinging grasp of the dark night approaches. "What do I do, Jeanne?" I fall to the ground, grasping my hands in prayer, asking God to forgive me. I rock and cry, and Jeanne sits in silence, rubbing my hair.

My tears have soaked the wool blanket. "Please, help me. I don't know if I can do this."

She lowers herself to the cold floor, arm around me. "This is a choice you must make for yourself."

"What would you tell your daughter to do?"

The tears now cresting her eyes, she tells me, "If I had the chance to kiss that little purple heart again and hold her in my arms, I would tell her to fight."

I close my eyes and weep into her embrace. Whichever choice I make, my life will never look the same.

My hands tremble. My eyes sting. I can no longer live in the shadows. I must cleanse my life of all that I've known to become what society tells me I must be.

.   .   .

The rules of Catholic France are clear. When one has gone astray and wishes to accept Catholicism, a public condemnation is required. One must denounce all other faiths and acknowledge the error in their ways before committing to the church that rules the land. Father is allowing me to take the first sacrament in secret, at considerable risk to him.

It's an unusually warm summer evening. I emerge from the shed once night falls. I wrap my arm around Jeanne as we walk behind the sisters, through the woods that surround the convent. My crisp white robe, the color of a dove's wings, billows in the breeze. My legs are as weak as a doe, and I turn to Jeanne, wanting her to tell me to run the other way.

She only smiles, nodding to me to continue. My bare feet claw at the earth. The dirt rises between my toes, cool and mossy. In nature I have God's ear, and I ask him to forgive me for the choice I now make.

Father appears, and I hesitate. I exhale, long and slow, the air rushing over my lips. The nuns take me by the hand to the edge of the Seine, where Father waits for me by the water lapping at its shallow edge. A grand yew tree shelters us, its trunk gnarled and aged.

Under the pale light of the full moon low in the sky, Father speaks of faith and commitment. "Through baptism, we are freed from sin and reborn as children of God. We become members of Christ, incorporated into the Church. You now will take the sacrament of regeneration through water." Father's voice is soft and loving, convinced by every word that he speaks as one believes in the trees and oceans.

The twirling unrest in my stomach is about to burst. Father reaches for a jug of blessed water. It is time. I lean my head back, looking up at the twinkling stars above. The water flows in a stream over my forehead, dripping down my hair and onto my neck. The cold water makes my hands tighten.

My twitching nerves soften through deep breaths, the quiet of the evening bringing me closer to a place I once knew, a place I once felt at home. Standing, the water drips down my temples.

I look at Jeanne, a motherly figure who sees in me her own child long gone, and Marie, taking in a heretic, sheltering me from the harsh world she helped create. My head throbs.

I turn to face the Seine. Tightness grips at my chest. It's not enough. I need God to speak to me, to forgive me. I walk the incline into the river.

My white robe wafts in waves as I lower into the rippling water. The thick mud pushes up through my toes. I turn and allow my body to immerse in the dark river, arms at my side. A chill flows through me, and my vision darkens. The water washes away the only thing that tethers me to my departed family, cleansing my body of its memories.

My eyes open to see the shadowy figures move above the surface. The light of the moon shines on my hair floating around me. I slowly exhale bubbles and wash away my sins.

Through the ethereal night, the light breaks through the black of this river, and I see my branded H, the emblem of my Huguenot family that will always be with me. A moment of quiet acceptance of all I've questioned, and all I've struggled to understand.

The presence of God embraces me, holding my hand and leading me to a new life, as the old one is washed clean. Love is always there. He envelopes me.

When I rise, my mouth gasps for breath and my body comes down from weightlessness. I walk along the rocky river bottom to the water's edge. My hair is wet against my face, and the thick cloth of my robe drips into the river. I long to dip back under the surface where God embraces me, but the earth now holds me, a reformed Protestant hoping for an easier life.

The sisters and Father Hyacinth smile, resting their hands in prayer. Jeanne places her hand on her mouth, her eyes happy that love for her lost daughter will somehow live on through me. I smile at those who saved me, and through tears, I am reborn.

A NEW LIFE

Outside the walls of this convent rests a new and terrifying world. I pull my sleeve over the symbol that will always be there, reminding me of where I started.

Marie arrives. "Isabelle, it's time to go."

"I have nowhere to go."

"Come, child. Don't be afraid," she says.

Marie leads me by the arm to the front of the convent, where Father Hyacinth stands beside a royal carriage, reaching out to me. Jeanne is here, smiling.

"Isabelle, you must flee. Master Dupre has woken up. He's still confused, but he uttered your name."

The royal carriage shines gold in the sunlight. My heart thumps against my chest. "Where will I go?"

Father Hyacinth says, "I've sent for assistance from a friend, an advisor to the King. Getting you out of this requires something more than I'm capable of."

The Royal driver stands rigid at the door to the coach, eyes fixed ahead. "Father, the Dupres just returned from Versailles. If your friend knows what I did to Jacques, I'll be sent to the rack."

"Isabelle, I trust that he can help you. He's a good man."

"How many men have done evil things while telling themselves they are good?"

Father sighs and nods to me with a smile. "I've requested your friend to accompany you." He gestures to Jeanne. "I told the Dupres she will bring you back to their home."

"And when I do not return?" I ask.

"She will tell them you escaped, ran away. She must return today," Father says.

My hand floats away from his and I face the coach. A black box with a curved bottom, embellished with the gilded crest of the Sun King, matching the gold glimmer of the large wheels.

"Will they punish you for helping me?"

"You let me worry about that. I answer to a higher power than that of Monsieur Dupre," he says.

"Monsieur Beaumont was right about you. You are a kind soul."

He smiles, in a surprised, delighted way.

With an outstretched hand, the richly dressed servant helps me to the rail. I duck into the small carriage. Jeanne follows. My faded robe rests upon the crushed crimson velvet of the seat. My hands run over the soft fabric and my fingers roll the golden tassels. Will the world I've entered treat me as harshly as the one that I've left?

The carriage drops suddenly with the weight of the driver, my stomach lurching with it, and the galloping of horses begins our journey. I lean forward onto my knees and wrap my hands over the open window, looking back as my friends wave me farewell. Tears roll down my cheeks again.

The bumping of the carriage is rough and nauseating. Jeanne and I don't speak. My thoughts race with memories of James and Maman and Grand-mère. I think of beautiful La Rochelle and the home I lost so long ago. The family I betrayed.

As we wind along the Seine, we enter the city center through the crowded streets. Le Gros-Horloge hovers above us, an astronomical clock on a towering stone archway. We pass underneath it, and I look out the open window at the shining blue and red and gold as it glitters in the sun. The Dupre house is within steps of this clock.

I fall back on the chair as we approach Le Palais Archiépiscopal de Rouen. This palace holds the church court and its prisoners. We arrive with a sudden stop and the clop of hooves marching in place. What would my fate be — jailed for life? Beheaded? Burned at the stake? This building is where a girl younger than me had her tribunal and met with a fiery end in the town square. Jeanne D'Arc lived and died with the courage of a lion, fighting for her faith.

For all her weakness, Maman never faltered in her convictions. And here I sit on this velvet chair asking the church I spent a lifetime fighting to save me. I feel ashamed and powerless.

A servant escorts us through the grand entry and up a dark staircase. The gold walls and beaded sconces sparkle. Through a long hallway, we come to a pale blue door. He opens it and bows his head. We step into the room, each of us with a slow exhale.

The servant asks us to have a seat, and Monsieur will be with us shortly.

The door shuts. Legs trembling, my knees give way like a sail without wind, and I grasp for the back of a chair. My head swims through a cloud. My hands glide along the edge of the braided wood trim, Jeanne assisting me to the gold chaise where I'm certain I will meet the fate of a foolish girl who thought she could fight the power of men.

The seconds drip by. An eternity passes when the door bursts open. A tall man saunters in. There are no officers with him, but several servants.

"Bonjour." He looks directly into my eyes as he tilts his head and smiles. The rush of servants follows him with trays of decadent food. Roast duck, candied fruits, creamed potatoes, red wine in crystal carafes.

"S'il vous plait." He reaches to help me stand. I take his hand, trying to control my shaking fingers.

A servant pulls out chairs, and we sit at the far end of a long wooden table as the other servants use silver spoons and gold-plated china to prepare our meals.

"I trust your journey was satisfactory?" His voice bellows through the large room. I nod yes, still unable to adjust to the people buzzing around us like bees.

"I am here on assignment from the King. Father Hyacinth sent word about your dilemma." He begins cutting his duck, gesturing for us to do the same. Jeanne and I glance at each other, shrugging our shoulders in confusion. "You are from La Rochelle, yes?"

The servants scurry out, leaving only one stationed by the door, hands crossed behind his back, eyes in a fixed stare. I stutter, "Yes."

"Much like Rouen, La Rochelle is an important town for the King."

I place down my utensils and straighten my shoulders. "Monsieur, thank you for this lovely meal. But I wish to know my fate."

"Pardon?"

Indignant, I carry on. "Father Hyacinth told you of my predicament."

"Yes, he did. An attack like that is a dangerous situation."

"Attacking a member of the nobility carries a punishment. I wish to begin immediately." My hands cross in my lap.

He lowers his utensils. "Mademoiselle Colette, you are not here to be punished."

I blink a few times. "I'm not?"

"No. The King requires your assistance."

"My...assistance?"

He continues eating and gestures for me to eat as well. "Are you familiar with the colonies?"

"America and New France."

"Yes. The new world is a challenge. We struggle to make it the thriving land we need it to be." He sighs and shakes his hand to dismiss the conversation. "It is complicated."

"The threat of Iroquois attacks and the lack of marriageable women make it difficult to populate the region. Men risk everything for a better life but find the frontier wild and lonely. You need them to keep the fur trade strong." The salons of Rouen debated this frequently.

"Aren't you a clever one?" He looks pleased as he sips his wine.

"Monsieur, I'm a servant with no references. I have no family, no money. I have nothing to offer the new world."

"Au contraire." His eyes begin to dance. "You are exactly what the new world needs."

Jeanne raises her eyebrows.

"As you say, the men are lonely and restless. We need strong women to join them in building our empire. The King requests that we find suitable women to help in this endeavor."

"So, you'll sell me to the highest bidder? Now I see my punishment."

"No, my dear." He tilts his head slightly. "You'll be paid... as a Fille du Roi."

A wave of disbelief washes over me. The words ring in my ears, the image too ridiculous to imagine. "Me? A Daughter of the King?"

"Precisely." He lifts his chin in pride.

"I don't understand."

"It's an honorary title. The world will treat you as one of the King's daughters. Your passage and accommodations paid by the Crown. You choose your best suitor and build a life with him as we settle the colony. You take as long as you feel necessary to find your right match. We pay you when you marry, and again when you have children."

"I choose?" I say, certain I've misunderstood.

"Yes, Mademoiselle. Any settler you like."

"And what if I do not find a suitable match?"

"You are under no obligation. We will not force you into anything you do not wish to do."

"Will the men of New France understand this?"

"You are under the King's protection entirely." He smiles. "You'll be making history."

I blink a few times, shaking my head. "You let the women choose the men? And then you pay them when they do?"

"That is correct. We need the settlers to be happy. If they send word back to France that the colony is dangerous or unpleasant, we risk losing more men. The fur trade is far too important."

"Wouldn't the King wish to send women of status?"

"We've been sending city girls for the past year, Paris mostly. Beautiful, young, from important families. They've been ill-suited for country life."

"And now you seek out peasants?"

"We've begun to recruit women from farms and working as servants. Orphans, and the poor. Young women who might be looking for a fresh start," he says.

"Women who have nothing to lose," I say.

He nods. "Yes, and young women who have the fight in them to build a colony. There are dozens of men for every woman, so you shall have your choice of husbands."

I've never had the choice for anything. "Why me, Monsieur?" My eyes lower to my lap.

"You are strong. There's a fire in your eyes. I see that as plainly as I see your beauty. You were brave enough to fight Jacques Dupre."

"I do have a rebellious spirit." Tightness grabs at my heart. "So I've been told."

"We need young women who can fight the new frontier with its very harsh winters and undeveloped towns. You must be prepared to work the land of your farm and manage your children. And you must be self-reliant. There will be no one to help you."

"Well, that is something I understand." I think back to all those years of hardship in La Rochelle, working in neighbor's farms and foraging in the woods.

"Another thing," he says. "You will marry in a civil ceremony."

"Not in the church?" This seems unimaginable.

"That will come later, if you wish. Marriage by a notary allows you to break your marriage contract should you ever find yourself in an… unpleasant situation."

We sit in stunned silence.

"Break a marriage contract? As in separate?"

"Yes. I must say, Mademoiselle, this is quite the opportunity for you, given that you come from such humble circumstances."

"It is a wonderful opportunity, and I'm so grateful." I put down my fork, and my shoulders raise toward my ears, the tension forming inside of me becoming too great to ignore.

"What could possibly be holding you back?"

"Leaving France means leaving behind my past, and everyone in it."

He nods a few times as if he understands. "Yes, it does. If you stay in Rouen, I cannot help you. Young Jacques will make you pay for your crimes. I encountered him while at Versailles. He has the darkness in his heart to wish for your destruction, and the power to see it through. Your ship leaves this evening for New France."

"It sounds like I have no choice."

"You always have a choice, child. The question is, will you make it with your head or your heart?"

.   .   .

Jeanne and I wait in a sitting room, staring at each other. "Jeanne, I can hardly believe something like this is possible."

"Nor can I."

"It's all so sudden. And terrifying." My hands wring together, squeezing the tension out.

The room is filled with ornate furniture with notched depressions in the shape of leaves and tapestries and oil paintings on the walls. None of this feels like where I belong — if there is such a place anymore.

I think of James kissing the skin on my forearm. A new man, a stranger, will see my scar for the first time. Touch me for the first time. I look out the window, tears puddling in my eyes.

Jeanne rests her hand on my shoulder. "Isabelle, please take this journey," she says. "Do it for me. Find yourself a new life, one with the freedom you deserve. Find the life I never could."

"A Daughter of the King," I mutter. "I spent my life as a Huguenot, tortured by the same people that now wish to use me."

The door opens, and servants arrive holding a large trunk. They drop it on the ground, the thud reverberating through the room.

"What is that?" I ask.

"A gift from the King. This is your trousseau," a man says. They bow their heads and leave the room. Jeanne nudges me forward.

Kneeling in front of it, I run my hands along the curved lid. The heavy walnut chest creaks open. My eyes grow bright. I gently pull out each item and examine them.

Two Coiffes, one ivory gauze, simple and pretty, another, pale blue taffeta with gold ribbon leading to its tails on the sides. A pearl-colored comb, thick and heavy, layers of ribbon and soft fabric. Sewing supplies to make dress details and handkerchiefs. Pristine scissors and thimbles without dents and the thinning of time like we had at home. Wool stockings without a stray yarn to be found and pointed shoes with a widened heel that has never touched the earth. Two knives, with long handles of mahogany. Sleek gloves with beading, and a hooded cape in crisp blue wool, lined with shiny satin.

"You deserve this. All of this. You are, after all, a Daughter of the King now." Jeanne picks up a box and opens it. "One hundred livres for your new life." She looks at me, eyes wide. "It's your dowry."

"Dowry?"

A large bright smile casts across her face. "What this means, dear girl, is that you have protection. You have the gratitude of the most influential court in the world. You have the rare opportunity to choose your husband, provide money for your young family, and you do it all on your own terms."

"What you are telling me is, I will have -"

We say together, "Power."

LE ST. JEAN-BAPTISTE

Jeanne helps me dress in crisp new clothing, a mustard yellow bodice with white ruffle trim and matching skirt. She envelopes me in a tight embrace as I hold back tears.

"No," she says. "No tears. I'll return to the Dupre's and tell them you escaped. And I will wake every day with a smile, thinking of your amazing new life as a Daughter of the King." The pride on her face stays with me, keeping me calm as I journey to the town of Dieppe.

The giant ship bobs and teeters. The St. Jean-Baptiste will be my home for the next few months. The summer sun lights the sails and ropes soar into the sky. The deep blue ocean looks almost black. A girl weeps next to me. She's about fourteen.

"Are you all right, Mademoiselle?" I ask.

She shakes her head "no" and leans forward as she retches at her feet. Gasping out, "I can't do this," she stumbles backward, crying. The first of the other Filles du Roi I've met. Not one of a strong constitution, it seems.

My eyes will never again gaze upon these rolling hills. My feet will never touch the ground of my homeland. My hands will soon hold a husband that I've not yet met. What happened to my people after exile? They don't know that I left my mother to die on a frozen hilltop, or that I traded my faith for a chance at an easier life. They don't know that I dreamed of a Catholic soldier who made me question everything. They don't know that I betrayed them all.

It's time to shed the hopes of a naive girl and begin my journey as a reluctant Catholic and Daughter of the King.

Our chaperone, Sister Marguerite, prepares us for boarding. "Come now, girls. It's a long journey, and we must get acquainted with our quarters." She lifts her head and raises her skirt from her feet as we gather in line behind her, like baby geese fluttering after their mother.

Men carry our hope chests that hold our trousseau. The girls fidget with their clothes. Their eyes large and nervous. There are men everywhere, leaning against the edges, sitting on the stairs. Some look us up and down, others stare off at the open sea.

Sister Marguerite swings the doors open. We follow her down the narrow stairway to the lower decks. In a line, we silently march, parading past the men who avert their gaze when Marguerite shoots them a stern warning.

"There will be four to a room. You may each take a bunk." She leads us down a dark hallway that smells of wet wood and human waste. The wooden boards settle and creak.

In my room, I meet Louise and Madeleine from Le Mans, and Elisabeth from Paris. We introduce ourselves, nervous about the three-month journey.

Louise is a short girl with a large bosom and an even bigger smile. Madeleine is not a beauty, but her pale, thin features hold something special. She wears a cream satin ribbon in her hair, a whimsical touch that offsets her seriousness. Elisabeth is beautiful. Her raven black hair is pinned back in natural waves of flowing curls that contrast her glowing blue eyes and milky white skin.

The Filles du Roi gather at the main deck, huddled together, a bond born of our common fate. This group of women France tried to toss aside now await their new life of power and freedom gifted by its King. We stand united in this shared adventure, quiet and courageous.

We lean over the edge as the Port of Dieppe becomes an image in our memory. Some weep as they bid farewell to the family they must leave, and the dreams they might have had. Others are content to say goodbye to a country that stripped them of every chance at a promising life. Me? I'm astonished and humbled. King Louis XIV, who tortured my people and exiled my family now calls me one of his honorary daughters. He gave me an extraordinary chance at something I never thought possible — to be a powerful woman in charge of her destiny.

.   .   .

Our first night aboard the ship, Madeleine cries into her skirt. Her cries meet the groaning boards of the ship, as waves rock us side to side. I smile at her, but she turns to the wall, drying her tears with the blanket.

We quickly learn the strict rules Sister Marguerite keeps. We perform chores and assist the men by mending their torn clothes. She keeps the girls in line, even the unruly ones who linger around the men, blushing and fluttering their eyelashes.

We have daily Bible study and prayer. We have classes in domestic life that set the girls into hysterics with a discussion of "wifely duties" and what to expect the first time you meet your husband's cockerel. The girls gasp in horror when the nun describes the act of childbirth.

She teaches us what our mothers cannot. She rarely cracks her rigid exterior. Her weathered face at first appears cold. Her tight black robe adorned with pristine white lace to the top of her neck.

She catches me staring at her left hand, which can't grasp her Bible, her fingers bright red and stiff. "It's an injury," she says.

"I apologize." I look away.

"It's all right, dear. One night the Iroquois attacked our camp. As I fled, I fell and broke my wrist quite severely. I hid in the forest until the settlers could come for me. By the time they reached me, my fingers were white. A healer fixed it, but my hand never did recover. I continue sailing between the colony and our homeland. It's my duty."

"I'm so sorry, Sister."

"We all have scars, Isabelle. But we must carry on, yes?" I nod. "Now, it's time for some rest. We have another stop at the end of the day."

I lie on my cot, tracing the knots in the wood above me into shapes of my imagination when the girls erupt in whispers. "We're here!" After several days on the ship, we're all eager to see something other than the lonely sea. We rush to the top of the stairs and hurry to the edge to watch the ship dock.

My mouth wide open, I whisper, "La Rochelle." My heart races with excitement. The sharp spire of the Lantern Tower greets my eyes first. Then, the medieval wall Henri waited for me behind, and the port where my father lost his life. My gaze lingers on the entry as the towering ship bobs smoothly through the gateway.

We float between the leaning St. Nicholas Tower and the rotund Chain Tower. The memories of my town feel so far away, and yet close enough to touch.

As the ship settles, the girls watch the preparation of barrels of goods and wait eagerly for the new Filles du Roi. I walk to the bow, leaning into the point, where I close my eyes. The familiar sounds of the port and the smell of the salty air bloom sadness from deep in my memory.

The streets I used to know and the houses I once looked upon now find me a stranger. Unable to set foot on this land, my place is in a new world I have yet to meet. I'm simply a visitor here, as I suppose I always was. The smell of wet earth brings me back to running through the hills as a child and our secret prayer circles.

Memories of my mother, grandmother, my sisters, Etienne and Henri wash over me. My chest tightens. My fingers grip around the railing, and my arms lock. The intensity knocks me to my knees.

My forehead leans against the wooden boards, tears stinging my eyes. My hands rest against the wet wood as the wind whips the strings from my coiffe against my face. In a crumpled mass, I grieve alone for the remnants of a life I once knew. This ship carries me between two worlds, neither of which are mine to call home.

On my knees, I pray. It feels different now, being a Catholic. My connection to God should be through priests and bishops and elaborate churches, but I still find him in the rush of wind and the cloudy sky. Here on this rocking vessel of souls desperate for a new life, I accept that my future belongs to the Catholic Church, my heretic past left in the shadows of La Rochelle.

A commotion gathers at the deck, and the grip on my heart softens. Sister Marguerite and four young women climb onto the main deck. The first three look like the rest of us — simple dress, shoulders raised in nervous anticipation.

Then the last woman. Her gown shimmers pink. The men gather, removing their hats and grinning. Elisabeth whispers that the woman is not a Fille du Roi. She travels to New France to marry a soldier.

A blush satin gown hugs the silhouette of her tightened waist, with loose billowing sleeves down her arms. Her blond curls rest in waves along her shoulders. She turns slightly, and in the light, I see a spectacular string of pearls.

Stepping down to the main deck, I push past the group just as she turns. Through a tightened jaw and a rush of disbelief, I mutter, "Antoinette."

"You know her?" Elisabeth says.

My heart sinks. "What I know is that my time on this ship just grew much more difficult."

She glides across the deck, her entourage follows, carrying several chests of her belongings. The salons of Rouen were right. We are shackled to poverty or privilege, a fate decided by God at birth. No one believes this more than Antoinette. She walks tall and proud, unlike the timid, uncertain posture of the peasant girls who've only known struggle.

She boards this ship knowing a wealthy officer awaits her on the banks of New France, in a home full of luxury and comfort. What do the rest of our futures hold? Stick homes on farms, where the whipping wind and freezing snow finds its way through the walls in winter. Working our hands bloody in the summer months while nursing babies and hoping they don't die.

We are orphans. Heretics. Poor. Frightened. The King gifts us money and beautiful clothing, and the chance to choose our husbands. These terrified girls, some as young as fourteen, take this daunting journey alone for the opportunity to change their God-given place. Antoinette? She will live the same life of privilege, just on a different continent.

Antoinette makes her way to her room and stands in the doorway to examine her new sleep mates. She orders one girl to straighten her bed and another to fan her. The girls look at each other, confused.

"Girls. We are about to start life in a new town. Would you not like to have the friendship of a soldier's wife? I will be prominent in the new society, and you do not wish to make an enemy of me, do you?"

The girls sigh and lower their heads, beginning their new role as servants to a soldier's wife. I watch from afar, remembering her years of torment from my childhood. I relish the sight of her in a wet, cramped, dirty ship.

They comply, as Antoinette snaps her fingers at her third roommate, a timid girl named Catherine. Her eyes flit about the room, shocked that anyone notices her. She scurries over to Antoinette like a tiny mouse, hands curled into her chest.

She whispers out a shy voice, practically balancing on her toes, "Yes, Mademoiselle?"

"You will be my little pet. Now find me some wine, and I will tell you all about the handsome soldier, Pierre, who awaits me in New France."

"Do you think she fancies herself the new Queen of Quebec?" Madeleine whispers to me.

"I think she fancies herself Queen of everything."

. . .

Antoinette and I have not acknowledged each other. I'm content to carry on that way. She remains in her room snapping orders at Catherine, or on the deck, basking in attention from the men.

This morning we gather in the storage space at the bottom of the ship, at a long table we use for sewing. Wine stored here spills onto the ground, puddling at our feet. The room is damp and dark, but these moments help us forget how lonely and scared we are. Louise keeps us entertained with silly songs and an infectious laugh.

The laughter fades when Antoinette enters, dressed in a crushed velvet gown in shining emerald green. Her elegant clothes now soiled with moldy wine that we saw rats swimming in earlier. The irony fills me with satisfaction.

Her lips purse and she studies the room. "Sister Marguerite instructed me to join you," she tells the stunned group. "Something about being friendly with my new neighbors." She can barely mutter the words from her pristinely rouged lips.

We glance at each other, sharing our displeasure, the way only women's eyes can do. She presumes us to be jealous of her, as she sits on her imaginary throne, pitying the peasant girls sewing for immigrants. It is quite the opposite. None of us want to be her. For once, we are hopeful as ourselves.

"Catherine, dear, where are you?"

She bounces over to Antoinette with an eager smile. "Yes, Mademoiselle?"

"What are they doing?" Antoinette asks as she circles us.

"They're sewing. Mending clothes for the men aboard the ship."

"Their hands will be rough, and their fingernails dirty. I thought they wanted to find husbands?"

"Come here, Antoinette. I will teach you!" Louise says, extending a hand.

"Ha!" Antoinette bellows. "I will do nothing of the sort."

Louise covers her hurt with a humble smile. A twinge of fury sparks in the deepest part of my belly, jumping and eager to explode into a raging fire.

"Poor Louise, you have no idea that your silly laugh sounds like a dying horse, and your figure is full like a grown swine." Antoinette's monstrous laugh fills the room as Louise's smile breaks like a rose without water, dropping its petals in the dirt.

My breathing becomes heavy, the tightness in my chest grips harder.

"No wonder you're friends with a dirty farm animal." Her laugh bounces in my direction. My vision turns red when I look in her narrowed eyes.

I drop the wooden plank in the metal bracket to lock the door from the inside. Marching toward Antoinette, my hand glides across the tabletop, eyes fixed on her entitled smirk. I swipe a blade off the table, squeeze it in my left hand and lower it to my side.

Her smile turns to fright as the other girls step back to allow my passage through them. Antoinette backs against the wall. Panic fills her big blue eyes and drains the rosy red from her now pale cheeks.

Louise steps aside and says, "Isabelle, I'm fine. It's all right." The nervousness in her voice grows when she sees the blade against my thigh.

I march directly to Antoinette, raising the knife to her head as the gasps echo from the girls around me. She shrieks, cowering against the wall.

My right hand grabs a fistful of her flowing mane, and I bring the blade up to the taut hair. I yank her head to the side. She recoils, helpless in the hands of the girl she once threw in pig manure. She pleads, "Please, Isabelle, no!" I lean in closer and tighten my grip on her hair.

Catherine tries to reason with my humanity. "Isabelle, if you take her hair, what will she look like for her soldier? You will ruin her chance to marry!"

I look wide-eyed at Antoinette, moving in close to her cheek. "He might think she got scalped by the Iroquois." I pull the hair tighter under the knife, forcing her ear toward her shoulder. Antoinette cries out, which prompts the others to as well.

A knock on the door. "What is the matter?" Sister Marguerite demands.

The girls become quiet. Antoinette's nervous breath warms my cheek. "Tell her we're fine." She looks at the door and back at me, breathless. "Tell her — before I rip the golden curls straight from your head."

She pauses. "We are fine, Sister." Her voice trembles. "Just learning to sew."

I grip her hair tight against her scalp, pulling her toward me. Her hair feels like velvet in my palm. "You have no power over us here. Your wealth and your privilege mean nothing." She shakes her head yes, searching for a friendly face among the girls. "The power you knew in La Rochelle is gone. Be kind, or I promise you I will steal our beauty, one cut at a time."

My eyes don't leave her face as I drop my hands to my side. Her luxurious wavy hair falls around her shoulders. She checks that I haven't snipped any. I step toward her. She flinches, her hands shielding her face.

Softening my stance, I throw the blade on the table. "We're all on this journey together. Not one of us has a family or a home to protect us. You are no different than every other girl on this ship."

I back away from her, my stare fixed on her trembling lip.

She looks around at all the girls staring at her. She gathers herself and motions to Catherine to unlock the door. She walks out, head high, with wet shoes, mussed hair, and trembling hands.

.   .   .

As sunset dances along the horizon, I stand at the edge of the ship to watch another day set on our long journey. The cold evening rests on my flushed cheeks and sprays of salty water mist my hair. I tuck my hands inside my gloves, relishing the cool air that feels like freedom.

Behind me, footsteps. "Would you really have sliced off my hair?"

Without turning my head, I grin. "Yes."

"I don't know whether to be horrified or impressed." She steps beside me. "You've come a long way from the shy little girl that used to scurry the streets of La Rochelle. However did they allow you on this ship?"

I take a deep breath and let the cold air calm me. "I converted. You may no longer accuse me of heresy."

She leans her elbows on the wooden rail. "You may have said the words, but you will never be one of us, Isabelle."

The sea grows darker as night descends upon us, pushing the orange glow of the warm sun behind its cover.

"So, no officer for you then?" she says. "Did handsome James decide on a woman with status?" She grins with pride for her nasty insult.

"Antoinette, I promise you that I am not the same girl you knew in La Rochelle. It seems, however, that you have learned nothing. We will be on this ship for another two months. If you want to make enemies of all of us, it will be a long journey for you indeed." I begin to walk away.

"Don't you think I know they all hate me?"

A moment of honesty in her voice. Stopping, I listen.

"They all hate me. Everyone. I know that."

"If you're looking for sympathy, you won't find it from me."

"I don't need your sympathy," she says. "People with powerful aspirations need not worry about friendship."

"Isn't it a lonely life? Knowing that you'll never be truly close to anyone?"

"What does lonely matter? We're all alone in this world."

"Where did you learn that?"

"My father," she says. "He has high expectations of me to be powerful and strong. I can't let him down."

"You can't be powerful, strong, and also kind?"

"He is not," she says.

"No, he is not. But you could be. If you choose to."

"My parents find me to be spoiled and impossible. When my father sent me off on this ship, his final words were, "You're now someone else's problem."

"New France is a chance for us all to start over. You can be different than your father."

She diverts her eyes, taking a deep breath of the ocean air. "Do any of us ever really know how to be different than what our parents tell us to be?"

"I don't know. But I would like to try."

ONE WICKED NIGHT

The blue sky turns to haunting shadows and blackened clouds. The night falls on us suddenly with no sunlight to float behind the horizon. The wind whirs in a loud hiss, and the waves crash around us. The storm approaching our fragile little ship stirs in me the emotions from the violin from the salon in Rouen. The feverish notes leave me breathless and worried.

The captain instructs us to stay in our rooms, sheltered by the darkened halls as the sea thrashes around us. The ship rocks side to side and up and down. Elisabeth, frozen with fear in the corner, falls to her knees, praying for survival. I close my eyes and try to drift away to the memory of James's embrace, but a sudden drop forces me to the ground and jolts me from my imagination.

Elisabeth prays and rocks, then stops to look up as water drips down from the low ceiling. She holds out her shaking hand to catch it drip between the boards and onto her pale white palm. We sit in silence, listening to the ship creak.

A sharp crash to the side of the boat throws us across the room where we land in a huddle against the wall, then slide back to hit the edge of the bunk. Screams, thrashing waves, thunderous rolls. Gripping the rail of the beds, we hold our place, looking to each other for comfort.

A sudden lift suspends us in air in a silent hover. Then a sharp fall back down. Any moment we may be swallowed by the sea. We keep our gaze on the stressed boards above us, sputtering with incoming water. The next crashing wave might devour us.

Louise crawls her way to a bucket, retching into it and sliding across the floor as she heaves. The rest of us crowd together, and through the hissing wind and angry swells, Madeleine yells, "I'm terrified of getting married! What if I don't like him? What if he drinks or hits me?"

"You won't marry anyone until you are ready. And if he hits you, we'll find you a way out," I yell as my legs slide away from my hands that grip the rail.

"Do you believe things will be better for us in New France?" Elisabeth asks.

"I think they could hardly be worse." We knock into each other.

"I can't read. Most of us here can't. How are we to understand what's happening?" Madeleine says.

"We don't sign anything until we know what's in the marriage contracts. We will write our own! If we do this together, we'll have more power."

"Whoever would have thought we would have the power to control anything?" Elisabeth says.

We all feel that truth.

A sharp drop. More shrieks and gasps and another round of retching from Louise. She lifts her head from the pail to say, "I lost my family in a fire."

We look to her, silent.

"I snuck out with a boy one night. The house collapsed around them as they slept. I lost my brother too." She stares at the wet planks. "The guilt eats away at me every second of every day. I confessed to my priest that I caused their death with my recklessness. He sent me here."

She cries, her large chest heaving. "It's why I put on a joyful face and a loud laugh. It's the only way I can hide the darkness inside me." She collapses in a heap, wailing. I hold my arm out to her, and she crawls toward me, lying on my lap like a child.

I hold her tight.

Madeleine begins. "My mother died giving birth to my little brother. There were already eight of us, and my father could not afford us all. Some were sent to family. He sent me here. I'm lost and have no home. I'm a burden to my own family, so off I sail to the new world."

Elisabeth adds, "Two lovely people raised me. But I did not belong. I was suffocating. Before I left, I found letters. My mother could never bear children and was able to adopt a child. I'm thankful for them, but I know now why I don't belong anywhere. My birth mother did not want me. I'm useless."

"Oh, Elisabeth, you're important to us." Louise holds her hand.

The ship rocks. The thrash of another wave hits the top deck, and the men begin yelling. A gush of water falls through the boards. We all gasp, and Louise asks me, "Isabelle, what about you?"

"I was born a Huguenot. I witnessed horrible things in the name of God. They exiled us from our home. My mother died. The only thing that gave me hope was the kindness of a young man named James, whom I will never see again. In Rouen, I nearly killed a nobleman. I had no choice but to take communion, convert to Catholicism, and board this ship. I left the hope of James on the shores of Dieppe."

Madeleine rests her head on my shoulder. "It seems we've all said goodbye to ghosts."

. . .

The stormy night we spent huddled together praying for daylight was nothing compared to the danger we now face.

We're sequestered in the first three rooms, two to a bed while the sick suffer in a heap of sweat and fever in my former quarters. Three men who boarded in La Rochelle developed a cough, and that familiar scarlet rash covering their bodies. Madeleine quietly shows me the patchy redness on her neck and whispers to me of her aching throat.

Sister Marguerite marches her to the room for the sick. We watch as they grow restless, and their coughs turn to painful groans. The terrified girls congregate outside the room where life teeters on death. Sister Marguerite covers her mouth with a cloth, hesitantly delivering water to the sick.

Catherine comes running. "Mademoiselle, it's Antoinette. She has the rash. She hides her cough for fear that you'll send her to die with the others."

"Hush!" Elisabeth shouts. "They're not going to die. They'll be just fine."

The group runs to Antoinette, curled in the corner, eyes like an innocent child. Her face is pale, her eyes glassy.

Marguerite examines her skin and instructs her to remove her clothes as her shift will provide more comfort. "I'm sorry, dear. You must join the others." She leads her down the hall as Antoinette mutters 'No,' repeatedly, pulling back from the sick room. She looks at me, desperation in her eyes. I gaze to the ground as she moves past, unable to tolerate her cries.

Sheets hang from the walls and between the bunks as makeshift beds for the men. Their lips turn dry and pale, their coughs weaken. We stand helplessly waiting to see who will survive and who will spend their last moments forgotten at sea.

As night approaches on day three, the coughs quiet. An eerie stillness settles under the weight of bodies succumbing to sickness. Groans and whimpers break the silence as their limp bodies shake with the ship's rolls. Sister Marguerite tells us to return to sleep. "If they live or if they die, it's in God's hands now."

The crowd begins to clear, and I stand alone against the hallway wall, feeling the strength of little voices grow loudly in my head. I've survived this once. I can survive it again.

"Isabelle?" Elisabeth says.

I close my eyes. My sisters, little Elisabeth and Anne, they whisper for me to help. I see my mother take her last breath on the cold, hard ground of the French countryside. Etienne screaming for freedom.

My eyes open, and I lean toward the door.

"Isabelle, no." Lousie grabs my arm. "You mustn't go in there. We need you."

I pull my arm from her grasp and enter the doorway. The sick and barely alive do not open their eyes. I drip a wet cloth along the men's foreheads and lips.

"Isabelle, please don't do this. You're welcoming death," Elisabeth whispers from the doorway. I carry on to each one. Their heavy eyes peer open and their mouths feebly crack apart to taste the water.

Antoinette's cheek rests against her shoulder, blond curls in waves around her darkened eyes. Her breath is shallow. Whistling. She still appears beautiful. I rest my hand on hers and wipe her forehead with the cool cloth. She startles awake, and through foggy eyes, stares at me in disbelief.

Without a word exchanged, I sit with her and hold her hand. She tightens her grip as she swallows tears that rest on her glassy eyes. Madeleine faces the other direction in the same bed, her breathing slowed. My sisters whisper to me that it won't be long now.

Madeleine's forehead is cold and damp. Her eyes barely float open, lost somewhere near death coaxing her into its dark embrace. She begins to shake, fear coming in waves of pleading looks. As much as I want to, I cannot save her. The girls start sniffling as I lift her weak shoulders off the pillow. I sit behind her, letting the full presence of sickness come to me.

"What is she doing?" a girl says.

"Isabelle, stop!" Louise cries.

I lean Madeleine's head against my chest and softly rub her hair, my hand flowing over the ivory ribbon she always wears. I rock back and forth, bringing her into my tight embrace. She rests her face against my arm and rocks with me as I begin to hum. The violin from the salon in Rouen plays in my head, and I whisper the painfully beautiful tune that echoed off those glittering walls.

Antoinette opens her eyes. I sing to the notes, soaring free along with the whispered tone of a violin I heard long ago. The music breathes as the notes lift Madeleine's soul and float it away on the air that dances around us. I say a prayer and ask my sisters to watch over her and keep her protected.

Her skin turns to ice and the tension falls from her limbs. Her head collapses into my lap. Tears stream through my flooded eyelids, and I whisper goodbye to another soul who never had the chance to live free.

The girls weep with us, standing in a crowd at the doorway. Antoinette lies silent across from me, tears rolling from her sapphire eyes. She pulls the sheet up to her chin.

The night claims two more victims, both men from outside Paris, and the others awake with clear eyes and grateful hearts. They wrap the dead bodies in linen tied at the ends, sealing in the sickness and remnants of the life they spent on earth. We gather at the main deck, and as the sun presents itself, several men lift the bodies to the edge. A spoken prayer rests on the wind. The orange glow warms us as the white forms glide through the air. They fly gracefully before they meet their watery end, where they will spend eternity, one with the sea.

The others shuffle away, emotionally raw from the difficult days that sit heavy on our hearts. The sea is calm. Rippling waves shimmer on its surface.

From behind me, a weak voice, "Why did you do that?"

Antoinette would never understand the sacrifice you make when someone you love needs you. My gaze stays on the water, watching the place where Madeleine entered drift farther away, leaving only her memory.

"Don't you know you could die?"

"Yes, Antoinette. I knew what I was doing."

"So, you would risk your life, for what? She died anyway. Nothing you could have done would have saved her."

"I couldn't take away her sickness or her fear. But I could make sure she didn't feel alone."

"But to risk your life…"

I turn to face her. "The image of her dying face will be with me for the rest of my days. The only thing that softens the sharp ache of losing someone is knowing your arms were holding them when they left this world. I suppose you find it foolish, but I would do it again."

A long pause with no words.

"I don't find it foolish, Isabelle. I find it brave. Braver than anything I could ever do." She shuffles away, wrapped in a blanket, her hair tousled at her shoulders.

Something flutters from the laces of my bodice, a small waving cloth swept up by the wind. Madeleine's cream ribbon. Holding it by one end, it dances in the wafting of sea air. It must have come loose and rested on me when I rocked Madeleine to eternal sleep. I release a deeply sad smile.

This delicate piece of satin holds the memory of a young woman with hopes and fears and dreams. She is gone. It reminds me how fleeting it all is. My new life begins with more memories than I have dreams. My hand rises to the air. The ribbon waves and bounces until the wind takes it. It flies up into the expanse of the sky, off to wherever lost things go.

ARRIVAL

Back in La Rochelle, the worn soles of my shoes shuffled flat and quiet against the ground. Now a Catholic, my shoes have heels, and the new soles clack against the wood boards of the top deck. My skirt drapes to the floor in flowing waves around my feet. The pointed tip of my shoe peeks out from the fabric. A floor-length hem for women who do not wade through muck and filth. Heeled shoes for the bright new members of society. Clean crisp clothing for a Daughter of the King.

The view of New France represents the birth of a new life for these adventurous, strong, slightly broken women. These outcast children are now a family, and together we must become women with husbands and children of our own. I had always imagined my life as a Huguenot warrior, fighting for truth until the day I die. That washed away with my baptism. I close my eyes and remember, one last time, the French hymns I will never hear again. My palms squeeze together, imagining the Geneva Bible I will never again hold. And my forearm, the one place my past is more than a memory.

The untouched land waves past us in the distance. Dense with trees and steep hills. Shades of green unfold in pointed treetops. This is more than a new land. Quebec brings memories of what we were and hopes of what we may become. The sacrifices we made, the ghosts we bid farewell, and the family we kissed goodbye. We believe that we can rise from the ruins of a desperate life. We light a fire in the dark. Our past does not define us, for here we are new.

The brilliant blue water carries us through the Gulf of Saint Lawrence and into the narrowing river that will end at our new home.

The ship approaches the dock. Elisabeth holds my hand and exhales a controlled breath. My heart races, our smiles hopeful.

Men line the port, smiling and removing their hats as we pass. We move closer to each other, our shoulders touching. My fingers grip the sides of my skirt to steady my shaking hands.

Sister Marguerite, controlled as ever, leads us in a line to Place du Marche. A cobblestone square, tall, steeped roofs. Big windows reaching into the eves. A French city an ocean away from France.

Merchants gather in their doorways to witness the parade of marriageable women. In a line, we stand with shoulders back and hair freshly coiffed, awaiting our turn to greet the man who inspired the Filles du Roi program.

I step forward to meet the first intendant, the governor, the first Bishop of Quebec, and some of the early settlers.

"Bienvenue au Canada, Mademoiselle." The intendant lowers his head as I curtsy.

They greet us individually, thanking us for our service to France. He welcomes us to the colony, and the crowd's applause startles me.

We travel to Monastère des Ursulines de Québec, the congregation that will house us. The girls watch our new town pass by, their eyes wide.

"Sister, why does the intendant call this Canada?" I ask.

"It's an Iroquoian word meaning village. The vast land in and around Quebec is called our village. Canada."

"Aren't the Iroquois our enemies?"

"The Algonquin and Huron tribes are our friends. The Huron also speak the language of the Iroquois, but they are not to be confused with the Iroquois people who align with the British and are quite dangerous. Especially the Mohawk," she says.

"I have so much to learn."

"We all do, dear."

Outside the town square are a handful of houses and narrow streets leading up the hill to the convent. The stone structure looks just like the Abbey in Rouen, except that people and children move about outside. According to Sister Marguerite, the Ursulines believe in dispersing in the community, rather than cloistering privately inside.

We pass a dozen little children with glorious straight hair, deep earthy skin, and glowing dark eyes. They're learning French songs and the unruly bunch giggle and point when we pass by. A little girl runs up to me and grabs my dress, to feel the softness of the silk.

Sister Marguerite produces a humble smile and welcomes us to her convent. She tells us of the indigenous children and how this is a school for young girls where they learn scripture, domestic work, and French culture. A school for girls. Whoever dreamed there would be such a thing?

Sister Marguerite boasts that her girls learn as much as they wish here. These nuns were the first brave souls to establish lives here. We all sailed the same dangerous journey to begin life again, terrified and hopeful.

The walls of our sleeping quarters are plain, except for a simple cross. We're so grateful to sleep where the floor doesn't move, and the ceiling doesn't drip on us. Antoinette demands the cot away from the window to limit the light on her skin. Little Catherine tiptoes behind her, ready and willing to serve. Catherine is tiny but perceptive. She walks as if she's trying not to leave a trace of her footsteps on the ground.

At night, after brushing and braiding Antoinette's hair, Catherine returns to her bed exhausted. Elisabeth asks her, "Why do you fuss over her? You're here to start your own life, not be a servant to someone else."

Catherine dismisses her with a smile and a shrug of her shoulders. We settle into our cots, a room full of women listening to the same whistling wind outside our temporary home, dreaming of a new life.

I drift to sleep, into a dream so vivid I can feel it on my skin. I walk the hills of France through a shroud of mist, barely able to see my hand in front of me. My feet plunge into something thick. Lowering to my knees, my hands feel the ground. Wet cold earth presses into my fingers. They crawl over something round. The mist lifts to reveal my mother's face eaten by maggots, her pale milky skin rotting and black where her mouth once was.

I drop her head and fall back with a sharp gasp. The back of my head hits something hard. I turn. Etienne, naked and still bound by his feet, hangs from the sky as his eyelids droop open, his deadened eyeballs opaque and still. Crawling away, my face hits someone's hand. The mist moves like a cloud, revealing Henri, emaciated, and begging for food. "Help me, Isabelle," he whispers as he pulls at my sleeve.

I cry out for someone to help, and a bright light floats toward me. Maybe it's James coming to rescue me. Through the mist, Henri's father stumbles, his body ablaze. He cries in agony as he reaches for me. Henri cries for his father. I reach to hug him, but he floats away with the fog. In the distance, James screams for me, but he never comes.

I wake with a tightened chest, the smell of scorched flesh in my nose, slapping my hands to rid them of maggots. My chest heaves. I close my eyes and breathe, waiting for my heart to stop pounding in my ears. Drawn to the halls of the still abbey, I walk through the peaceful silence, the cold stone under my stocking feet.

In the great hall, candlelight flickers. Catherine sits near the faint flame, sewing a tear in Antoinette's stockings. With a sigh, I join her.

"Good evening, Isabelle. I've just about finished. May I help you with any mending?"

"Catherine, it's the dark of night. Why aren't you sleeping?"

"I don't sleep much. There's too much to do. I hope to find a husband, but until then, I will help anyone who needs me."

"You're from La Rochelle?" I ask.

"Yes." She remains focused on her stitching. "It seems you and Antoinette have a complicated past."

"We do."

She lifts her eyes to me, "She tells me you both lost someone. James, was it?"

I pause. "Yes, I suppose we both did lose him."

"You came from Rouen. When did you leave La Rochelle?" she asks.

"Five years ago."

She places down her needle and thread. "The exile?"

My neck tightens with the memory.

"It's not proper to say, but what they did was simply horrific. I wish I could have done something to stop it. I was just a child, though." She catches herself and looks back at me. "I'd be branded a traitor if anyone heard me say that."

"Your secret is safe with me." I smile. "Tell me about your family."

"I took care of my father. He suffered from a cough, spending his days in bed. My mother died years ago, so I cared for my six siblings."

"That's so much for a young girl." Catherine is only fourteen.

"They needed me. If I did not feed and dress the children, they would be helpless. I could not allow it." She shakes her head with closed eyes. "When my father died, my aunt took the children. I was old enough to manage myself and left without anywhere to go. And now, I'm here."

Catherine serves Antoinette because she had no one left to help, and without it, she might starve. Her tiny frame might hold the biggest heart of anyone here.

"Do you still have family in La Rochelle?" she asks.

My head drops, and I shake my head. "I have no one left."

"You have us."

"Yes," I say, "that is true. Maybe I was waiting for the wrong people to rescue me."

"Isabelle," her hand rests on mine. "If there is one girl here who does not need saving, it's you."

I smile before wiping my teary eyes. "You will soon have a husband and a whole mess of children to manage. Please choose a man who appreciates how special you are."

We sit in silence in the empty expanse of the hall lit only by the dwindling fire and twinkling stars persisting through the black night. The Daughters of the King have arrived in Canada, and together we face the new world.

. . .

We wake to a flurry of activity. One by one the nuns lead us to a private room. The sister shuts the door and clasps her hands at her hips.

"Do you understand your purpose here, Mademoiselle Colette?"

"Yes."

"To marry and have babies and assist in populating the colony."

"The expectation was clear. I understand." The tightening in my throat forces me to swallow.

She paces, looking at her feet. "Are you of true virtue, Mademoiselle?"

My neck muscles twitch, my temples throb. "Of course I am."

"Good. Your new husband will expect a certain kind of woman."

"I was under the impression that we have a choice. The King's subject made clear that we may choose not to marry."

"Are you planning on joining the Ursulines?"

"No, I'm not."

Each stride causes her rosary to jingle at her hip. "Then you should not be a foolish girl. There's no future here for a young woman without a husband. Stay true to your purpose. As soon as you choose a suitable man to marry, you'll find yourself with a farm, a home, money. That is the only future you should be dreaming of."

"I believe there's more to life than satisfying a husband. We have a larger role to play."

"Ah, a dreamer," she says. "You came here for freedom from your circumstances back in France. You thought you could live without responsibility or purpose."

"I never live without responsibility or purpose."

"If I may provide you with some advice, child." She did not wait for me to agree. "This land is wild and dangerous. Iroquois attacks are common. Wolfpacks attack women on their farms and houses go up in flames in the dead of winter. The snowfall is unending and brutal. As strong as you believe you are, you will not survive here without the protection of a family."

"I've lived without a family before." I turn from her to stop the tears from rushing to my eyes.

"You might think I'm being unfair. Cruel even. Let me tell you that your future here is as uncertain as it was in France. The English side with the Iroquois. You can be certain wars will be in our future."

"Then why bring babies into the mess?"

"Because that is what we do, Mademoiselle. We have children. They bring hope in an otherwise difficult world." She brings her hands in a prayer position to her mouth. "I've seen the young women who long for something they left in France. Someone, perhaps. They hold off the settlers, the dream of a long-lost time pulling them to a place of desperation and loneliness. I've also seen them returned, their chosen man begging for a different wife."

"They can do that? Return us like spoiled wine?"

"Sadly, yes. Our purpose here is to ensure a successful program. Happy marriages, prosperous citizens who bring more little French boys and girls to our village. We fulfill our promises. To the church and the King."

Promises. What does that even mean? I've broken every promise I've ever made. "I will consider all my options."

"You have two hours. The settlers will be here then."

"Two hours? We've just only arrived."

"I told you. Promises."

HOPEFUL SUITORS

The walk to the barn heightens my tension with every step. The girls are giddy. They whisper to each other about men and marriage. Hope and excitement. The sun beats down on my skin, a soft breeze fluttering a loose curl in my face. I stop to fix it, holding myself in the still afternoon where a hummingbird rattles its wings, feeding on a field thistle.

Promises.

"Come, Mademoiselle Colette. Do not dawdle," the sister says.

With a deep inhale of the warm air, I step into the barn. The other girls are lined up along the long wall, equal distance apart, as the nuns fuss with their dresses, their hair, and pinch their cheeks into a rosy blush.

I take my place. Dust particles float in the air, the scent of moist wood and hay lingers. My heart races and I can still hear that hummingbird beat its wings, ready to take flight.

"Now girls, the men will be here shortly. You will meet with each one of them, converse for five minutes, then we will move them along to the next girl, and the next. If at any point, you wish to choose one, step forward and alert us."

"What happens then?" Louise asks.

"There's a notary waiting in the next room. Once you sign your contract, you're free to start your new life."

Just like that. You choose a man from a crowd. A stranger who doesn't know your past, your fears. Your scars.

"Isn't this exciting," a young girl says to me.

I force a smile.

The doors open. A crowd of men with wide eyes remove their hats, peeking over each other's shoulders to gawk at the barn full of marriageable women.

The nuns lead the first group to spots marked in the dirt, a few feet in front of each of us.

A man stands before me. When he smiles, all I can see is the gaping hole where his front teeth should be.

"Hello, Mademoiselle."

"Hello."

He says his name, where he lives, and the size of his plot. I don't focus on his words. All I can see is the dark cavern in his mouth.

Next.

A man with a flowing mane of facial hair that reminds me of a horse's tail. It's probably as dirty as one, too.

Then a man old enough to be my grandfather. He tears up discussing his late wife and I soften to him. Until he asks if I would like to take his wife's place. The washing is so difficult to manage.

I hold back a very deep sigh.

A man who fidgets and scratches at his temple as he stutters out his name. Then the name of his friend. He peeks out a field mouse from his pocket as twitchy as him.

Louise screeches when she glimpses the little creature.

Two nuns hurry over and hook his arms. They lead him away as one says, "Monsieur, we told you not to bring the mouse."

My hand covers my mouth, stifling a laugh, then a cough to cover my outburst. I gather myself, smiling to greet the next settler.

His shirt is crisp, buttoned to his neck. An embroidered jacket perfectly tailored to his tall frame pleats at his waist.

"Greetings, Mademoiselle."

"Hello."

"I have a home in town. No need for a farm because I have plenty of money. I import textiles from France. Silk, wool, taffeta."

He has deep brown eyes, a wide jaw and manicured hands.

"Your name, Monsieur?"

"I should think you care more about my station than my name." He straightens his jacket.

"I do not."

The girls all glance at him, their attention on the tall man with beautiful clothes and money. He notices them staring at him, not bothering to continue to speak with me.

As soon as he moves along to the girl next to me, she waves her hand to the nun. "I choose him."

They follow the nun into the small room where she will learn the man's name on the marriage certificate. The nun places a layer of lace over her head as they disappear behind the door without a word passed between them.

A quiet boy. A handsome man who emanates the scent of brandy. A strapping man in his fifties who does not break a smile. I pass on them all, but other girls decide they are perfect for them. Off they walk to the back room. Lace coiffe. Marriage.

I catch a glance at Louise, her bottom lip puffed out. Poor thing is at the end of the line. The men that make it to her are the castoffs. The men deemed not worthy of a wife.

The afternoon sun turns the room hot, stifling. The doorway shines like a star where the air moves and birds circle and trees sway.

The last of the men move through the line, now dwindled to half its size.

"Well done, girls," Sister Marguerite says. "If you did not find your husband today, don't worry. You will have many more chances. Come along."

Another afternoon interviewing potential life partners in a hot, stuffy barn. A deep knot forms in my stomach. Then I step outside. The rush of cool air, the open space. The hope that freedom still rests at my fingertips.

I may never find another James. What I will grasp for is the chance to breathe free without rules. A new life in a new land. Maybe, someday, I'll fall in love.

· · ·

This morning Antoinette floats along, telling the girls that she will meet her new husband today. "He's been waiting for me for so long. I can't wait to present myself. Catherine? Where is my gown?"

Catherine lays out the gorgeous crimson robe with black lace. Antoinette smiles as she runs her fingers along the skirt. "Oh, Catherine, I'm so happy."

"And I'm happy for you, Mademoiselle."

"My father tells me Lieutenant General Beaugrand is one of our finest men. I had hoped to receive letters from him, but Father tells me the correspondence between France and the colony is still rudimentary." She holds the gown up in front of her, waving the skirt to the side and practicing her curtsy.

"Yes, I've heard that can happen." Catherine presents the shiny black shoes with a red heel.

I turn to leave. The air is thick with perfume and vanity and my mind begs for a cool breeze.

"Isabelle, wait. Will you come with us today?" Antoinette asks.

"Why would you want me to escort you?"

"We've been through so much together. I want a friend by my side."

"You have Catherine."

"Catherine is not my friend! She's my lady's maid," she says as she pinches her cheeks in the reflection of the window.

Catherine tries to hide the hurt in her eyes.

What Antoinette wants is to parade her soldier in front of me. "Why don't you ask someone else."

"But I have no one else," she says.

I swallow my bitterness. "All right. I'll go with you."

When we arrive at the town square, the intendant gathers with a group of settlers, making plans for a brewery, and discussing the potential of New France. Sister Marguerite presents with a smile. "Good day, Monsieur."

"Sister Marguerite! Lovely to see you. Are these some of our new citizens?" He gestures to us.

"Yes, Monsieur. Mademoiselle Lamarche has come to find her soldier, Lieutenant Beaugrand. She would like to meet him and discuss their marriage ceremony."

"Oh yes, of course, Mademoiselle."

He bows his head. "Your father wrote to me many times. He speaks highly of your commitment to the colony. Please, allow me to find him."

"I thought letters were difficult to send?" I whisper to Catherine, who shrugs.

Antoinette fiddles with her dress as she smiles at passersby. She waits for the man she will spend her life with, knowing only his name. Am I the only one that finds this process absurd?

"It will be all right, Mademoiselle," Catherine whispers to her.

"Of course, it will!" she snaps. "Why wouldn't it be?"

Catherine shakes her head and looks to her feet.

Sensing something, I look behind me. A soldier moves toward us, his eyes boring into me like fire. He's tall, and his long legs remind me of a spider crawling along the dirt, sticking to the ground as they move. A chill runs up my neck as he approaches.

"Well, aren't you lovely." He circles us. "Are you the new Filles du Roi?"

Antoinette smiles. I lower my head, gaze to my feet.

"Yes, Monsieur," Sister Marguerite acknowledges. "This is Antoinette LaMarche, from La Rochelle." He bows his head. He moves past Catherine as if she is invisible and turns directly to me. "And this is Isabelle Colette, from La Rochelle. Girls, meet Mestre de Camp, Colonel Bastien Leroux."

He steps closer and I flinch. His fingers rub together, like he's rolling a pebble between them. He speaks near my cheek, "Mademoiselle Colette, it's a pleasure to meet you. You are a true beauty." His breath whistles through his nose.

"Bonjour, Colonel Leroux." My eyes leave the ground only to look at Sister Marguerite, whose posture stiffens.

"Mademoiselle Lamarche is here to meet her suitor. Nice to see you, Colonel Leroux." She pulls us away.

"Mademoiselle Colette, I hope we meet again."

As he creeps away, Sister Marguerite whispers to me, "Stay away from that one."

The intendant returns with a young man, tall and handsome, hair a wavy chestnut brown. His bright eyes glitter in the sunshine, and his smile makes even Sister Marguerite blush. Antoinette practically lifts off her feet. She turns to me and smiles.

She whispers, "Look, girls, the Lieutenant is just as dashing as I'd hoped he would be."

"Antoinette, may I introduce you to First Lieutenant, Pierre Beaugrand. He's one of our finest men." The intendant presents him to his new bride with a satisfied smile, then dismisses himself back to work.

Antoinette drops one shoulder and flutters her eyelashes. He greets her with his hat against his chest and a bow of his head.

"Mademoiselle, my father's letters told me all about your beauty and commitment to married life. He's delighted that your father has arranged this union."

"I am ever so pleased to meet you, Lieutenant. I'm eager to move on from my harrowing journey," she says with a demure smile. "Is our home ready for us? I'll start planning a ceremony immediately. Two days should be sufficient."

"That quickly?" he says. He loosens the collar of his uniform.

"Father has arranged for payment and arrival of goods as soon as we sign our marriage contract."

The Lieutenant clears his throat. "Mademoiselle, our home is not yet completed. I'm sorry if my father has misled you. I've been busy with military commitments and I simply was not prepared."

She forces a smile. "Of course. I understand completely, Pierre."

Our eyes grow large, and I tighten my lips at hearing her address him by his Christian name.

"I would never pull your attention away from your military duties."

"Very kind of you, Mademoiselle. I'm quite busy at the moment." He looks back at the office.

"We shall marry in two days' time and I can stay at the convent until our home is finished. It won't be a problem."

His neck muscles tighten, and he clears his throat. "Well, pleasure to meet you, Mademoiselle."

Small beads of sweat form on his brow. He pauses, looks around, then turns on his heels to rush back to the office.

"Catherine, my dress is not grand enough. I need you to make it sparkle."

"Yes, Mademoiselle," Catherine says.

"More beads. More lace. More everything." Antoinette commands as they hasten their stride.

We hurry after them. I glance back at Bastien Leroux, leaning against a wall, his foot propped behind him. His smile drips much like Jacques's did after he would rub his body on me. I turn to walk with the girls, scratching the back of my neck.

"I must look perfect tomorrow. We'll set a wedding date. I'm sure of it," Antoinette says.

"Maybe he just needs more time," I say.

"Hush!" Antoinette yells as she turns to me. "What would you know about marrying a soldier?"

My fists tighten. "I know that people need to feel connected."

"Well, this *is* a land of new opportunities. I've found my husband, and I hope that you find yours. I don't doubt that even your plain face can find someone here in the new world." She turns and hooks her arm in Catherine's.

My arms straighten. My teeth bite together.

"Careful, child, you don't want to carry hate in your heart," Sister Marguerite says.

"I don't hate her. I just don't understand her wickedness."

"This new beginning is difficult for everyone, Isabelle. Be patient with her. We are all trying to get through the challenges God presents to us." She sighs in Antoinette's direction, "Some just do it with less grace than others."

. . .

The first meeting with the settlers was such a disappointment, I can't imagine doing it again. The girls have devised that the men who've been here the longest get first introductions. I can see why those men had not yet found a wife. The second round arrives tomorrow. At least we will meet in the garden, as the weather is sunny and bright. The girls laugh and whisper, while I stare out the window, watching the birds circle the trees.

"Goodness girl, it's been years. He's gone," Antoinette says.

"You know nothing of my feelings. Go away."

"I don't understand your need to live in the past. You were never meant to have James. Why don't you prepare to find yourself a nice immigrant? A simple man whom you can live blandly ever after with."

The sun filters through the window and dances on her face. "I'm sure you're nervous about your upcoming wedding."

"Why would I be nervous?" She straightens her shoulders.

"The same reason I don't want to choose a husband from a crowd of strangers. We all feel it. Maybe you should take a walk outside. The fresh air is very calming."

"I don't need to calm myself, Isabelle. My life is turning out just as it should be."

"That must mean you were never meant to have James, either."

"I suppose not. The Lieutenant is far more than what Monsieur Beaumont could ever be. Pierre is loyal to the Crown, and he will be loyal to me. He's far better than that traitor from La Rochelle."

"You're planning a wedding, it's best to wash your memory of another man."

Antoinette pulls at her skirt and floats off to dream of her promised husband. Elisabeth places her hand on my arm. "She really is a vile woman."

"All she knows is how to demand what she desires. It's fear that makes her act that way."

"I didn't know she feared anything."

"We all fear something, Elisabeth."

"Why do you continue to be kind to her when she's nothing more than a nasty wench to everyone?"

"I don't know." I sigh. "I think that behind all that miserable vanity is a little girl who's more frightened than anyone understands. She's also the only person left from my past."

Catherine completes the final touches to Antoinette's wedding gown. She secures a sapphire and gold brooch to the rounded neckline of the bodice tightened against Antoinette's bust.

"Ladies, this is what it looks like to see your dreams realized. I've always known that I will marry a handsome, powerful man, but Pierre is something special."

The girls roll their eyes and sigh. Still, living in a convent under the watchful eyes of the nuns can be quite dull, and everyone enjoys the excitement she provides. Catherine helps her don the elaborate gown.

"Why marry so quickly?" I ask Antoinette. "Don't you wish for more time to prepare your wedding and complete your home?"

She whips around. "I want Pierre. And he wants me. He might be resisting, but men are often scared, weak creatures. They need us to teach them how to be strong."

"They want to choose their futures, just as we all do."

She tightens her fists, exhaling as she closes her eyes. She shakes her head and tells Catherine, "More pearls!"

The dress has a billowing white skirt. The porcelain satin shimmers in the light, with detailed stitching of leaves the color of pale pink hydrangea. The soft romantic sleeves and overskirt shine with a hint of champagne when the sunlight hits it just right. Antoinette admires herself in the reflection of the window.

I sneak out for a walk in the garden. It's reminiscent of the Dupre mansion. The moths visit the bright yellow buds of evening primrose, and the sweet perfume of purple lilacs float from the violet blooms. Brushing the soft petals of sunflowers help me forget that soon we'll be surrounded by snow.

A horse's gallop diverts my attention. The intendant arrives. He dismounts, straightens his jacket and marches to the front door of the abbey. I follow behind him, tuck myself behind the arch, and listen.

"Our young Pierre has abdicated his position with the Carignan Regiment. He renounced his French allegiance. He's gone."

"Oh dear," a sister responds. "Why would he do such a thing?"

"He's gone to live with an Algonquin tribe," the intendant says.

A dashing Frenchman living among the Native people, learning Algonkian, and spearing fish to avoid a marriage with Antoinette. This is truly a land of surprises.

"I tried to dissuade him, but he's fallen in love with a Native woman and decided he can no longer live the life his family set out for him. That includes Mademoiselle Lamarche."

"It's all so shocking," Sister Marguerite says.

"If they married, her father would have handed over the shipping rights for La Rochelle's wine and salt trade. His father will be furious. The Lieutenant has let us all down. Please, give my condolences to the girl." He bows his head and departs.

I slip behind the nuns as they hurry through the foyer. They pull Antoinette away from her dress fitting and sit her down. She stuns in her wedding gown, the soft light of the fire behind her.

"Dear, we have some news," Sister Marguerite says.

"Why do you all look so solemn? We should be joyous."

"Mademoiselle, Lieutenant Beaugrand has left," she says.

"Left? Where has he gone? I'm sure he'll return soon. Our wedding is tomorrow, after all."

"There will be no wedding," Sister says.

"No. No. You are mistaken." Antoinette shakes her head.

"The intendant just now delivered the news. The Lieutenant has chosen someone else to marry."

"What do you mean he will not marry me? That can't be. His family promised my father!"

"Yes, dear, but he has chosen to leave his French allegiance behind."

"That is absurd. He'll come back." She fiddles with her dress, avoiding the nuns' worried eyes.

"Antoinette, sometimes God presents us with challenges."

"Don't speak to me of God. I want the husband promised to me."

"Antoinette, he has gone to live with the Natives," Marguerite says.

"What?" she says with a forced laugh. "Why would he do that? That's ridiculous."

"He's decided to marry an Algonquin woman."

Antoinette blinks several times, tilting her head. "No Lieutenant in the Royal Army would dare walk away from his responsibilities."

"He already has, I'm afraid. He's gone," Marguerite says.

"You're telling me that Pierre left me for a woman with no status or money or power?" After a few shallow, rapid breaths, she hurls her chair across the room. "I did not come here to be humiliated!" Her screams echo off the chamber walls.

"Mademoiselle, if you could just take a breath. We can pray and ask God for guidance."

"I don't want to speak to God. He has betrayed me."

The girls peer around the corner, eyes wide. Antoinette reaches her hand to the front of her dress, grabs a handful of pearls and rips them from her bodice. The little gems bounce and ping onto the stone floor like raindrops. Antoinette continues clawing at her dress, hair flying and eyes wild.

The girls run over, stopping her from damaging the dress more. Antoinette looks down at her brooch. Ripping it off the dress, she holds it up to the light. "I will have my revenge." She opens her hand, and the brooch plummets to the floor, where it breaks apart.

"Antoinette, please. We have a relationship with the Natives. We teach their children. I know you're upset, but please keep an open heart."

"I won't forget this." Her voice cracks. She turns to the nuns. "What am I to do now?"

They fold their hands in prayer and avert their gaze.

I step up to her and hand her a coiffe. "You do what the rest of us will. You meet the men and find a husband."

"What?" she scoffs. "Marry a hunter who lives in a stick home?"

I cross my arms in front of my hips. "Careful, Antoinette. You're one of us now."

She throws the coiffe at my face and marches off to the garden. I watch her through the window. Somehow from the back of her perfectly curled hair, I can tell that she's crying.

Catherine lowers to her knees, picking the pearls from the ground one by one, wiping her tears as she works.

The girls all have a heavy look in their eyes. Worry splashed across their faces.

No amount of wealth or power or status can protect us from sadness. This, we all have in common. Heartache bounces about in our lives, casting its shadow wherever it pleases.

A BRAVE SWALLOW

The settlers of New France are working men. They hunt caribou and fish for their meals and build their homes from stones and sticks. Dirt settles under their nails and their skin darkens where the sun colors it. They're capable and strong yet, they can do nothing but line up in front of these young girls and hope to be chosen.

We gather in the garden, take our spots. Elisabeth says, "Are you scared?"

I shrug. "If this group is anything like the last, I don't think you have anything to worry about."

"Antoinette spent hours on her hair and wardrobe this morning, tiring poor Catherine before the day even started."

Antoinette wears a pale pink satin dress and matching hat. She straightens her stitched stomacher and puffs out her décolletage. She says, "I'm sorry, Louise, that you don't have the attributes I do to gain the attention of these men. Despite that, I'm sure you will find someone to take you in."

Louise lifts her chin, eyes focused on the sky to stop the tears.

I lean toward Antoinette. "Don't make me threaten your hair with scissors again."

Antoinette tightens her lips and turns from me.

It's a warm summer day, and the leaves bleed a touch of yellow, hinting at the change of seasons drifting toward us.

The crowd of men arrives, younger than the last. They brim with confidence and pride, ready to parade their colors like a fully displayed peacock. I roll my eyes and watch the clouds drift in and out of shapes above me.

The nuns forego the formal lines and allow us to mingle as a group. Their eagle eyes scan the garden, circling us as the men approach. Several girls dart to the youngest men, others stand back, their faces blushed red.

I clasp my hands and sigh, turning my attention to a small bird. He bounces on a thin branch, twitching and watching us.

A broad-shouldered young man appears, his hands behind his back, each step long and exaggerated. "It's called a cave swallow."

"Oh?"

"You can tell from the pale orange on their bodies. They're brave. They stay into the cold fall, long after other swallows fly south."

"They like the taste of danger, I suppose."

He smiles, a hint of trouble in his eyes. "My name is Andre Boucher."

"You know all about the birds, Monsieur Boucher?"

"I spend a lot of time in the forest. I've learned their calls and habits. It helps me navigate."

My neck flushes hot when he runs his hand through his thick golden hair. My chest swells like the ocean tide, causing me to take a deep breath.

"Might I know your name, Mademoiselle?"

"Isabelle Colette."

"Pleasure to meet you, Mademoiselle Colette. It appears you have a few interested suitors." He motions to a group of men with hats removed, smiles wide. They nod. They're eager. Hungry even.

I look back to his eyes. Deep brown. Reserved. "Would you like to walk with me?" I ask.

His face breaks into a half smile. "Yes, I would."

We stroll through the garden, weaving through the crowd of laughing girls and anxious men.

"I'm from Nantes. Came here two years ago for a better life," he says.

"And is it? Better?"

"Canada is a welcome change from the struggles in France." His smile softens the roughness of him, lighting up his dark eyes with a touch of wildness. "Where did you come from?"

"La Rochelle."

He takes a quick inhale and turns to face me. "La Rochelle. Not far from my hometown."

"And here we are. On the other side of the world, trying to make a new life."

"It's untamed here. Wild." His mouth curves into a tilted smile. "But that is what makes it exciting."

The glint in his dark eyes sparks something in my belly. My heart quickens. I turn my gaze to hide my smile.

I notice Antoinette. The men walk past her as if she's invisible.

"Don't you find it odd? To begin a marriage this way?" he says.

"The men don't seem to think so."

"They're lonely. Happy for a chance at a family," he says. "They don't care how it happens."

"And you?"

He lifts his eyes to the sky and takes a deep breath. "I'm on an adventure."

"And is there room for a wife in that adventurous world of yours?"

"For the right one, yes."

I scan his face. His wide, angular jaw, his full lips. His reddened cheeks look like a boy, but his chest and shoulders are all rugged man. He smiles when he sees me staring at his chest. A devious smile that reminds me of Henri.

"The girls are lonely, too." I trail my hands along the pink rhododendrons. "They're all eager to settle into married life."

"But not you?" He walks beside me.

"No, Monsieur. I'm not eager."

"You aren't like the other girls, are you?" he says.

"I suppose not."

"Look at her, for example." He nods to Antoinette. "You are nothing like her."

"No, I am not. Why aren't the men approaching her? Antoinette is the most beautiful girl here."

"The most beautiful woman in the world is of no interest to these men."

"I thought it is of interest to all men," I say.

"The settlers need wives who'll work the land and build a life together in this difficult place." He rubs the back of his neck. "The last thing they want is a fussy woman who'll complain about the cold or fall apart at the first sign of struggle. One look at her tells me she would be nothing but another difficulty to manage."

"She certainly can be difficult."

"Most men here want a strong woman to share their life with," he says.

"Not a well-bred noblewoman draped in satin?"

"Canada is not merely a new land. It's a new way of life." He raises his eyebrows and tilts his head.

I bite my lip to stifle a smile. A deep urge overtakes me to grab his hand and run into the forest. Disappear into the deep green thicket of trees where the birds sing and the wind howls. Run free, away from responsibility and promises. I have stepped closer to him and once I notice, I step away and straighten my shoulders.

"I see some have already chosen a settler." He motions to three girls signing their contracts under the arches.

"That will make the nuns happy."

"Would you like to walk with me in town tomorrow?" he says.

"Weren't you expecting to find a wife today?"

"No. I was hoping to meet someone interesting." He leans to my ear, "And I have."

His breath brushes my ear, sending a rush of life through me.

Once I catch my breath, I say, "Perhaps you can show me more of this wild land."

"It would be my pleasure. Tomorrow?"

Louise's laugh catches my attention. I turn to see her leaned in toward a man, her hand on his chest.

"Is she a friend of yours?" Andre asks.

"Yes. She is."

"Tell her to be careful. That man is known for a mean temper."

"Thank you. I should pull her away then," I say.

"Tomorrow," he says with hopeful eyes.

"Yes. Tomorrow." I lift my skirt and walk to Louise. I glance over my shoulder for another glimpse of Andre. He hasn't moved. He shoots me a smile and I smooth my skirt, trying to shake off the weakness in my knees.

$\cdot \quad \cdot \quad \cdot$

Back at the convent, the girls chirp like baby birds who've found their first meal. The nuns are exasperated but let them release their girlish excitement. I wrap myself in a cape and walk outside to rest my ears from the chatter.

I stumble upon Antoinette, weeping. As I tiptoe back toward the convent, she calls out to me, "Isabelle, you aren't going to take your opportunity to put me in my place?"

My feet halt. "No. Unlike you, I don't delight in other's pain."

"Oh, yes, you do. I know you must have been bursting with joy to see me left standing alone. You think I deserve it."

"Antoinette, you aren't meant for these men. You won't be happy baking bread in the fireplace you built, hands covered in ash and hair dusted with dirt."

"But my soldier didn't want me. He traded me in for life with the savages. Am I so awful that even men who have never met me want nothing to do with me?" She stifles tears.

Her life has fallen apart, and she's terrified that even farmers don't want her. When she feels frightened, she acts like a wolf in a steel trap. I need to keep her angry claws from scratching at the fragile Louise or soft-centered Elisabeth.

A long, slow exhale prepares my heart to open. "I've been left by everyone I've ever loved. I lost my parents, my sisters. Henri and Etienne. The only man I've ever cared for is gone. I was an outsider in my town. In my own home. I belong nowhere. Not in the Protestant circles that are vanishing, not in a Catholic mansion. Not even in an abbey of women fulfilling promises to their King. Interest from a lonely settler doesn't take away any of that pain."

Her eyes soften and for a moment, I see the little girl from La Rochelle. The one who smiled at me. The girl she was before her family clawed their way through her kindness.

"I have money and power to offer. And they still don't want me."

"The settlers don't want that. Besides, you're meant to choose. Not the other way around. You can have your choice of any man here. Without your father's demands."

"Just as myself?"

"Yes."

Her tears turn to whimpers. She lifts her face toward me with a twinkle of hope. "I doubt that's possible. I need a strong man."

"There are plenty of those here. You will find your husband, and he will be important and handsome, and better than any man you could meet in the gardens of this convent. Better even, than in La Rochelle."

"A new kind of power." She casts a relieved smile.

"There are plenty of soldiers living here, and more arrive every month. I'm certain you'll have one of them as your husband, with a grand wedding for the town to celebrate."

She looks into the black night, "Maybe I can still find what I'm looking for."

"Hopefully we all can." I tighten my cape and turn toward the abbey, but her hand reaches to my shoulder.

"Isabelle, do you still long for James?"

I freeze. My eyes lower and I remember his kiss. His freckles.

"I thought so," she says. "We were children back in La Rochelle. In a fight against our families. We both thought our only way out was through a handsome soldier."

"Our lives were hardly the same," I say.

"I know. But you were always so brave. You didn't need him. Even if you thought you did." She wraps her arms around herself and sighs.

"He teased a different life. One where I wasn't threatened and terrified all the time."

"James could not have changed that for you. He was kind. But he was also weak. Anything you wanted you would have had to find yourself."

Tightness grabs at my stomach. "I thought I had when I converted and came to Canada."

"I don't believe that," she says.

"What's not believable about wanting a better life?"

"When we were children, I used to watch you," she says.

"What?"

"I would hide on my father's ship and watch you from the deck. I was too frightened to be near all the activity. But you, you were always running around with that untamed friend of yours."

"Henri," I say with a smile.

"One day, I saw him steal salted meat from a barrel meant for trade. You created a scene so he wouldn't get caught. Pulling at the dock worker's shirt begging for bread."

"I don't remember that."

"You risked yourself to help him, and still managed to prevent the worker from beating you." She sighs. "I told father how I wanted to be like Monsieur Colette's daughter, brave and wild."

"What did he say?"

"He slapped me. Told me I should never aspire to be like a heretic. Called me childish and demanded I prove myself worthy of the Lamarche name."

"Oh." My shoulders curve forward.

"I set your hair on fire the next day."

Tears rise and my throat stings. I want to hate her for all she's done to me. For what she was a part of and what she allowed. But I remember who she really was. Before this cruel world broke her. When we were innocent, hopeful children who didn't care which Bible we held.

"It was never enough," she said. "He sensed my weakness. I've not earned my place in our family. I often wonder who I'd be if I had loving parents. I'm sorry that I hurt you."

A breathless grip seizes me. My eyes ache from holding back tears. "Antoinette, you can change any time you wish to. Your father isn't here to control you."

"I have an obligation to the LaMarche name. An obligation for power. I marry to strengthen his trade. Anything less will be a failure." She stiffens her posture.

"Might you learn to be powerful without hurting others to get there?"

"My dowry is dependent on two things. Protecting my father and protecting his money. There's no use for softness. Weakness topples giants. So he says."

A mockingbird sings from a tree in the darkness. I search the black sky for a glimpse but can only hear his echoes in the distance. I think of Andre. His coy smile and broad shoulders. His wild eyes.

"Isabelle, James never could have come for you."

Shaken from the image of Andre, I square my shoulders and tighten my jaw.

"His father punished him," she says. "He sent him to fight in the Spanish Netherlands to prove his loyalty to the Crown."

My fists tighten and look away. "What happened to him?"

"He was captured. No one's heard from him since."

I open my mouth to scream at her, but she raises her hand.

"I know I should have told you. But what good would it have done? You aren't like the rest of us, Isabelle. You're wild and free. Don't let the past hold you back."

Her figure fades into the darkness of the abbey.

How long have I held onto a dream that has never been possible? I think back to La Rochelle, to the girl I once was. Full of fight and bravery. I intended to bleed Protestantism, fight for my people, and force change.

I failed.

The mockingbird carries his song into the inky sky. The breezy summer evening is like a whisper on my skin, like it might float me away to nothingness. Freedom is all I've ever wanted, but now that I have it, I may have no soul to fight for.

.   .   .

Sister Marguerite insists that she chaperone my time with Andre. "You are a Daughter of the King, Mademoiselle."

The term still makes me shudder. Back home, the King orders Protestants beaten and killed, yet I am one of his chosen ones. I scratch at my neck with the thought, a feverish itch that climbs over my skin.

"Yes, Sister."

James is a prisoner of war, sent as punishment for helping me. It's my fault he's lost in the Spanish Netherlands. Possibly killed. I did this to him. And now the smile of another man makes my heart race. A deep pain settles inside of me, the bitter feeling of betrayal. I long to breathe the fresh air and experience the wild of the forest. Where these thoughts don't smother me.

My hand grazes the rough bark of the trees as we pass, and the wind brushes my face. It softens the aching restlessness crawling through my mind. When I see Andre's smile, everything softens a bit more.

We stroll past the merchants' stalls and the shops in the town square, Sister Marguerite close behind.

"Tell me more about you, Monsieur."

"I have a good life here. I've built a nice home close to the river, where I can fish and hunt. There's never a lack of food in Quebec."

"In France we often traded bites of bread and cheese to survive." The words slip out like water through a crack. I shake my head to rid the painful memories. "Please, tell me more of your work with the Natives."

"I've grown to see many of them as family. The military men don't understand that we've stolen their land and forced our French ways on them. The Natives know nothing of our King but benefit from trade with us. France needs their cooperation to make the fur trade successful. It's a complicated world I navigate."

"Canada has been good to you, it seems."

"When I walk through the forests, smell the trees, and listen to the river rush, I know there's no better place for me," he says.

"Most of the girls work to perfect their sewing skills and chatter about babies. All I want is to fly open the door and run into the forest and breathe in the biting cold of the fall mornings." I catch myself, tightening my lips.

"That can be arranged," he says, "I like that you want adventure." We flick our eyes between each other and the ground.

"Tell me, Monsieur, are the winters as terrible as they say?"

"That depends on your view of terrible. They are miserably cold. But the quiet of snow and the crunch of ice under your shoes. The thrill of a still forest. It's a freedom I never felt in France."

"Dangerous, too."

"Well, if the cave swallow can do it, so can I."

His cheeks redden into plump rounds as his lips pull into a smile. His eyes glint with flickers of sunlight. A lightness like a breeze wafts through me, landing at my thumping heart.

"Well, what do we have here?" The familiar spider movements creep toward us.

"Colonel." Andre's posture stiffens.

"Bonjour, Mademoiselle. We meet again." Bastien circles me like prey. "We had a lovely encounter a few days back." He steps closer to me and whispers, "Didn't we, Mademoiselle."

Sister Marguerite links her arm in mine.

"Andre Boucher, yes?" Bastien says. "You live close to the river. Spend a lot of time with the savages." He flashes a smile crowded with yellowed teeth.

"It's vital to the fur trade that we maintain strong relationships," Andre says.

Bastien's snarls. He turns to me, rolling his fingers. "Mademoiselle, might I call on you tomorrow? Show you the real Quebec."

"I'm afraid I'm quite busy tomorrow." I shoot a glance at Sister Marguerite.

"Colonel, Isabelle is busy attending to chores at the abbey. Now, we really must go. Au revoir." She rushes me away, Andre at my side.

"When that man talks, it feels like a dragon breathing fire on me," I say

"He's as corrupt as they come," Sister Marguerite says.

"He's had his eye on me for a while, "Andre says. "He's eager to shut down individual trade with the Natives. He wants to control the shipping rights."

"The struggle for power extends far beyond France," I say.

"It extends everywhere humans are," Sister Marguerite says. "You girls would be wise to choose men that strive for stability. We live in an unpredictable land, and it's only going to get wilder."

NAVIGATING A NEW WORLD

The girls that haven't married grow restless. It's all they can talk about. Some have met with their choices, taking time to get to know them. Others have already signed their names and left with their ox, chicken, pigs, cow, and barrels of salted meat — and a stranger in their bed. The King gifts them the beginnings of a farm, and fifty livres to start their new life. Then, it's onto the immediate task of having babies. The more you have, the more money you receive.

"I can't take it anymore, I'll marry Francois tomorrow," Louise says.

"Louise, I told you he's known for a temper. Why would you jump into marriage with him?"

"Because he's the only one that wants her," Antoinette snaps.

Louise lowers her head. "I don't want to be left alone here while everyone else marries."

"Does he have a home for you?" I ask.

"I don't know."

Catherine says, "I might choose Charles as well. He has no money, but he seems kind."

I shake my head. "Girls, we must be smart about this."

"Most of us can't even write. We're not smart," one girl says.

"None of you are ignorant. If you can put an X by your name, you have the power to decide your future. We choose our husbands. They do not choose us."

"But we're here to be wives," Louise says.

I kick off my shoes and lift my skirt to my knee, stepping onto a sturdy wood chair in my stocking feet. Their hopeful eyes stare back at me.

"We were brought here to fulfill a promise. In exchange for our sacrifice, the King gives us power. Don't waste it by giving in to childish insecurities. We're women now. We decide what we need."

Elisabeth stands. "We're just happy for someone to care for us. What else do we need?"

"To start with, a house. You will not accept a marriage proposal from a man who has yet to build a home or has one built primitively just to secure a bride. You'll say no to any contract you please and ask the men any question you wish. Does he drink? Does he gamble? What are his views on the colony?" My hands clasp together at my chest. "Ladies, this is your future. Our needs become the needs of your family for years to come."

Antoinette stands. "Isabelle, you're asking these girls to want something they've never known. You think them capable of power?" She releases a dismissive laugh.

"Yes. I do." Holding my skirt off my feet, I steady my hand on the back of the chair and jump down, face to face with her. "We are all capable of power."

Catherine asks, "Isabelle, will you marry Andre?"

A pain slices straight through my chest. "Forget about me. I care about you. All of you. I made a promise to someone long ago that I won't break."

"Oh, Isabelle, James is gone. When will you realize that?" Antoinette folds her arms.

"My promise was to my grandmother. To find a path to courage, and I'm going to start with these girls."

"Change is not possible, Isabelle," she says. "We all still live by the same rules that have long governed our place in the world. There is no sense in hoping to change the will of God."

"You believe God has determined that you dress in fine linens and sleep on satin sheets, while he has relegated us to freezing nights and empty bellies."

Antoinette nods. "The Sun King was predestined to rule the most powerful empire in the world. He was born into the throne, being in power at such a young age. Why would God place him there if it is not what the world needed?"

"Why would God place me here if it is not what the world needed? He's kept us together all these years. I've seen you change. So can these girls."

"I demand more from my life because I know that I'm entitled to it. You fight for scraps because you've always been poor. You have nothing in your mind, so you have nothing in your hands."

"France made me poor. People like you held me there."

"Maybe God has forsaken you, Isabelle. You betrayed who you are, didn't you?"

Fire shoots up my arms and I bite down hard to control myself from slapping her. "Has he determined that you are so unworthy of comfort that your own family trades you for shipping rights, and your husband leaves you for a Native?"

The girls gasp again. A twinge of regret bites at me.

Her arms drop to her sides, her eyes rimmed red. "My family will continue to support me. What do you have? Nothing."

"Which means I have nothing to stop me from dreaming. God put me here because I dared to believe that I'm more than a helpless peasant."

"I believe I'm to marry a powerful man, just as my mother and every woman that came before us has done."

We circle each other.

"God gave us pain, but he also gave us the power of resilience. He gave us the strength to let go of our past and demand a better future. Out of every peasant and every orphan, the powers of France picked us. This new world is ours to shape. I know that these beautiful, strong women have the power to make change in this new world." A pause, and a glare at Antoinette. "The power God has granted them."

The girls rise, clapping.

Antoinette steps back, rubbing her hands together. "Be careful, Isabelle, the only thing more dangerous than fear is hope." She sulks away. Sister Marguerite paces in the hallway, flashing me an approving smile and a bow of her head.

.   .   .

The leaves have turned to the rich crimson and gold of fall. The sun glows with a rust hue, much like the mornings I ran between homes, my Bible sewn into my skirt. I slip out of the garden as the girls learn of harvesting and preserving for winter months. Nature still beckons me, to the silence of walking amongst the trees.

The fear of the dragoons is no longer with me, but Quebec City carries its own dangers. As I crest a hill, Bastien appears.

"Pardon, Monsieur." I turn back toward the abbey.

His hand slithers around my arm, resisting my forward pull. "No need to take off. I've been hoping to speak with you."

I turn slowly to face him. "What about, Colonel?"

"Well, Mademoiselle, the Filles du Roi are under orders from the King to marry and start families in Quebec."

"I'm aware of that."

He leans to me. "I wish to marry you."

My heart sinks. "Why would you want to marry me? You're an officer. I have nothing to offer you."

His hand rests on my cheek, my face twitching from his touch.

"You have much to offer me." His voice is slow, like rain dripping down a window. He runs his long bony fingers through my curls while I stand rigid.

Flashes come back to me of Jacques's bloody face.

"I am powerful here." His voice is smooth and controlled. "You can have the life you could never dream of in France."

"There are other women who are a better fit for your needs." I pull my head back and shake my hair loose.

"What I wish for is the most beautiful woman in New France."

"That is not me, Monsieur."

"I assure you, it is. I can offer you beautiful things, a stately home, and protection." He leans close as the back of his fingers glide along the curve of my neck.

Flinching, I say, "Again, Colonel Leroux, I'm not the right girl. I cannot marry you."

"Surely, you would not pass on the opportunity to marry a powerful leader of the Royal Army. I can offer you a life better than any immigrant can."

"It is entirely my decision whom I marry. By orders of the King." My eyes squint. My shoulders straighten. "And I do not want you."

"You don't want to make an enemy of me, Mademoiselle."

"Need I remind you that I am protected by the King. If you will please let me pass."

"No. The King is not here. He is an ocean away and he's very grateful for my service. It would be a shame to have you sent back to France for failing your duties here. Tell me you'll marry me," he says.

"Let me through." I tighten my arms at my side.

"Don't be a fool. You need protection here in the colony."

"A fool would marry for status. I have no interest in your power."

"Your little friend Boucher is not who he seems," he says with a roll of his fingers. "You will be in a dangerous world with that man."

"My life is none of your concern, Colonel."

"Maybe it should be."

"Or you'll send me back to France?" I square my shoulders and do not back down to his stare.

"Don't tempt me."

"I have no interest in tempting you. Now let me pass."

He steps aside, arm extended. I lift my skirt and run back toward the abbey, worry boiling inside me.

His laugh echoes through the trees and hangs in the air, my feet striking the ground feverishly. Through the quiet he yells, "I have all the power here."

. . .

Elisabeth greets me when I rush through the doors of the abbey. "Goodness, are you all right?" she asks.

She leads me to the kitchen, handing me a goblet of wine while I try to rid my mind of the Colonel's bony fingers. "I'm fine."

"Good. Now tell me about Andre," she says with a smile.

"He's lovely. My time with him seems very natural and…" I stop to catch my breath.

"Yes?" she urges.

"When he looks at me, I feel as though excitement rests just below the surface. I want to trust him."

"What are you scared of?"

Colonel Leroux was just trying to scare me, I tell myself. "That I will get my heart broken again, just like I did with James."

"But Andre is here. He's real."

"Yes." I shake the worry from my mind. "Now, tell me about your suitor," I ask.

"He has a lovely home just outside of town, a fully stocked farm, and he's kind to me."

"That's wonderful. I think you are making a wise choice."

"I need more time, but I feel good when I'm with him. You inspire me to take a chance."

"He's a soldier?" I ask.

"He was. He left the French army for a simpler life here in Quebec. He doesn't wish to be involved in fighting with the Iroquois and hopes to live in peace with them. You were smart to tell us to ask about their views on society."

Just then, through the door bursts Louise, crying, hands shaking. "Goodness, what happened?" I ask.

Her eyes dart between us.

"Louise, it's all right. Tell us what happened," Elisabeth urges.

"I... I snuck out with Francois tonight to tell him I would marry him. He pushed me against a tree and kissed me."

"All right. What then?" I ask.

"I didn't want to act impure before our wedding day, so I pulled away. He...he grabbed me." She rubs her arm.

My fists tighten. "And then what?"

"And then when I told him to let me free..."

"Yes?"

She lifts her hand to her brow and pushes aside her mound of dark curls to reveal a shining crimson welt on her cheek.

"Oh, Louise, you poor thing," Elisabeth says.

"You must never speak to him again," I say.

"We're to be married tomorrow! I can't leave him now."

"You certainly can. We were promised the right to break contracts," I say.

"The girls that break them are shunned. No one wants them after that."

Elisabeth and I exchange worried looks. "Louise, send word to him that you're ill and wish to postpone your marriage contract. We need time to figure out how to protect you."

"Isabelle, I just want to be a wife."

"Not like this, you don't."

.   .   .

We gather in the dwindling afternoon sun to learn about medicinal herbs to dry and use during the long winter months. Sister Marguerite displays freshly picked juniper and lobelia. She teaches us how partridge berry and raspberry leaf tea help our bodies prepare for childbirth in the months before the baby arrives. Movement behind the trunk of a red oak steals me attention. Sneaking away from the group to follow the flutter of the leaves, Andre's mischievous smile beckons me.

When Sister Marguerite turns her attention to a bloodroot flower, I run behind the wide trunk, hidden by the scarlet leaves that hang on the long branches. Andre smiles, biting his lower lip.

"Come." He holds my hand.

"Where are we going?"

"You'll see."

He pulls me by the hand. We run from the convent, my heart racing, my auburn curls fly in the cool breeze. Once under cover of trees, he lifts me to his horse, his strong arms placing me softly on the saddle. He positions himself behind me, adjusting the reins. I only have a moment to feel his legs tighten against me when the horse rushes forward, sending my heart lurching against my chest.

We bounce together as the horse gallops through the trees, turning west along the St. Charles River, past glistening silver spruce and tall spindly pines. I close my eyes as we fly through the trees, the autumn air sharp against my cheeks.

Andre whispers in my ear, "You told me you longed to run into the forest and breathe in the biting cold of the fall mornings."

My eyes sting from the sharp air. I fall back into his strong chest, the exhilaration of the forest swirling around me. The air prickles my lungs like needles. Andre's stubbled cheek brushes against my ear.

The horse slows as we reach a pathway under a grove of white birch trees. As the horse trots, Andre's chest rises and falls against me. Above us is a canopy of soft fluttering leaves the color of dandelions. The gold and sunflower treetops perch high above the crinkly white trunks, spilling out onto the branches beside it, shading us from the glow of the amber sun. The horse clops through the white trees, its hooves wading through a forest floor of butter yellow that matches the leaves above.

Andre pulls back to stop the horse, which lets out a tuft of mist from its nose into the cool air. Andre's boots hit the ground, and he reaches for me. He slides me down, his hands curled around my hips, my feet lightly rustling the leaves that cover the earth. He wraps his hands around my waist. My stomach tightens, leaning toward him.

He leads me deeper into the honey-rich foliage.

"It looks just like a painting." Spinning in a circle the blur of yellow floods my vision like sunshine. The trees aren't withering, but alive and exuberant.

"It only looks this way for a short time," Andre says. "I steal away to the forest every moment I can as the brilliant colors soon fade to the dark of winter. Its beauty is fleeting."

My stomach flutters as he steps closer to me, his hand reaching for mine. "Thank you for bringing me here," I say.

The golden woods light up Andre's rugged face. He watches my eyes take in the beauty of the forest. We hold hands facing each other, our bodies moving closer. His face nears mine just as a gust of wind flies through the trees, rustling the branches.

The wispy yellow leaves take flight and dance through the air, falling around us as they float on the wind. They fall like feathers, landing in our hair and on our shoulders. We release each other's hands, bringing them together, palms up, to collect the fragile little leaves shaped like spears. I hold one up to watch the light flicker through its veins. "Beautiful, isn't it?"

Without turning his eyes from me, he says, "It's remarkable."

. . .

The yellow birch leaves fluttered through my mind when I woke this morning. My desire to run is stronger than ever. But today my feet find themselves eager to run toward him. I slip out of the abbey quietly and rush to Andre's house in the hazy morning fog.

We walk the woods around his house, discussing the adventures of colony life. He tells me about arriving in Quebec after being knocked unconscious in an accident on the ship. "I arrived with no money and a wicked headache. The local tribe of Huron found me sleeping along the water, so they took me in. They taught me to trap furs and accepted me as one of their own."

"How did you progress from trapping to trading?"

"The Chief learned to trust me, demanding that I negotiate their trades. The Frenchmen agreed, reluctantly, but I remain the sole trader for the

Huron. And I still trap. The thrill of walking alone in the quiet forest, it's where I'm at home."

My cheeks bloom with heat. "Being alone in nature is the only place I've ever been able to breathe free."

"That's why I chose to speak with you that day at the abbey."

"How could you possibly know that? You picked me out of a line of girls who all look the same."

He shakes his head with a knowing smile. "The other girls were nervous. Fidgeting their hands and rocking on their feet. I was beginning to think it was a mistake, looking for a wife this way. And then I saw you. Still. Strong. Your eyes scanned the men, then went back to staring at the treetops. To that lonely bird on a bouncing limb. I knew there was an adventurous spirit in you. And I was right."

I turn my face from his, fighting his stare. "Are you ever scared? Out here alone?"

"Sometimes," he says. "But I've lived my life always in some sort of struggle. At least here I have a home and friends to protect me. They keep watch, hidden in the forest." He gestures around him. "There are eyes everywhere among the trees."

"It's been a long time since I've felt like part of a family." Memories begin to bubble and grow but I quickly tamp them down.

"That's one thing about New France. We can all be reborn here. Did you leave family?"

"No." A catch in my throat. "They're all gone."

"We both arrived alone. Hoping for an easier life." He shifts toward me.

"And now you have it. An easier life. Freedom. Why stifle that with a wife?"

He tilts his head, furrows his brow. "There is no freedom in a lonely heart."

Warmth ripples through my limbs. Liquid gold envelops me and all I can see is his dark inviting eyes. "You're lonely?"

"Aren't we all?" he says.

"I was too busy trying to survive in France to feel loneliness."

He steps so close that his chest touches mine. "And now?"

His breath warms my lips. "Now I have a taste of what I've always dreamed of."

"Love?" he asks, hopeful.

"To fly free."

His head yanks back from our almost grazing kiss. His cheeks pull slowly into a grin — one of devilish intrigue. He steps back from me but reaches for my hand. His neck is rough and dark red, illuminated by the filtered sunlight through the trees. His stubbled chin looks coarse, but his touch is soft as velvet. My lips long to pull him back to me.

"You're a wild swallow, Isabelle Colette."

"Wild at heart. Just like you." My lips ache to taste his mouth on mine.

I drop my hand from his. This swallow can't fly. Not yet. The faintest memory of James tethers my feet to the ground. I can't seem to wash away the guilt that's stuck to me like a cobweb.

A BEGINNING AND AN END

The gray of morning rolls in through the windows of our room as Elisabeth fixes another girl's hair. She chose her husband yesterday, and today she will leave the abbey as a wife. Elaborate wedding gowns are for the wealthy. This group wears their cleanest frock, adorned with hopeful eyes looking toward a brighter future.

Louise carries on about their future babies playing in the woods together. I face my reflection in the window. My pale skin. My green eyes. It's like looking at my mother. It snaps at my heart, sucking my breath into the cold air.

I've failed everyone.

"Your suitor will be here soon," Elisabeth says to the young girl. She smiles broadly and the other girls gather at the glass doors to wait for her soon-to-be husband.

Elisabeth stands beside me. "Are you all right?"

I grab her arm. "How do we let go of our past and jump into life with a man we hardly know?"

She looks at the girls standing at the window. "Everyone marries into the great unknown."

"I've made so many mistakes. Hurt so many people." Tightness grips my throat, my shoulders wind up to my ears.

"We've all made mistakes. Forgive yourself. You deserve to be happy."

"I was so desperate. I betrayed my family, gave up my faith. I turned away from everyone I loved."

I catch my breath and rub my eyes clear of tears. A swallow chirps in the trees outside. Elisabeth rests her hand on my shoulder.

The girls are in a crowd gathered at the open doors, clamoring to see into the courtyard. Antoinette, impatient, pushes her way through the whispering crowd. "Goodness, girls. It's only a settler."

At the entry, Antoinette stands still. She turns slowly to stare at us. I shake my head in confusion. With the girls surrounding me, I step outside. Antoinette's eyes are wide, her mouth open.

Past her, a man stands at the other end of the courtyard, propped on one side by a cane. I can't make him out, so I step out, into the hissing wind. The deep copper hair. The tall frame. The protective chest I once buried my face in.

"James?" I whisper.

My chest heaves, and the world around me fades away. It's him and me standing with only earth between us, the world that once divided us, now crashing us together.

He was a memory for so long. Now he stands so close that I can see his curls flying in the wind. The vision of him across the courtyard leaves me frozen. It feels impossible.

He sees me, a brilliant smile fills his face. The earth releases its grip, and I take a step, afraid he's a mirage that could float to dust. Another step leads to another, then my legs release into a run. I don't slow down, crashing into him, arms wrapped around him, grateful and relieved.

"You're alive." My body remembers his as a familiar but distant memory that's come back to life.

"I am." His hands hold my cheeks as he lowers his eyes, and his forehead touches mine. Time stops. The gray clouds open and rain patters the rooftops.

"What are you doing here?" I ask.

"I came back for you, just as I promised."

Mud begins spattering my dress, rain moistening my face, feeling the touch of the man I thought was gone forever. A man I thought I killed with my selfishness.

Sister Marguerite yells at me from inside, "Isabelle! Come here at once!"

I ignore her. James's shining blue eyes welcome me back to them. Comforting. Protective. Real.

"I never stopped dreaming of the day I would be back in your arms," he says as he leans toward me again.

His lips almost to mine, memories of Andre push their way through. I pull back and look to the mottled sky to catch my breath. "You survived a war."

"Only because of your memory. You saved me, Isabelle."

I am also the reason his father sent him there.

He runs his hand through my hair. "I'm here. After all these years. I'll never leave you again."

My stomach tenses. It's all too much. James is alive and stands before me in Quebec. An injured Catholic soldier. Ready to pick up where all the pieces shattered apart.

"Sister Marguerite is calling. I should go."

He smiles, scanning his eyes over my face. "I'll wait."

. . .

The raindrops drip on the stone path with a soft beat. On the other side of the parlor window, James paces. He limps, leaning on his cane. The way he winces makes pain churn in my stomach.

Elisabeth slides next to me and we watch him. "Is it really him?" she asks.

"It really is."

"So why are you in here?"

I turn my face from her and swallow against the gritty pain in my throat. "Andre."

"Oh. Of course."

"James was supposed to be gone forever. A foggy dream. Memories."

"And now that he's here?" she asks.

"Memories are gone. He's real, reaching out for a promise I made to him years ago." I watch his hair fly in the breeze. No longer the bright shining glow of copper it once was. It's dulled. Dark. Like a clay pot soaked in water.

"Is that a bad thing?" she says.

"I was so young and naïve back in La Rochelle. I thought I needed him to save me."

"You don't need to be saved anymore, do you?" she says.

"No."

"Then tell him that."

I rub my eyes to stop the tears. "He was sent to war. He sacrificed everything to help me."

"It's all right if your feelings have changed."

"I don't know if they have." A long slow exhale does little to calm my racing heart. "I was certain I would never feel close to another man. Until

Andre." I close my eyes and let the memory of racing through the forest sweep me away in a breathless escape. "He's wild and free and unpredictable."

"A little like you," she says with a smile.

I turn to face her. "My wild heart has led me to betray everyone. I don't know if I can let James cross an ocean to find me and not give him the life I promised. Andre is brave and strong. He will be fine."

"But will you?"

My eyes roll up to the ceiling. Dark wood panels with dancing shadows of dark clouds. Tears crest my lids, but a deep breath halts them. I lower my head to her. "I don't know."

I enter the courtyard alone, my hands trembling and cold. James waits under cover of an arch, the rain dripping onto the ground around him. His posture is strained. Twisted to the side as his elbow braces his waist.

I grab hold of my strength and lift my head. "James."

He turns, his face thin and angular but he still finds a warm smile. "I'm here. We can finally start our life together."

I bite my lip, tighten my brow. "The girl you knew was merely a child. I was desperate. I'm not the same person you left in La Rochelle."

"Neither of us are the same as we once were." He looks down at his cane. "I certainly am not."

My stomach tightens hard enough to force a moan. I shake my head. "What happened to you?"

"The Spanish will stop at nothing to get to France's secrets."

I step closer to him. "They tortured you?"

He begins to speak, then stops. "It's all in the past."

I reach for his hand. Covered in ridges and depressions where scars have knitted over wounds. "You fought back."

"What choice did I have?"

"Your father sent you to fight. Because you helped me. These scars are because of me." The anguish rolls up on me. So fast, it tumbles me like a wave and spits me out to the sand.

"None of this is your fault. I made my choices." He intertwines his fingers with mine. "Besides, you're no longer a Huguenot. You finally converted."

"I had no choice, either."

His hand cups my cheek, the tough ridges of his scars press into my skin like a sharp knife. "Nothing else matters as long as we're together." He leans close, kisses my other cheek with a soft press near my temple.

He rubs his hip and shifts his weight. His pain makes my heart sick. I close my eyes and remember our secret meetings in the forest. His kiss. His smile. The hope I held through all the heartache.

He pulls back and says, "If you're mine, I could want nothing more." He wraps his arm around my waist. "Let me protect you, just as I've always done."

I soften into his embrace, like a hug for the frightened girl he first met. His scent reminiscent of life before. His touch somehow connects me with my past. His lips rest on my neck and I know that I cannot break another promise.

"Walk with me," he says.

"You look to be in pain. Should we sit?"

"No. I want to take in the view with you of our new home."

The sun lowers its eyes as it turns toward night. We walk to the edge of the enormous cliff that lies just beyond the convent. The sky stirs with ribbons of pale pink that move into lights dancing, turning the color of a bright red rose tinged with saffron, and the wind flutters my dress in waves around me.

Overlooking the enormous St. Lawrence River that carried me from my homeland, James holds both my hands in his. He kisses them. "Be my wife, Isabelle. Let's forget everything from the past and start a new life. Together."

Forget my past. It is so entrenched in my being, I'm not sure how to do that. Much like the decision I made under the moonlight on the Seine, marrying James means saying goodbye. Forever.

The rich glow of the now ruby sky lights up the sea. Everything I dreamed of since exile is here in my grasp.

"I can offer you beautiful things. Protection. You may walk in the sunshine and breathe free. Isn't it just as you always wanted?"

"Yes, I suppose it is."

I turn to the fading sunlight and wonder where Andre is.

His fingers reach deep into my curls. His eyes so hopeful, so certain. "Leaving you was the hardest moment of my life." Tears rim his eyes. "These scars, these broken bones, none of them will hurt as long as you are with me. Hold me. Be my wife. Just as we always dreamed it could be. I need you."

His blue eyes reflect the sun, shining like a prism and dulling the ache inside me. "Yes. I will marry you."

He pulls me tightly into his chest. My body turns rigid, worry heavy in my gut. I lean my cheek against his chest and stare out to the blue expanse of the ocean.

James shifts uncomfortably. "There is nothing more I need. Just you."

I let him hold me. The Catholic wife he has always dreamed of.

DON'T LOOK BACK

The notary presides over our union. The sun hangs low in the late fall afternoon as the amber light tumbles through the window of the dark room. Gone are the vibrant colors of autumn, now the trees stand bare. No fluttering yellow leaves under which to fall in love. No golden sun to warm our skin. Only the cold blowing wind before the snowfall. James holds my hand, caressing it. As the notary announces us married, I turn to Elisabeth and Louise and force a smile. The tears crest my eyes, and I look at James. He's kind and loyal. This was the right thing to do.

Elisabeth waves goodbye, her hand on her heart and a sadness in her eyes. I swallow the regret that simmers in my throat, nod my head, and extend my hand to James. He helps me to the carriage, his bright blue eyes focused on the trail ahead. I turn from him and watch the abbey fade into the distance.

A high-ranking officer has traveled to France, permitting us to stay in his home, thankful for James's sacrifice to the Army. James leads me through the door to the two-story home overlooking the town square. Beaver pelts drape the chairs and stacks of wood climb the walls next to the stone fireplace.

"Some wine," he says. He pours from a decanter into two goblets and grimaces as he lowers to the chair.

"Are you all right?"

"Of course. I'm fine. Now tell me about your journey."

"It was difficult," I say. "Long and terrifying. How did you find me?"

"Father Hyacinth. On my way back home after I escaped, I stopped to see him secretly, to ask what happened to a girl named Isabelle." He smiles. "He told me how he helped you land in the good graces of the Sun King, how you sailed to Canada. I prayed I would reach you before you married and forgot all about me."

"I have never forgotten you." I tug at the tightened sides of my dress. "And your time in the Spanish Netherlands?"

"I spent two years in a prison cell, prodded for the secrets of the French Army. I never imagined I would see my homeland, or you, ever again. The French officers finally arrived, breaking down doors and killing guards to drag us out."

"Oh, James, I'm so sorry." My eyes lower to his leg. The way he shifts his weight to the side. The way his back curves.

"It's all over. I'm here now," he says.

He runs his fingers through my hair, brushing my cheek with the back of his hand. Thoughts of Andre creep up and I shut my eyes to push them away.

We spend hours catching up on lost time. He tells me of the exile, and the bodies strewn about the streets, bloody and broken. His punishment for helping us was a savage attack from the dragoons. "My father handed me off to them to teach me a lesson," he says.

I tell him of Jacques's attack and the kindness of Jeanne and Clement and Father Hyacinth. I recount Maman's death and my baptism in the moonlit waters of the Seine. How Madeleine died in my arms. "I sometimes wonder if I'll ever find the peace I long for."

"Darling," he says, "that's exactly what we have here. No more trouble. Only happiness."

"Yes, happiness." The rooms grows warm.

"It's a shame you didn't convert back in La Rochelle. All that time lost when we could have been together."

I take a deep breath, staring into my glass.

He places his hand on mine. "My capture. My injuries. They all could have been prevented." he says.

I shoot my eyes to the fire. The glowing heat of flickering red.

He leans to kiss me. Hesitant, I pull from him. "Nevermind," he says as he scoots closer. "You are here now. I'm here. Nothing else matters."

"What is your job here, James?"

He sighs, frustrated that I'm resisting him. "Protect the fur trade. Until my hip heals, no battle."

"The fur trade?" A knot tightens in my stomach. He'll meet Andre.

"Oh, Isabelle. You're growing nervous for nothing. I promise you, I'll be fine. I don't want you to worry anymore. I'm here."

His smile is painfully handsome. His shining eyes reflect off the flickering light of the oil lamp and for a moment I remember what it felt like to be close to him.

He stands and reaches his hand out, pulling me into him. My hands hesitantly reach for his chest. I close my eyes, trying to settle into the softness of his touch. He removes a satin ribbon from my hair, placed by Elisabeth for my wedding day. He moves my curls aside, kissing my neck softly. My body melts, the touch of someone feels so foreign and impossible. Andre was right, maybe I was lonely.

His hand rests on my cheek as he takes in the scent of my hair. His body feels different than it did years ago, leaner, the spaces filled in with rigid muscles. My chest tightens, and I look into the eyes that I once felt lost in. It's him and me by the light of the fire, feeling our way through closeness after years apart.

I hesitate again, and he leans in to kiss me. A husband kissing his wife, consummating marriage. Yes, I can do this.

I remove his jacket, my eyes scanning his shoulders. I untie his shirt, watching him lift it over his head and slide it down to the floor. My hands run over raised scars on his chest and stomach, where they burned him. My body tightens. The wave of guilt ready to crash me into the ground again.

He lifts my chin with his finger. "They don't hurt. Not anymore."

"You didn't deserve this."

He grabs me and kisses me. My stomach does not flutter the way it used to. My knees don't go weak as they did with Andre's kiss. Still, he is gentle. He keeps kissing my neck and chest as I try to relax in his hands. He unties my bodice and removes my gown, leaving me in my shift.

I untie the ribbons on the front of the white linen, looking at him with nervous anticipation. He waits for my readiness. The shift slides off my right shoulder and his eyes dance with intrigue. I drop the other shoulder, and as I release my hands, the final cover of protection falls to the ground, leaving me as bare as the trees prepared for snow.

He inhales, his hands curving around my hips. His hands run along my waist over my shoulders and down the skin between my breasts, then he kisses my collarbone. He removes his breeches, leaving me frozen. I've dreamed of this moment for so many years. And here I stand, feeling only the cold air against my skin.

He lowers me to the fur rug by the fire, his touch gentle as a breeze. Our naked bodies knock together, feeling like stones tumbling. He lies on top of me and finds his way to push inside, causing me to gasp in pain. My open mouth rests on his shoulder.

"Are you all right? Should I stop?"

I shake my head no, determined to push past the pain that Sister Marguerite assured me would happen. He moves gently, rocking back and forth. I try to relax as she instructed me to do. As his lips and tongue entangle with mine, the searing pain inside me lifts. My back rubs against the scratchy fur. With each push, the sting lightens. He groans and I inspect the freckles on his cheeks. I can't see his blue eyes, his lids are shut tight.

He keeps thrusting. He wraps my legs around him and buries his face in my neck. My gaze lifts to the wood beam above me. There are cobwebs that need clearing. I'll do that first thing in the morning.

A final thrust and he falls heavy on me, a deep sigh escapes through his falling chest.

When it's over, I feel wet and sore. We lie together, bodies moist, his breath pronounced. Heavy. My head rests in his shoulder, his lips on my forehead.

"Isabelle, we have the rare opportunity not often seen in the world."

"What is that?" I ask as he covers me with a fur blanket.

"To marry for love."

I turn my back to him, watching the smoke rise from the blackened logs of the fireplace. "Yes." My throat stings, and I quietly wipe away a tear.

· · ·

My first morning as a soldier's wife.

"Come, my dear." James extends his arm toward the Notre-Dame Church in Place Royal.

"What are we doing?"

"Mass. What else would we be doing?" He laughs.

"I don't see why-"

James interrupts me. "Isabelle, you are no longer an outsider. You are a subject of the King. A Catholic member of New France, just as I am. We will stand before our town and become part of this world. Come." His hand on my back, he pushes me into the stone building.

The air is cold inside the stone cathedral. My heart thunders in my chest and I look to James for reassurance. We have Mass at the abbey every day. Being here, in front of the town, declaring my place in the church sends chills up my neck. My head grows lightheaded.

"Well, it's certainly…" He pauses. "Simple. I suppose it fits the country life here. I'm sure that will all change as we build our city."

Each step on the gray stone makes me shudder. I look back at the light in the doorway, but James guides me forward. We take seats and wait for the priest to begin. He stands before us in silence. His gold robe glitters in the light. His hands are pristine. Not a fleck of dirt under his nails. He turns to the altar and begins to preach in Latin. I trace the stitching on the back of his white robe. I don't understand his words, so I watch the way his clothes move, the way they float across the floor. The clanging of rosaries echoes off the walls. The nuns and Jesuits pray in the dirt with fellow worshipers. This is too close to La Rochelle. Too much like the day Etienne died.

James doesn't look at me. The incense fills the room as the priest swings the thurible attached to metal chains. The air smells sweet and thick, and the back of my knees grow wet. I reach for James's hand, but he pulls away without a glance.

"It would be improper," he whispers.

My breathing tightens. Everyone around me stands and sits and stands and sits while I hold the edges of the wooden pew and perspiration gathers on my forehead.

"Isabelle, please. You must participate," he says.

I close my eyes, and all I see is Andre's smile. I feel the rush of wind over my cheeks as we run through the birch trees. "I am not well. Excuse me."

The light beckons me. Draws me to its open air. I stumble, holding the pews to steady my weakened legs until I can emerge into that bright yellow light.

Free from the stifling church, my legs run as fast as I can make them. Both hands gripped on my skirt, I fly through town. Back to the abbey where I can steal a horse and ride to Andre's house. I need to see him. Feel him. I need to know if I made a mistake.

At the stable, at the front gates of the abbey, is Andre. I step toward him, breathless and full of excitement.

I want to scream his name, but he stands still, his hands folded and gaze at his feet. He begins pacing, rubbing his forehead. The gates open.

Out walks Louise, a smile on her face and Marguerite behind her with a sack of her belongings. She steps up to Andre and smiles. He reaches for her hand to lead her to his horse. The same horse that carried me to the birch grove. The same hand that touched mine.

Louise turns to Sister Marguerite and returns to the abbey to say goodbye to the rest of the girls. My legs quiver, walking toward Andre as if a wind could pluck me from the ground and float me away like a dandelion.

"Andre?" I say, my voice pleading.

"Isabelle." He says my name without a wisp of magic. Flat. Lifeless.

"What's going on?"

"Louise and I signed a marriage contract. I'm about to take her to my home. As my wife." He looks down with a deep breath.

"You married Louise?"

"Yes."

"Oh." I can't speak. I can't find the words.

"You married a soldier, I hear."

"I did." My tongue stumbles over the words.

His cheeks shape into rounds with a forced smile, but they aren't rosy red. They look pale. Like the rest of his face.

"I should have told you. I'm sorry. It's just that he escaped a war and came to find me. I promised so many years ago, and I couldn't bear to hurt him." I wish he would interrupt me, so I don't have to say the truth. But he doesn't. He hears every word. So do I.

"You've always had the power. Not just as a Daughter of the King, but with my heart. Yours to choose or to deny. I wish you nothing but happiness."

"No, Andre." My eyes fill with puddles of tears as I step toward him.

"Louise needs protection from the man she almost married. I know how much you care for her. I'll give her a good life," he says.

"I don't know how to forget you."

"Then don't." Andre turns from me and waits by the door.

When Louise appears, she sees me and smiles. "Hello, Isabelle. Isn't it wonderful? We are both finally wives."

They walk away to his horse. Louise's hair bounces against her shoulders.

Andre holds Louise's hand. He turns to look at me over his shoulder. His heartsick eyes disappear into the afternoon light.

Andre rides off into his new life with his new bride. My chest squeezes against my heart. The ground pulls me down with a thud. My hands slam into the dirt and pebbles, and I weep.

What have I done?

.   .   .

The morning feels strange, the harsh light of the October sun shining on our bed, my husband next to me. The thought of Andre's lips and hands touching Louise sends fire through me. It grabs at my stomach and I must turn from James until it stops hurting.

"Good morning, my love." He kisses the back of my neck.

I rub my eyes and roll to face him. "Good morning."

"I must report to my superior officer this afternoon. But first, I want to show you our land."

"Our land?"

"Yes." He smiles. "The snow will arrive any day, so I've asked them to begin on the house immediately."

"I didn't expect that so soon."

"The King is very grateful for my sacrifice. He granted my transfer request after my rescue. He made sure to contact the intendant to secure the best parcel of land in thanks for my bravery. And a position in the regiment, of course."

"Yes. The fur trade." I look away.

He tells me of his long journey to New France, accompanied by a consultant to the sovereign council who passed the time teaching him Iroquois and educating him on tribal customs.

"I've much to learn and little time to learn it." He kisses my forehead. "For now, let's see our new home."

The flat parcel sits high from the river. The clearing rests against a backdrop of dense trees. They've completed the foundation and are preparing to set the walls.

"It's lovely," I say.

"Yes, it is a wonderful spot. The river's close with hunting out our backdoor. My father has commissioned the builders, paying them extra for an expedited completion. I have asked that they build a storage shed for meat, and a barn for a milking cow and chickens so we may have fresh food year-round."

"Your father? You still speak to him after what he did to you?"

"Of course." He tips his head to the side. "Loyalty."

"Does he know it's me you came here for?"

He hesitates. "He believes my station here will benefit him in the future to have eyes in the colony. I sent him a letter about a lovely Catholic girl who will make a fine wife. That is all he needs to know."

A familiar twinge of unease creeps up my neck. I am not enough as Isabelle; I must pretend to be an unnamed Catholic girl.

"The only reason we have soldiers stationed here is to protect us from Iroquois attacks," I say.

He ignores me, looking up at the trees.

"Why would your father take an interest in the region?"

"Isabelle, there is no use in causing trouble for our new life. Who knows why my father does anything? What matters is that you are finally mine. Let's leave the past in La Rochelle."

My body turns rigid. A faraway memory drifts into my mind like a feather. James's sister, hungry for independence from the controlling men in her life.

The patter of hooves catches my attention. We turn to see a carriage led by a servant. The horse comes to a stop, the door opening. Outside steps Colonel Leroux.

"Bastien," I whisper through gritted teeth.

James wraps his hand around my waist and pulls me close. "Careful, Isabelle."

Bastien straightens his jacket. "I could not wait to meet my new officer. James is it?"

"Yes, Colonel, "James bows his head. "Have you met my wife?"

He sniffs with his thin lips tightened against each other. "Yes, Madame Beaumont. A pleasure to see you again."

He looks us both over. The rolling of his fingers speeds up.

"It seems there is happy news to go around. I would like you to meet my new bride." He opens the door to the carriage and assists out a hand covered in a black glove. The familiar emerald green gown flows out, and I see her emerge with a smile as satisfied as a cat who has caught a live mouse.

"Antoinette?"

"Hello, Isabelle, isn't it wonderful that we are both starting our happy lives?" She turns to James, her face turning sour. "Monsieur Beaumont. Back from the Spanish Netherlands, I see."

He nods politely, "Madame Leroux."

She forces an accepting smile then flutters her eyes at Bastien.

"I've married the most beautiful woman in the colony," Bastien says.

I pull her aside as the men begin chatting. "What were you thinking, Antoinette?" I turn to look at his lanky body, leaned backward, fingers smoothing the tips of his pointy mustache.

"I don't believe I need your permission. We met with the priest this morning. He married us in a private ceremony with the nuns witnessing."

"I don't understand, why did you marry him?"

"Careful, Isabelle," her voice snaps. "That's my husband you're talking about."

"He's not what I would have thought you wanted. He threatened to send me back to France if I didn't marry him."

"I see," she says. Her voice tips up high at the end of her sentence. "You think every man desires you, don't you?"

"Of course not."

"He's the most powerful man in Quebec. I have spent too much time interested in handsome and charming." She flicks her eyes to James. "It hasn't served me well."

"You could have any man in Quebec."

"I think we've seen that isn't true." She smooths her hair in place and checks her dress for wrinkles.

"Don't you want to fall in love?"

"Please, Isabelle," she tightens her gloves. "Don't bore me with your childish idealism. I need a powerful man, and he needs a woman to see his potential. We're a perfect fit. My father's shipping connections in La Rochelle are highly coveted. I offered Monsieur Leroux an opportunity."

"And what of you? Are you happy?"

"My power is solidified. Bastien is strong but needs training. He is too wild, too unpredictable. In time, I will mold him to his potential."

"You're getting everything you've always wanted then."

"As are you, it seems." She flicks a glance at James.

"Please, Antoinette, you're more than what your father says you are. I believe you can-"

She holds up her hand, head turned from me. "I am starting my life as a powerful woman in New France. I don't want to speak ever again about weakness."

"There's more to life than power."

Her eyes shoot back to me. "No, there is not. Not in my world."

The men saunter back.

"Darling, shall we?" Bastien assists her in the carriage, the horse hooves clapping against the thick mud.

"Unfortunately, they seem to be a perfect match," James says.

"More than you know. With the LaMarche connections in La Rochelle, she can dictate what items arrive from France. And she is now married to the man who will demand control of our port. They just might try and destroy the Natives and the rest of us in the process."

"None of this is your concern now." He raises my hand to his lips for a soft kiss. "You are a soldier's wife."

I am much more than that. But I simply smile and nod, my insides burning like fire.

A DUTIFUL WIFE

Antoinette and Bastien have solidified their power on both coasts of the Atlantic. They march through town, buying up all the goods that are already scarce. It's rumored that Antoinette demands work from local artisans, paying them a fraction of what they ask. Any glimmer of softness in her has been snuffed out by the taste of power.

James asked a local Jesuit missionary to help him understand the troubles that face the colony. He organized a meeting with the local Huron tribe to discuss the matter with the tribal Chief. As we prepare the horses for the ride, James says, "Cold weather is setting in. I assume you prefer to stay warm by the fire and wait for me?"

"I'm of no help to anyone staring at a fire all day."

"Very well," he says with a deep sigh.

We arrive at the Huron settlement near the river. Strips of bark weave over each other into braids and sheets that form the long rectangular dwellings. The Natives gather in clusters, draped in beaver pelts and porcelain beads. The clan Chief greets us. A huge, strapping man with dark eyes and a weathered face. He welcomes us with a warm smile.

"Welcome," he says with a bow of his head. "We call ourselves the Wyandot, but you call us Huron. You are welcome in our home."

"Pleasure to meet you, Monsieur," I say.

"Please, come join us," the Chief says.

"I hear many of you converted to Catholicism," James says.

I shudder with his intrusive question.

"Yes. Many including myself have. But we keep our traditions and way of life."

We walk through the small settlement, past longhouses with trails of smoke out their door and groups of women peeling squash and laughing. A low rumble of grunts and whispers catch my attention. At the edge of the camp, a giant black bear paces in a stick enclosure, throwing his head around and clawing at the ground. A young girl, no more than fourteen, stalks the perimeter. Slowly, softly. She walks sideways, bending her knees, her arms waving as she whispers to the beast.

"Black bears are an important part of the Wyandot diet," The Chief says.

"Why is he in a cage?" I ask.

"We will keep him for two years. Feed him and let his body grow thick before we kill him for meat."

"And the girl?" She crouches low to the ground, leading the bear to lower with her. They stare into each other's eyes.

"Naira. She has a way with the animals," the Chief says. "Come, let us gather at the fire."

He leads us to a longhouse. My eyes linger on Naira and her bear. Young, intense, brave. Inside the longhouse, beds line the walls, fish and meat hang from the interior beams. Families live happily amongst each other, children run about screaming and laughing. We sit, and an older woman offers us a bowl of game and maize.

We bow and smile.

"Thank you for meeting with me today," James says.

"It's a lovely camp." My eyes scan over the happy group sitting on the ground and working together. "Such beautiful families."

"My people have fallen in great numbers. We've lost land, fought battles with the Iroquois and the English, relocated and moved as our people starved. We've settled in Quebec, where we've found friends." His French is sharp, without the familiar rolling poetic sounds. His words seem to come from his throat rather than his nose.

"The French have saved you many times, I hear." James puffs out his chest.

"We do not need saving, Monsieur," the Chief says. "We've been at war with the Iroquois long before your people arrived."

"Of course." He shakes off the Chief's response. "We would like to help you, how can we keep trade strong between us?"

"We are untrusting of many of your leaders," the Chief says. "Their choices make us question their intentions."

"I see." James does not meet my gaze.

"There is another matter of great importance to us." The Chief extends his arm as the woman who offered us food leads a young boy from the dark recesses of the longhouse. He's about five and hesitates under the shadows in the corner.

As she nudges him toward us, he moves into the light, and the shadows fall away. The right side of his face is burnt, the scar extending onto his neck. His right hand has only a few stubs where fingers used to be. His ear is gone, leaving only a mangled mass of flesh adhered to his charred scalp. There's no hair, and his right eyelid rests tightly in place, leaving only a faint glimmer of his dark shining eye underneath.

"This is Nadowa." He speaks to him in Iroquoian, urging him to step forward.

The little boy bows his head and says, "Hello, friends."

I look past his scars and focus on his little angelic voice and sparkling eyes. I kneel to the boy and ask if he would like a gift from his new friend Isabelle.

He looks to the woman, who agrees, and I remove my cross necklace. This symbol that started my journey into a new world has been around my neck since the day I put it on at the Dupre house. As I unlatch it from my neck, I glance down at my forearm, then back at him.

The necklace glimmers gold in the light as it turns in a circle in front of him. He smiles and puts out his hand as I lower it into his palm. His face lifts into a half-smile, bound on one side by rigid tissue. I smile at him, and he bows and says, "Thanks you, lady Isabelle."

Tears well in my eyes. Nadowa runs to hold his new charm to the light to watch its reflection on the wall.

"What happened to him?" James says.

"His father was a great warrior, full of promise. He fought alongside me against the Iroquois and was a master hunter. I hoped he might be Chief of our people one day. Our tribe was dying from disease and famine and bloody attacks. He, like many others, found the inebriants given to us by the French traders soothing to his wary nerves. He drank the brandy more and more, without regard to his family or his people. He stopped hunting and spent his time sleeping or vomiting. He became aggressive and disruptive, and his wife came to me, worried about her children. So, we confronted him."

"What did he do?" James says.

"He threw his baby in the fire."

His words feel like the crack of a whip against me. My throat tightens, my breath gone with a gasp.

"What happened to this man?" James says.

"He was exiled. No longer welcome in our home."

"I see."

"The colonial men push it on us. They use it to weaken our men and strengthen their trading power. These inebriants are unknown to our people, and it does strange things to us. It has ruined families and placed us in a position of weakness."

Just as Bastien wishes it to be. I open my mouth to speak but James squeezes my knee.

"We must live in peace with the men who stole our land. They give us this poison. Many wish to do us harm. The Jesuits advocate for abolishing the trade as we have seen the effects firsthand. We trust them. And Monsieur Boucher."

My heart races with the mention of him. "How is the practice continued?" I ask.

"There's a battle between the members of the sovereign council. Some town leaders look the other way when alcohol finds its way to tribal clans, while the religious leaders are strongly against it. Your Bishop advocates for removal entirely, but he meets resistance from those who write the laws."

"Who is ignoring the rules for distribution?" James asks.

"Your governor believes it necessary for your growth, and his focus is on fighting the Iroquois. He is a military man, he believes in strength and power. The shipping companies of La Rochelle demand payment upfront, often delivering diluted or spoiled items, and the governor looks the other way. Colonel Leroux is known to get our people so drunk that they pass out. He strips them of their hides and abandons them alone in the forest to die."

My jaw tightens, holding back words, as James's hand is still firmly on my knee.

"We have an alliance with the Frenchmen we can trust.

"Thank you for your honesty, Chief. I can assure you I'll work toward a resolution to this matter."

"You are always welcome with us." He bows to James and then to me.

He escorts us back to our horses. I stay behind to watch Naira, grateful to have James's grip off my leg. She glides like water, flowing and powerful. The bear seems to hear her, but she doesn't speak. She's tiny but commands the wild animal through whispers in her eyes.

"Isabelle, come." James says, agitated.

I pick up my skirt and follow him, but not before Naira turns to watch me. Her long braid rests over her shoulder. She bends her knees, palms to the sky, and bows her head to me. My stiffness lightens. Naira's eyes flick up to me, intense and strong. She has spoken to me. What she said, I'm not sure. Images flash through my mind and my heart races. Flying past trees, rushing along water. Sliding down a snowy hillside. I feel breathless. Then, a smile. Andre's smile.

I shake my head from the image, exhilarated.

Naira bows her head, a slight smile creeping across her face. James marches me to the horses. I close my eyes to feel the rush again.

．　．　．

"Why did you stop me from speaking?"

"Darling, you don't understand how the world works. It's always best to keep your true thoughts close to your heart. It's how you gain leverage against people."

My back stiffens. "Certainly, we don't need to gain leverage against the Wyandot?"

"Of course I do. It's my job."

"Do you keep your true thoughts away from me?" A deep thumping begins in my temples.

"Don't worry yourself with my troubles."

"Am I not your wife? Isn't it my duty to lessen your troubles?" The tips of my earlobes flush hot.

"My job is to protect you. It's all I've ever wanted to do." He holds my hair in his hand. "You're so beautiful. Back in La Rochelle I dreamed that one day, you would be mine."

"How is your sister, James?"

"My sister? What a thing to bring up. She's the same. Wild. Childish. Has not yet learned to live by responsibility."

"Responsibility to whom?"

"To her family. She has no idea what sacrifice means. Now, enough of that selfish child."

"Do you still live by responsibility to your family? The father that turned on you. Had you beaten and sent to war?"

"We need not discuss such things. Leave the pain in the past, darling." He sighs and rests his hands on my shoulders. "You're not the same girl you once were. You don't need to remember such a difficult time."

My heart quickens when I think of the girl I used to be. "I'm not so different."

He smiles widely. "Now you are a proud Catholic, a Daughter of the King."

My eyes squint. "I wouldn't say I'm proud. I regret many of my decisions."

"Those decisions brought us together. I'm grateful to see you take your place in the world. No longer the Huguenot who hides in shadows." He hands me a goblet of wine. "I only wish you could have seen it sooner."

My hand tightens into a fist under the folds of my skirt, and I close my eyes, breathing away the tightness rising in my throat. He kisses me, his soft hair tickling my face.

"I'm here now. You may settle into the quiet life you've always wanted."

He begins kissing my neck. A quiet life. Does James know me at all?

. . .

I return to the convent to visit with the girls and ensure that they keep a wise head amid the wave of settlers eager for a wife and her dowry.

I see Elisabeth, and we run to each other, my feet leaping from the tiled floor. "Oh, Elisabeth, how I've missed you."

"Enough of that." She leads me to a quiet corner of the convent. "Tell me about James. How is it being married?"

"I still feel like I'm getting to know him. We are different people than the ones that met in La Rochelle."

"Have you thought much about…"

"Yes. How can I not?" I close my eyes and shake my head, pushing Andre from my mind. "The memory will fade soon enough."

"And your marriage bed?" she says, her eyes wide.

"Just as the nuns told us it would be. Painful. A little scary."

"How do you think the nuns know about such things?" Elisabeth looks around. "Certainly not from the Jesuits!" We erupt in laughter and then catch ourselves, hands cupped over our mouths.

"Is it still painful?" she asks.

"No. It is still awkward though."

"I long to feel the comfort of a man that I love someday. I hope to find happiness, just as you have."

The muscles in my neck tighten. "Yes, I am fortunate." I wonder if my smile is convincing. "Enough about me. Let's speak with the rest of the girls. I want them to know they have a choice and to use it wisely."

. . .

James hands me a glass of wine then kisses my cheek. We continue to settle into our lives as a married couple.

"How is the new position coming along?" I ask.

"I've been watching Bastien. He meets with the sovereign council often and I can see he's brewing something in secret. He can feel me watching him, so he's careful."

"What do you think he's up to?"

"I'm not sure. He's lying to cover something up."

"I don't doubt that," I say.

"Antoinette controls all goods coming from La Rochelle. She demands higher payment and forces them to take inferior goods. If they complain, she refuses them access to the boats."

"Her father's doing, no doubt."

"You've heard of the cabarets in town?" he says.

"The homes that turn into a tavern at night?"

"Yes. Most are harmless ways for families to make extra money, and they welcome the newcomers to meet those already established here. There is one, it seems, that Bastien frequents."

"Why is that a concern?"

"The governor runs it," he says.

"Intriguing."

James begins pacing the room. "I've heard rumors that they store an excess of grain while farmers reported a lean crop this year." James stares into the fire and rubs his chin.

"So, the Native population and the farmer's livelihood are at risk if we don't protect them. We must do something to stop them."

"I will figure something out. This is nothing for you to get involved in." James waves his hand.

I place my hands on his chest. "They won't back down. Not unless we force them."

"Meaning we take a great risk and make enemies of them?" he scoffs.

"They already are our enemies. Now begins the battle for who will attack first and loudest." I kiss his neck, softening his agitation.

"I promised to protect you. Let us stay quietly in the background." He runs his hands along the back of my neck. "Leave them be, and I'll find a way in time."

I allow James to undress me as my mind brews with ideas. He kisses my chest and I arch my back, remembering Andre's touch.

He leads me to the bed, where he lies on top of me. I let him move me as he wishes. This is what a wife does, after all. Our naked bodies next to each other, his hand on my stomach, his breath on my neck. A hollow crater cracks open inside me.

"Why are you so distant after we make love?"

I teeter on the edge of that crater. When I look in his eyes, the softness spills out of them. The need for my affection.

The fire pops and warms the room. I move my hand over his scars. "I'm sorry for everything you went through."

He covers his chest with the blanket. "The sounds of the fire sometimes bring me back. They would stick their swords in the flames, then grind them into my skin to force me to talk."

I cover my mouth and try not to cry.

He looks past me into the darkness. "When they broke my hip with a rock, I had to sit in a cell. It wouldn't heal. No room to walk or move. Just blinding pain every moment of every day. I would stare at the wall and think of your emerald eyes."

My hand rests across my open mouth, tears streaming down to my chin.

"No, darling. It's better now. Please don't cry." He pulls me into his chest. A raised scar rubs against my cheek, forcing images of the sword that pierced him and the cries he must have released. I begin to sob.

"Please, Isabelle. Just spend the rest of your life holding me, and I promise I will be whole."

The deep shame starts to cover me like a black cloud, shutting out the light and air. My husband needs me. I promised him. To survive, all I must do is forget everything I was before now.

A NEW DISCOVERY

While James works, I meander through the town square. Colored shutters frame tall windows. Sloped roofs and narrow streets. Merchants gather and laugh. Horses pull carts of cabbage and pumpkins, maize and sacks of green peas plucked straight from the ground of the gardens all around us. No huddled peasants, no children hiding in the shadows. The elite walk together with immigrants in the center of the streets.

I eye Antoinette as she parades through the square in a gown of shining taffeta with lace sleeves. Atop her head is a hat so tall, the ostrich feathers barely make it under the doorway of the textile shop. Behind her, Catherine fiddles with Antoinette's dress to help her into the shop.

"Catherine, what are you doing?" I hold her in the street.

"Madame needs a lady's maid she can trust. I can't let her down."

"You were sent here to find a husband and receive a dowry and begin a new life. If you wish to be a servant, you could have stayed in France. Is this the life you want?"

"Isabelle, I can't leave her. She is so lonely."

"Oh, Catherine, please don't trust her. She craves nothing more than power and control."

"I'm not naive about Antoinette. I know she has a dark soul, but that is precisely why she needs me." She places her hand on my arm, "Not everyone is as strong as you."

"You're stronger than you know," I say.

"I was speaking of Antoinette. I've always been strong. And I use that strength to help those who need me. Is that not what you do?"

. . .

Unable to take my mind off Catherine, I arrive at the abbey to teach the girls to read. Some days I teach the young Native girls, others the Filles du Roi.

Many of the Filles are not interested, saying they merely want to find a husband and get on with the business of making a home and having babies.

Sister Marguerite welcomes me to sit by the fire with her. "Madame Beaumont. How is married life treating you?"

"Very well, Sister." My mind still hums from my easy walk alone through town.

"I can see that." Madame grins as she sips her tea. "It's wonderful that you wish to stay and help us, but you must get on with your own family. I presume you'll be having babies soon."

I fuss with my dress to control my nervous hands. A tea of white turtlehead flower keeps me from becoming a mother. A secret amongst the Native women is now my secret too.

"Until then, I've much work to do here. How is the Filles du Roi program? Has it been successful?"

"Magnificent! The girls are already beginning to have children."

"That's wonderful. The King must be delighted."

"I'm sure he is," she says.

"You don't correspond with him?"

"No, only through the intendant."

"We could bring more women here to settle in New France. I am sure he would be proud to hear about the success of the program."

"Yes, I suppose he would," Sister says.

"Imagine how strong our community could be if we were to bring ships over every few months?"

"Yes. We would need to find larger housing, but I would think more marriageable women would only strengthen the colony."

"Wouldn't you agree that the country girls are better suited for life here?"

"They certainly handle the harsh seasons and farm life better than those from the cities. I would agree they're more resilient."

"Imagine hundreds more women coming to support New France, and the legacy we would leave for generations."

"Madame, you're quite persuasive."

"I'm merely supporting an already successful venture by the King."

"All right, then. I'll communicate our needs for more women. Country girls. Peasants. This is how we'll grow our colony."

Madame relaxes in her chair, satisfied with the grand idea that the women of the Ursuline Convent will change history. "You're doing God's work, Isabelle. It's admirable."

"I simply want more girls who wander the streets of France cold and hungry, to have a chance at more. Just as I did."

.   .   .

At home in the evening, I prepare dinner. James greets me with a warm smile. "My dear, Isabelle, I have some wonderful news."

"I do, as well. Tell me more."

"Our house is complete. We may start our new life." He holds my hands in his.

"That is wonderful news."

"All I want is to make you happy."

He kisses me. I am a wife.

"Now, tell me of your news," he says.

"I spoke with Sister Marguerite today, encouraged her to send for more Filles du Roi. I explained how the peasant girls are better suited for life here and how we need hundreds more to help the colony succeed."

"It's wonderful that you find things to fill your time. Soon enough, you won't need to bother with all that. You'll spend your time as a mother. Just as it should be."

"I'm not with child."

"It's only a matter of time. You must be eager to fulfill your purpose."

"My purpose?" I pull back.

"Of course. A woman best serves her man by keeping a successful home, just as my mother did. Certainly, there's no better way to honor God than by sharing a bed with your husband and growing his child." He holds his hand against my cheek.

I want to tear the door open and run into the forest, but I bite my lip hard enough to taste a drop of blood hit my tongue. It tastes like copper.

"I think it's time we perform a church union," he says.

My hands tremble. "A church union?"

"Yes. We followed the silly rules of a civil union. It means nothing. Not until we marry in the eyes of God."

I search for something to say that will not anger him. Why wouldn't I want to marry my husband in the church?

A frantic knock begins at the door. I exhale, relieved.

"Isabelle! Are you home?"

"Louise?"

James opens the door to Louise, eyes wide and filled with tears.

"Come in." I lead her inside. "What happened?"

"Andre is missing."

I lose my breath, grab my stomach. James looks at me, head cocked to the side. I realize he's noticed my reaction. I steady my face. A look of concern only, but inside I crumble to dust.

"He's been missing for two days. At first, I thought he stayed out longer than expected on one of his fur trapping expeditions. But today, one of the Huron men came to my door and presented me with this." She reveals Andre's hat, dirty and torn.

"What does he think happened to him?" I ask.

"He believes the Iroquois captured him. He was close enough to their territory. Somewhere he shouldn't have been. He's so brave."

My hand tightens against the back of the chair. "Why would they want him?"

"He's a valuable fur trapper. I suppose for his skills."

James is calm. As if we're discussing a stranger.

"James, we must get him back," I say.

"Please help us." She cups her hand around her belly, pulling the layers of skirt taught to reveal a small bump. "I'm expecting our first child. I can't do it without him."

My heart stops. The room spins as if I might faint.

James grabs Louise's hand. "I need him as much as you do, Louise. Without him, my position to keep trade flowing with the Natives becomes very difficult."

"So, you'll help me? Ask the military to save him?"

"I'll find a way. You should rest. I don't want you worrying. Your focus should be on becoming a mother." James shoots me a look before retiring to our bedroom.

I hold her hand. "We'll get him back, Louise."

"Isabelle?" She looks at me with heavy eyes. "I must tell you something."

"What is it?"

"I did something awful."

"How awful?"

"The day that James arrived in Quebec, I ran off with that boy again, the one who hit me." She shakes her head, her dark waves of hair trembling. "He hit me again. Harder this time. He shoved his hands up my skirt."

"Oh, Louise." I reach for her, but she stops me.

"He threatened me. Demanded that I marry him, or he would hurt me worse. Then, I found Andre outside the abbey, waiting to see you. He saw me and realized what had happened. I begged him to help me, to protect me. He told me that he loved you."

"I don't understand."

"I told Andre that you've always loved James and now that he returned, you two would marry. I told Andre that you made your choice and that you did not want him."

I turn from her, my cheeks fire hot.

"I'm so sorry. It was the truth, wasn't it? You've wanted James since the day we left Dieppe. I was scared and desperate and Andre is so strong and brave. I needed him to save me."

I close my eyes and breathe slowly. I made my choice. Andre made his. Still, I can't bear to look at her. Her little belly. "What matters now is that we get Andre back. You may stay here for the night." I continue upstairs.

"Isabelle?"

The stairs creak when I stop moving.

"I'm glad to see you happy."

The words catch my heart like a fishhook.

In our bedroom, James watches me, his face warmed by the glow of candlelight.

I force myself to appear calm. Unfazed. "Will you really ask the military to help?"

"No. They won't risk men to save a fur trapper. Especially not one whom they see as more Native than he is French."

"He is from Nantes."

"Here, his loyalty is to the Natives. I meant what I said. I do need him. If the Huron and Algonquin refuse to trade with us, I will have failed. I would lose my post, forced back to La Rochelle to work for my father."

A wave of sickness washes over me. "We must find a way to bring him back."

"Isabelle, this is not a matter of your concern."

"Yes, it is!" Heat rises up the back of my neck. *Calm down.* "We have to help him."

"For Louise?" he says slowly.

There's a knowing in his eyes. One I can't bear to look at.

"Yes." I place my hand on his cheek. "And for our future children. I can't go back to La Rochelle. Please."

He stands tall, stretching out his painful hip. "I'll do it myself."

"The snow is set to arrive any day. It's dangerous."

He pulls me into his chest. His jacket buttons press into my cheek.

"I'm coming with you," I say.

"You'll do nothing of the sort! You promised to stay out of trouble."

"I promised to help the girls. They were my family before you came back to me."

He steps away from me, shakes his head and places his hands on his hips. "I won't risk your safety."

"You'll be there to protect me." My heart thumps. I've just asked my husband to save the man I cannot rid my heart of.

"Are you worried about Andre?" His neck flushes, mottled with spots of red. "Is there something you aren't telling me?"

I can see his chest pounding. "Louise needs my help. I can't let her down."

The faintest taste of copper still floats on my tongue.

NAIRA'S COURAGE

"Won't you stay home?" James says as we pack our horses.

"No." I see the concern on his face. He still doesn't believe me about Andre. "Your leg. I worry about you. We can do this together."

"What if you're with child? It's not safe."

Chills run up my arms. "I've survived cold winter nights before. I can do it again."

"I wish I could change your wild ways."

"I believe you should stop trying." I face the horse and squeeze my eyes shut. A deep inhale of sharp air stings the inside of my nose and throat.

Galloping hooves approach. The Chief arrives with a girl — the one who speaks to bears. Beads and leather ties spangle her sleek hair. Animal hides and fur boots drape from her petite frame.

"Greetings, Madame Beaumont," the Chief says. "I offer for your journey, our young Naira. A tribe of Huron approaching a Mohawk camp would incite a bloody battle. Naira's skills can help him escape quietly."

"Oh, that's very kind of you, but we do not want to put her in any danger," James says.

"I will not be in danger," Naira snaps. "I'm here to help you."

"I don't understand." James almost laughs.

The Chief answers, "Naira is our most accomplished explorer. She knows the terrain and how to navigate to avoid the enemy. She's a skilled hunter and can wield a tomahawk with unmatched precision. She will be your protector."

James smiles at the Chief with a bow and throws me a skeptical look.

"We need Monsieur Andre back to resume trades," the girl says. "Just as you do."

Naira's skin glows in the sun, her dark eyes solid as stone. James pretends to hide his limp, rubbing his hip when he thinks I'm not looking. Our fate now rests in the hands of this young girl as we set out into the desolate, wild forest.

We gallop at a steady pace, set by Naira and her obedient horse. We stop briefly for water then carry on, as rest must wait until camp for the night. After a full day of riding, my body is sore and my mind races with notions of Mohawks in the shadows, stalking us like prey.

We arrive at a clearing near the water, where Naira ties up her horse and steps through the trees, looking for signs of hidden eyes. James builds a fire, and I set out our beds of rolled fur. The ground is icy, and the wind whistles in my ears.

Harpoon in hand, she disappears into the forest. We warm ourselves by the fire, listening to the whispers of the night.

"I hesitate to see how this child can be of any help to us," James whispers. He winces, trying to find a comfortable position.

"She seems quite skilled. The Chief would not have sent her if she weren't up to the demands of the journey."

"I'm here for both of you," James says.

Naira returns sometime later, holding her speared fish in one hand and a limp rabbit carcass in the other.

She sits without a word and begins to slice into the rabbit, handing James the fish to clean. She works with precision and focus. She's no older than me when I began to walk the streets of La Rochelle alone, yet she bears no resemblance to that girl.

"Why do you watch me?" She asks as she tears into the flesh of the animal, ripping off its skin and piercing its belly to place over the flame.

"You fascinate me," I say.

"My people are very different from yours." She speaks without eye contact.

"You're so young to be so accomplished and capable."

"I owe it to my father. I'm his only child, and he began teaching me from the time I could walk. I spend my days learning to hunt and track animals, and nights connecting with the spirits of the forest."

"The spirits?"

"Yes. Nature is our gift, and it speaks to us if we're willing to listen. I am fulfilling my tribe's wishes. Nature and the spirits guide me."

"You aren't afraid?" James asks.

"No. We are all placed here for a certain time. There's no use in fighting for a different outcome."

We eat our meal of freshly caught fish and game, chewing on greens from the forest to aid in digestion. Naira instructs us to sleep.

James pulls me into him, covering our bodies with bear fur. He hugs me tightly as Naira dances by the fire with soft feet. Her movements like a babbling brook. She burns dried herbs, swirling her body in the smoke. Her body is low to the ground, her movements quick. Her long braid flies through the night, her body illuminated by the flickering fire. I watch her until my eyes grow heavy, drifting away to sleep in James's warm embrace.

The morning finds the ground covered in frost, my cold body rigid despite being close to the fire all night. Naira instructs us to pack our horse and be on our way. We need to reach the nearest Algonquin tribe. James stands tall and clears his throat, reaching his hand for me.

We move deep into the forest, and after hours of riding, my legs grow numb and my back aches. Naira comes to a quick stop with her hand up, instructing us to do the same.

"What is it?" I ask. "Is it the Mohawk?"

"Quiet," she says. "The forest moves. I do not know with what."

She steps down from her horse and nods at us to follow. We walk through the silence, leading our horses. The birds caw, and the trees rustle through a blanket of wet air. "A storm is coming. We must stay here," she says.

She uses sticks and rocks to form a shelter with deerskin and places the fire under cover of pines so the incoming rain will not dampen the flame.

"We wait here until the rain passes. We can't stay for long. We're vulnerable to the Haudenosaunee, so close to the British lands."

"Haudenosaunee?" I ask.

"That is their name. You call them Iroquois. The aggressive tribes like the Mohawk are part of the Haudenosaunee alliance."

"Why do we call them a different name?"

"The same reason you call us Huron. We are Wyandot. The French call us the names that suit them."

The wet air turns to mist and the mist turns to raindrops. We huddle under the deerskin, the melody of rain hitting the leaves like the flicking of harp strings. The cover of conifers and pines creates a sea of darkened green that rattles in the wind.

"James, are you scared?" I ask.

"No, I just worry about you. I want to rescue Andre and return him to his wife." He pulls me into him.

"You have been through a great deal to get here," Naira says to me.

"Haven't we all?" said James. "Your people have seen their struggles."

She looks at me with fierce eyes. "The white man stole our land and our voices."

My stomach aches. I understand living with no voice at all.

"My family adopted Christianity, but I refuse to attend the white man's school for girls. I have everything I need in the forest where I can breathe free."

Tiptoeing through the forest as a young girl, speaking to God through the wind and trees. Prayer circles in the dark. The memories push their way forward, crumbling the wall I've built around them.

James pulls me tighter. "Sometimes, we do what we must. What our leaders demand of us," James says.

"Yes. But we must never lose sight of who we are inside."

My breath is gone. I pull from James and warm my numb hands by the fire, trying to hide the stabbing pain in my chest. Eyes closed, the darkened room of my mind unlocks. The hum of the forest quiets. My mind washes blank — black and empty — and a Protestant prayer bubbles to the surface.

Home. The stabbing lifts. My breath returns.

"Rest now. We leave at nightfall." Naira sharpens a stick into a spear, determination in her eyes.

The pelting rain drifts me to sleep.

Naira's whispering voice pulls me awake. "Come now, the rain has stopped. You both must be quiet. No loud noises. Our enemies are always looking for someone to scalp."

We slosh through the wet ground, the bottom of my wool dress covered in dark mud. I fuss to lift the skirt while Naira moves freely, her fur lined moccasins glide over the terrain without difficulty.

We lead our horses through the marshy ground and watch for signs of movement. A whooshing sound whips past my face. My horse releases a loud wail. I turn to see an arrow cut into the flesh of its belly. Another arrow cuts the air near my chest, landing at the horse's ribs. It wails again, and Naira grabs my waist, throwing me to the ground. James rushes toward me, crawling on his belly.

"What is that?" My heart hammers against my chest.

"Mohawks. Wait for my signal, then both of you will run behind the large boulder and wait for me." She retrieves an arrow from her sack and readies her bow. She crouches with bent knees, hiding behind a fallen tamarack tree. With a loud wailing call into the night, she waits for movement and pulls back the arrow. "Now!" she yells. She releases her grip. The stick wavers through the air.

We run hand in hand to the rock, James dragging his damaged leg. We slide through the wet mud. Just as we reach the boulder, James's foot gives way, rolling his ankle. He slides down the muddy hill into a depression twenty feet below. He puts his hands up to motion that I should stay where I am.

I turn to see Naira take the sharpened stick she made this morning and stab it into the horse's neck, twisting it until the beast stops moving. She grabs the reins of the remaining horses and sends them down the hill toward James. She slides behind the rock as another arrow flies past us.

"When I call to you, run along the tree line until it brings you down to the water. Do not run up the hill." She slides on her side down the muddy incline. Flat on my stomach, I watch helplessly as she helps James to his horse.

Naira points west and slaps the backside of the horse, tethered to the other. They move as if they understand her voice. James looks back at me as the horse carries him away.

She climbs through the dirt and mud, covering her deerskin dress in darkness. She pulls out another arrow and takes position behind a tree. "Be ready."

"Where did you send him?"

"To the village where he'll be safe."

She takes position, with a recoiled arm and a tight grip on the string of the bow. She sees movement and releases her fingers, her body and eyes still. She does this as she simultaneously roars, "Now."

I run as fast as my feet will move, my heart racing, my boots sloshing through wet, heavy earth. I pull up my skirt and wade through the muck and maneuver around fallen tree limbs. The lights of the village flicker below. A wave of relief washes over me, which quickly dissipates. There's movement on my left. Shadows of black and gray. Quiet steps fill the night air.

I run up the hill as Naira instructed me not to do. I have no choice. I move swiftly, the full moon shining its glowing light through the trees. The movement advances, coming closer, and every moment I wait for an arrow to slice my back. My foot catches on a branch, my hands and face thrust into icy mud. I stumble forward, falling again to my knees. My wobbly legs fail to carry me up the hill.

Alone and stalked without the steely confidence of Naira for protection. The noises grow as I sit breathless, preparing for the onslaught of red-faced Mohawks closing in on me. I crawl back into a corner, surrounded by rocks and a cliff down the other side. My breath hovers in the white mist, my heart thundering into my throat.

A whimper escapes my lips, floating into a cloud in the cold night air. From the shadows emerge four figures low to the ground, dark silver and white. The shadows part. A pack of wolves, fangs out, stance low.

Massive dogs with tall ears. Their mouths are open, the guttural growls seep out with the fog of their warm breath, saliva dripping from their sharpened teeth. They creep toward me, breaking apart to circle me on all sides. I grunt and grab a rock, holding it in the air. They slink closer, subtle growls rumbling from their throats. Images flash in my mind. Their teeth pulling shards of my bloody flesh as James hears my screams from the nearby village. I begin to cry as they inch near me, their lips snarled up to bare teeth.

A swift arrow pierces the eye socket of the wolf closest to me. I turn to see Naira crouched behind a tree above us, bow in hand. The other three wolves are stunned, and Naira takes her opportunity, jumping down, holding a tomahawk raised above her head as she flies like a hawk. She lands beside a wolf, slicing the ax through the air and across his neck, leaving the head dangling. A second slice severs it completely, its head rolling on the ground. I recoil from the bloody head at my feet, its ears pointed up and full of white hair.

She spins like a dust cloud, severing its tail, sending it howling into the forest. The last one stops and bows down to her, inching backward, its eyes never leaving hers. Scattered wolf remains surround me. A head, a tail, a full body on its side, one eye lost to an arrow. Naira stands in the middle of it all, her tomahawk extended toward the sky. Her braid has loosened, her raven locks flying in the air around her face. A beam of moonlight through the trees meets the blade. I swallow, intimidated by her power. She is terrifying and beautiful.

"Come. We must get to the water." She helps me to my feet, which stumble as I follow her. As my heightened fear settles, my limbs feel shaky and feeble. I hold a tree trunk to find my strength. The mist in a cloud around me, I move to follow Naira, who glides through the trees like a swan across water.

We arrive at the river. Through the trees, the village lights flicker.

"Aren't we going there?"

"No." She grabs a canoe, made from birch bark raised high on the sides. "Get in."

"I don't understand. What about James?"

With a sigh, she holds her hand out to gesture for me to enter the boat. I do as she asks. My hand rubs the roughness of the bark, reminding me of the birch trees and Andre. The stillness of the water ripples as the canoe sends tiny waves on either side of us. Naira makes it clear that we are to be silent. She directs the canoe, and the lights grow faint, eventually disappearing into the twilight. Down the river where the tree line recedes from the shore, she places the oar in her lap.

"The wolves..." I mutter.

She holds up her tomahawk. "This is one thing I take from the Europeans. The iron blades are more useful than ours made of deer antler."

"You're skilled with the bow and arrows."

"Those men were likely watchers for the Iroquois. They report back to their tribes, when travelers near their settlement and guard the woods north of here."

"Then why are we not in the protection of the Algonquin village?"

She squints her dark eyes, searching the trees for movement. "They will not attack this village. They need them for trade. They will hide in the trees and attack anyone who leaves."

"Which means we would not be able to reach Andre."

"Not for many weeks, and the incoming snow will make it impossible. We must carry on into the mouth of danger."

"And we must do it without James."

She tilts her head to acknowledge my words, then lowers it as the wolves did, and scans the area, on watch for danger. "We do this ourselves."

I sink into the front of the canoe, wrapped in fur. Naira settles into the protection of the high walls of the boat, eyes focused on the water ahead of us. Her dark skin shimmers through the reflection of the night bouncing off the water. I close my eyes, the cool air rushing over my face.

Water lapping and birds taking flight into the rustling trees lull me to sleep under the protection of this young girl. All the threats in our world do not intimidate her. She carries on the journey of her tribe with unwavering courage, showing the rest of us what it means to light a fire in the dark.

THE WHITE OF SNOW

My hair crackles with ice as I push my way up to sitting. The canoe is on land, and Naira crouches at the water's edge, her whittled stick raised in the air, her eagle focus waiting for the moment to strike. With a swift stab into the water, she pulls out a speckled fish, writhing as the scales shine in the sunlight. She throws it in the leather sack around her shoulder.

"Time to head into the forest. Be on alert," she says.

I nod with eyes wide, sliding my gloved hands into the side seams of my filthy skirt, tucking them into the hidden pockets. My steps follow hers, emulating her movement. Hours go by with nothing spoken between us. Every stick crack or bird song sends my heart racing.

The wind picks up, and she gestures for me to stop. She grabs my hand and rushes me up the hill, jumping over its crest and behind the tree line. She rolls to her stomach, and I do the same. My eyes dart between her and the land below us.

Suddenly, a line of horses trotting. Atop them are men with feathers in their hair, red grease swiped across their cheeks and eyes. A man staggers, tied behind them, a rope around his waist. It's a young boy, about the same age as Naira.

"He's their prisoner," she whispers. "They're heading back to their village. We're close."

"What do we do?"

"We follow them." She jumps over the ridge, sliding down the hill. I carry on behind her, my feet now aching from the cold and the long hours of walking with soft feet.

Near twilight, the Mohawks arrive at their village, a large settlement with multiple longhouses. The group is loud, like the wolves that howl and holler into the night on the outskirts of Quebec City. At a safe distance, Naira examines the layout, scanning the edges.

"See that hut?" She points to a cloth tent with a guard pacing its entrance.
I squint to make it out. "Yes, I think so."

"I think he's there."

"How do you know?"

"Their prisoners must prove their bravery. If they find them to be useful and strong, they bring them into their family. They begin to trust them and give them their own hut."

"And the ones they don't trust?" I ask.

"They scalp them."

I turn away, shaking the image from my mind.

"We will head into the forest for the night and plan Andre's escape for tomorrow," she says.

"Back to the forest?"

"We need to build a fire, and we must be far enough that they don't see the smoke."

Settled in a sheltered area deep in the forest, we sit by the fire, warming our frozen toes and hands. Naira uses a stick to draw the layout for the village and describes how she will create a distraction while I assist Andre into the forest.

"Do you believe he's still alive?" I say.

"They would not kill such a skilled hunter."

"Yes." I look away, into the dark.

"Monsieur Andre spoke of you many times."

I try to hide my flushed cheeks.

"He asked the Chief to see that the forest watchers keep you and your husband safe. Mostly against Colonel Leroux."

My chest tightens, and I close my eyes, bracing my arms to the ground.

"We need him," she says. "He's one of the only white men we trust. When the Jesuits came to the Chief to ask for protection for Monsieur Beaumont and his wife, I knew my responsibility was to save him and protect you."

The tightness moves to my neck, and I rock ever so slightly to stop the tears from falling. Naira prepares the fish she caught earlier today.

"Are you ready for tomorrow?" Naira asks.

"I'm no match for your skills. I worry I'll slow you down."

"Why do you not see your strength? We're all born to this earth, not to the people around us. Everything you need is already in you."

Her deep black eyes are pools of glowing light, the reflection of the flames dance in their darkness. "I've never been allowed to be what I know is inside of me." The words shock me, so painful they feel as if they cut as they come out.

"Ah, and there is your struggle." She looks up from her fish, hands still slicing, but a smile creeps to her face. "Fear must not hold you back."

I run my hand along my wrist and begin to scratch. "How do you face awful things without fear?"

"You don't do it without fear. You do it in spite of it. That is strength."

The memory of the bricks, the worn Bible in my fingers. Prayers by candlelight. Foggy midnights and whispered French hymns. Hand in hand with Henri. The memories tumble over me, heavy and deep. The weight could crush me. The vision of a time before I gave in to fear.

"I see people in colors, revealed in an array of shining light."

A deep breath lightens the vice on my ribs. "How do you mean?"

"James, he is the color of earth. Grounded. Loyal. The strongest storm does not loosen his roots that are deep within the ground."

"Yes."

"His loyalty can push him in the wrong direction. He cannot see when those he cares about use him for their own interests. He cannot see outside the view he has always known."

"And me?"

"You are bright green," she says.

"Green?"

She nods. "Green like the leaves that grow at the top of the trees. You take nutrients from where you came from and move toward the light of the sun. It was the earth that gave you footing."

"James."

"Never forget the strength a leaf must have to take the heat of the sun and the whipping of wind."

"You're saying I will get hurt by my need to be in the sunlight?"

"The taller a tree grows, the farther away from earth it lives," she says.

I stare at her, thinking back to the birch trees and the delicate leaves of fall.

"The earth wants to hold you. It's in their nature. It thrives on protection. It cannot help itself. It will pull you back home where it can protect and hold you."

"Maybe I want to be held."

"You want that no more than you want shackles. The green leaves that shine in the sun need to feel free. Only you know how to find that freedom."

Tears sting my eyes. "What color are you?"

"I am white. The color of snow. I come and go where I am needed and cast a presence around me. I know that I am fleeting, just like winter."

This girl, she's still a child, yet holds the wisdom of an old oak.

"Do not be sad for me. When my brightness fades to water, I become one with the earth. It will be like coming home," she says.

In the distance, high-pitched screams. "What is that?" Shivers crawl up my neck.

"They killed someone."

"Andre?" My voice quivers.

"We will find out tomorrow."

She sinks into the fur, taking a much-needed rest. I also find my eyes falling into slumber, my mind filled with visions of the green leaves of Spring shivering in the golden light of the sun.

· · ·

"Wake up. We move now." Naira whispers in my ear. Flurries of snow swirl in the dark sky and fall softly on the ground. I dust the flakes from my hair and tighten my boots, layering fur over my shoulders.

"The first snowfall."

"We must get him this morning before the sun rises. Soon, the snow will make it impossible to pass." She gestures her head to indicate it's time.

I follow her, watching her nimble body move through the trees, one with the earth and the snow. Bright white snowflakes dust her black hair like stars. She pulls me down behind a rock.

"There." She points to the hut. "See the guard? I will distract him while you enter the hut and see if Andre is still alive."

I scan the settlement. "Why don't you go?"

"He will not come for me. He will for you."

"I don't understand." I shake my head, the nervousness in my belly growing.

"Andre needs you. I need you," she tells me. "It's at the edge, you can hide behind the trees." She draws a line in the dirt, indicating where to hide and the path that I will take Andre out through the forest. "Go high first, walk along the ridge where you can track movement. Follow back to the boat hidden in the trees and take the canoe back up the river. The earth is wet and thick in those areas. It will be partially frozen now, making it much safer by boat."

"Will you meet us?"

"Go on, and do not wait for me. Once you're back at the village with James, you will be safe from there. They'll help you return to Quebec City."

My hands tremble. She gestures for me to move. The sun begins to cast a faint glow from behind the horizon, illuminating our path.

At the edge of the Mohawk camp, we sit and wait. The silence heavy around us, I take a deep breath as my skin flushes with heat. I clasp my hands together to stop the shaking.

"Are you ready?" she says.

I shrug my shoulders and furrow my brow to indicate that no, I am not ready, but what choice do I have?

She moves where I can barely see her. I wait. The only sound is my breath and the snow falling around me. She appears at a lower section of the camp, moving toward their supplies. She moves smooth as liquid, pushing a pail ever so gently then returns to the trees. The wooden bucket teeters effortlessly back and forth, barely making a sound until finally, it falls to the side, hitting the ground with a bang.

The guard takes notice and walks over to investigate. From the trees, Naira gestures for me to move. I circle the back of the hut, careful to watch for the guard. Opening the curtain, I see Andre, asleep on his side. I come to my knees and place my trembling hand near his face.

He jolts awake, pulling back from me. "Isabelle?"

Breath returns to my chest, strength growing in my legs. I struggle to find words but do manage a smile.

He is alive.

I peek out of the hut to see the guard walking toward us. I rush back inside and look around to find a place to hide. Against the pole that frames the flap, my back leans into the cloth wall. Andre lies down again, pretending to be asleep. The cloth moves to the side, his arm pulling it in front of my body as he looks inside. I turn my head and close my eyes, frozen.

He closes the opening, and my body softens.

"What are you doing here?" he asks.

"We must go. Naira is helping us."

"The Huron hunter."

"Promise you'll come with me." I must resist the urge to throw my arms around him.

He nods, yes. We peek out through an opening as the guard paces the grounds.

"It has been too long," I say. "She should have returned by now."

Andre and I wait at the opening of the hut, listening to each other breathe, glancing at each other. Then suddenly, the sound of a commotion. The guard moves to follow the noise.

"Now," I say. We run behind the hut and into the forest, up into the trees. My heart races like a stampede of wild horses. We crouch behind a tree to see Naira, dragging a white-tailed deer into the camp. She drops her tomahawk and puts her hand in the air. The men grab her and take her to one of the longhouses.

"What will happen to her?"

"They'll take her to the clan Chief," he says.

"And then what?"

"She's buying us time. We have to go." He pulls me forward.

I pull back from his hand. "No. I won't leave her. I have to go back for her."

"Isabelle, if you return, you will only put her in more danger."

"No." I begin crying. "I can't leave her here."

"You must. What did Naira instruct you to do?"

"To take you back to the river."

Andre softens his grip on my hand. "Then that is what we must do."

I leave Naira in the hands of the enemy. She laid herself out as sacrifice for us. I long to run back and save her. The idea that they might extinguish her bright white light leaves me breathless and aching.

Few words spoken between us, we move through snowy fields and freezing forests, and paddle against the river dotted with ice. Andre steers the canoe, his cheeks dusted with rosy patches.

"You could not have saved her," he says.

"I wasn't brave enough. I should have gone back for her."

He places the oars down. "Isabelle, if the Mohawk captured Naira, I promise you, it was part of her plan."

"I don't understand."

"She's a cunning and fierce warrior. She let them take her," he says.

"To save us?"

He shrugs. "Maybe."

"If she is so fierce, why wouldn't she fight? Come with us?"

Andre leans into me, "The Mohawk honor bravery. If she ran with us, we would all be branded cowards and they would attack us. If she stays, she has a chance to prove herself worthy of becoming one of them, giving you and me a chance to escape."

"And what happens to her?"

"She offered herself as a trade for me. By proving she is unafraid to die, she hopes to become one of them. They will either kill her or admire her too much to lose her."

As dark approaches, we climb the hill into the forest, finding shelter among the trees. Andre places the fur down by the fire as the sky turns black. "Here." Andre hands me a sack of dried meat Naira left in the canoe. He gestures for me to sit near him.

"Louise is worried about you," I say.

"I'm sure she is."

"Congratulations on the baby." The words sting like the slow press of a needle in my flesh.

He looks down. "Yes, well." He doesn't finish the sentence. "And James? How is married life? Are you happy?"

"Yes." I nod, my voice breathy and strained. "I'm so glad you're safe."

"Why did you come with Naira?"

"I needed to see you. Needed to make sure you're safe."

"Thank you for helping me," he says.

The snow turns to wet slush, putting out the fire every time Andre lights it. The freezing night settles on us. We lay by the remains of the fire, darkening to smoke. Andre pulls me into him, his arm wraps around my waist. "It's all right. I need to keep you warm." His breath brushes over my ear.

My body shivers, and my heart races. Andre's strong arms around me make me think of James, and I pull back.

His face falls. "Maybe I can try the fire again."

His hand slides from my hip, and I catch it in mine, looking up at him. He lowers back down, moving the fur to form a pillow under my head. I pull closer, the curve of his chest against my cheek. My hands tuck into my chest, and his arms envelop me in a protective embrace where the cold doesn't hurt, and the guilt rests far away in the distance.

Andre exhales, his bristly face buried in my hair. My body wants his touch. I lie still as the last of the light extinguishes. Stinging tears roll down my face, cold as ice.

. . .

I wake in the curve of his neck, his skin rough against my cheek. His breath cycles in and out, warming my cheek with every exhale. I close my eyes again, the dreamy sensation of his hands on my back and my hip. I run my nose along the line of his chin and let my mouth rest on the skin below his lip. His eyelashes, long and still. He groans like a dream pulls him awake.

His eyes open, struggling to focus. I lean into him, his soft lip pulling mine down to open my mouth. Just as I fall weak into his touch, he closes his mouth, pushing me away.

"Isabelle, no."

The sensation still pulls me toward him, and I grab his jacket. "Andre."

"No." He pulls away completely, bringing me crashing to the earth. "You made your choice. And he waits for you to return to him." He stands, turning his back to me.

"Why don't you ask me?" I say.

"Ask you what?"

"Do I wish it were you." I stand and wait for him to look at me.

"Because it doesn't matter. All that matters is that you chose him."

"I was scared. He came back from war damaged and full of hope to find me. I owe him."

He puts his hand up to me. "This is of no help to anyone. You chose your husband, and I chose my wife."

"Do you love her?" I ask.

"Do you love James?"

We stare into each other's eyes. Water drops off the ice in the trees, falling from the frozen branches, dripping onto the pool of ice on the ground.

He takes a step toward me. "Tell me you'll leave him, and I will take you in my arms right now."

James's wounds. His scars and the fear in his eyes at the sight of fire. A promise to stay by his side forever. Louise and her baby.

"See, it brings only pain to think of what might have been." He picks up a dry, brittle leaf and holds it up. "I prefer to remember you under the floating leaves of the birch grove watching me fall in love with you."

My shoulders sink. A wave of tears overtakes me.

"I keep you as a memory. When I lie in the arms of a woman I do not love, it helps me feel less alone."

I open my teary eyes to see Andre, his back to me, looking into the morning forest dusted with snow.

FEEDING THE FLAMES

We stop at the crest of the forest, looking down at the Algonquin village. Andre begins to walk down the icy hill, holding out his hand to me. I take it, letting him lead me to stable ground.

"Andre." I stop walking.

He hesitates, not wanting to look at me.

"Did Naira ever talk to you about colors?"

"Yes."

"She tells me I'm bright green, like the leaves of a tree." I wait for a response, but he says nothing. "What color are you?"

"Blue."

"Like the ocean?"

"Blue like the hidden flame of fire. Below the surface of the angry red and orange lies a subtle blue core, quietly feeding the heat."

My heart thumps, hard and fast. Before I can speak, Andre has turned away again. We approach the Algonquin camp. The warmth and light of their fires reaches out, carrying us into the welcome arms of friends. When we enter a longhouse, I see James. The weight of the journey finally crashes into me, and I fall to my knees, weeping.

James limps over. He helps me from the ground, leading me to a bed near the fire, covering me in layers of fur. A woman with kind eyes arrives with a bowl of hot broth. She smiles through missing teeth and hands me the bowl.

I long to be back in the forest, lips touching Andre's. My eyes remain on the bowl to prevent them from drifting to him.

"How did they treat you?" James asks Andre.

"They didn't kill me. They killed several men while I was there. It involves an entire ceremony that lasts hours." He shakes his head, trying to rid his mind of the memories. "They put me to work, hunting and trapping, and preparing meat."

"Louise will be so grateful to have you back," James says as he pulls me closer.

"Yes," he says with a wavering voice. "I'm very grateful to all of you. And to Naira." He clears his throat and puts down his bowl. "There's something you should know. Bastien ordered my capture."

"Oh?" James says.

My hands tighten at the mention of him.

"He wants to hurt the Native's trade, and I stand in his way. I'm a threat."

"He is an evil one." James shakes his head.

"But it seems he's doing more than that."

"What do you know?" James leans toward Andre.

"He's been secretly supplying the Iroquois with weapons to fight the Huron and Algonquin tribes."

"Why would he do that?" I ask.

"To expand trade and power on all sides of Quebec City and Montreal. He wants to weaken France's hold on the colony to insert his power over the settlers. He's trying to fund a war, and he's doing it with money and weapons from the King."

"We have to stop him," James says. "But how? My commander won't believe me."

"We need to figure something out, or we might be caught in the middle of a bloody war," Andre says.

"Well done, Monsieur." James stands. "I need to speak with the Chief." He leaves the longhouse, and when he's out of sight, I lower next to Andre on his cot.

"That's why you didn't escape," I say.

"What do you mean?"

"There was one guard. You know this land better than anyone. You could have fought, and yet you stayed in that tiny hut, cold and hungry."

"They would have come for me. I would be risking too much. I had to prove my bravery, knowing one day I would find the right time to escape. And it finally came."

"You had valuable information."

"Yes. And if they killed me, no one would be able to stop Bastien. Now, thanks to Naira, we can stop him."

Andre clears his throat and looks down. He pulls his hand away from where it rests next to mine. I stand and look down at him. He settles in for the night, hands behind his head, and gaze up at the tall ceiling of the longhouse.

The night grows silent. James lies next to me, pulling me into him. I think of Naira's shining face smiling at me, telling me that the snowfall will be her whispering to me, reminding me to shine brightly into the sun.

. . .

We gallop home in awkward silence. Louise and her tiny belly collapse into Andre's arms. I turn to pet my horse, remembering Andre's neck and his lips. The waves of delight that rippled through me at his touch. The way he looked at me in the birch trees. The way he can't look at me now.

The men shake hands. Andre helps Louise to their horse, mounting behind her, his strong arms protecting his wife and baby. They trot off, Andre barely glancing out the corner of his eye at me.

James leads me inside, holding me closer than usual. The fire warms the icy air in our new home. The memories of the forest crawl back to me again and again, despite how I push them away.

"We succeeded in bringing Andre home. Why do you look sad?" James asks.

"Naira showed me what true bravery is. She's unafraid to die. And unafraid to live."

"She's from a different life than us. I'm sure she will be fine and find her way back home." He reaches for the wine.

My hands tighten into fists underneath the fur blanket. "Naira was a warrior. And now she's a prisoner."

"Darling." He puts his hand to my cheek. "It's all over. Please rest. I long to see you by the fire, mending clothes, happy and relaxed. A little belly like Louise's."

My face burns hot, but I force a smile. He must never know that in my mind, Andre is kissing me. Running through the forest with me. Making my heart race.

"What are we going to do about Bastien?"

"The Attorney General protects him, and the King believes him to be loyal. He sent correspondence thanking the governor for his commitment to the colony. How the fur trade is growing across Europe because of Monsieur Leroux's successful management."

"But he's stealing from the Crown to push out France's control. Surely the King would remove him if he knew?"

"Yes." James says as he paces the room. "No more ships are leaving for the winter months and getting word to him will take too much time."

Careful and hesitant, as always. James sprinkles water on the fire, just as he's always done. The snow swirls through the hissing wind, increasing from soft flutters to an angry gale. Naira's voice whispers in my ear that everything I need is already inside me.

"The group of unassuming Filles du Roi had no idea the power that they would have in the colony. Maybe we can help."

"What help could a group of marriageable women be to me?" he says with a laugh.

Biting my lip once again and clawing at the fur over my lap, I see so clearly. James, the earth that holds me down.

. . .

"Sister Marie!" I wave her down when I arrive at the convent, wet and cold from my sled ride over the mounds of fresh snow.

"Oh, Madame Beaumont. You're looking lovely. Here to teach today?"

"Of course, Sister. I am here to help." I grab books from her hands. "How are the young girls doing?"

"Just fine, dear. The young ones are quite unruly this time of year. They're eager to get outside and play, but the weather..." She shrugs and smiles toward God.

"I hear you had a terrifying ordeal recently. Poor Louise was worried sick. You did a wonderful thing, dear. God has shined his light on you."

"I'm grateful to be home. Have you spoken to Madame Leroux?" I ask.

"No, she's become quite an important woman since her marriage. I pray for her happiness."

"Yes, we all do." *God, please do not strike me down for lying to a nun.* "Have you had a chance to report the success of our program?"

"Yes! The intendant has agreed to several hundred more girls in the spring. Isn't it wonderful?"

Happiness flutters through me. "Goodness, it is. Wouldn't it be lovely to host a dinner celebration? Madame Leroux would be delighted to show off her new home. She told me she is eager to see her friends again. The intendant would delight in seeing his young Filles du Roi and their new husbands. We can all hear more of the program and how we can help its success."

"That is a lovely idea. And Madame Leroux agrees?"

"Absolutely. I will settle on a date with her later today. Might we invite the Bishop as well?"

"Lovely idea, Madame." Sister waddles off with a grand smile, ready to shape young minds.

I walk away from the convent that just a few months ago saw me holding court to rally the inner power of our orphaned group. I now bite my lip when my husband speaks of my wifely duties and bearing his children. Quiet, submissive. I let my husband touch me while I dream of another. I long for a man who no longer longs for me.

. . .

As we dress for dinner at the Leroux's, James marvels at my new robe, one he purchased for me. It scratches at my skin, the fabric hot and tight. Lush and scarlet red with soft velvet and white pearl accents.

"Now you look like a proper soldier's wife," he says, hands on his hips.

What would society think if they knew that under this beautiful velvet, my flesh wears the branding of an outcast? Hiding against the walls in the salons of Rouen and wading through rat-infested water at the bottom of a ship felt more comfortable than being stuffed into this vice.

"Why was I chosen?"

James steps back to exhale and asks, "Chosen for what?"

"I was an outsider. No money, no power. Born into a country where heretics are tortured, and the poor remain impoverished. Out of all the girls like me in France, why was I chosen? Why did a priest who knew I lied about who I was, save me from jail, or hanging? Why didn't I die with my sisters or Madeleine?"

James holds my hands, kissing the backs of them. "You are my courageous Isabelle. You were always meant to be mine."

"As long as I became what you needed me to be."

He scoffs. "You were wise to convert. Being Catholic affords you safety and keeps you close to me. As it should be."

"I converted because I had no choice."

"You knew that being a Huguenot was not your destiny. That was your mother's dream. Now that you are on the right side of society, you can realize your destiny. Stability. Protection. You have everything a woman could want now. Not like when you were one of *those* people."

My fingernails dig into the soft velvet. I married a stranger. I gave up everything out of fear and desperation. I traded faith and loyalty for comfort and safety. I let him pull me to earth, controlling me, slowly suffocating out the flame of who I know myself to be.

A silent Protestant prayer settles my mind. A mind whose restlessness grows yet again.

"Now, about our church union," James says, his back to me.

"Yes."

"I will arrange for an intimate ceremony. In the Church for the town to see and recognize." His eyes still have not met mine.

"Might we wait until spring?"

"Spring? Whatever for?"

"Well," searching my mind for reasons, "I would like Elisabeth and Louise present, and Sister Marie. It will be difficult for them to attend in the deep snow of winter."

He sighs. "Do not ever say I'm not kind to you. Fine then. As soon as the snow melts. You know I just want the best for you?" He caresses my face.

"I do."

He hesitates. "Darling, you have been afraid since the moment I met you. All I've ever wanted is to take that fear away. Make you whole."

I am already whole. It is the world around me that is in pieces. James wants to set me free by clutching me in his hands. "I know you mean well, James. I just need a bit of freedom."

"Someday, you will wash away the memories of who you used to be. You just need to stop resisting. Let go of that scared Huguenot. She no longer serves you." He takes me in his arms, my face buried in his protective chest that now stings of betrayal. "Be the woman I always knew you could be."

"Inside, I am the same woman I've always been. And I don't need you to make me whole."

His mouth tightens, his eyes wide and angry.

"Love me as I am or not at all."

Our sleigh ride is silent, the wind rushing in my ears and the pain biting at my heart, unable to tolerate James's touch. We arrive at Antoinette's home through the blistering cold, our faces flushed with ruby hues and my chest tight from the freezing air. We shelter our horses, and Catherine greets us at the door.

"Bonsoir, Monsieur and Madame Beaumont. Lovely to see you."

"Catherine, please, you mustn't be so formal."

"Madame would not approve of casual discussion." Catherine's face hangs heavy.

"Ah, bonsoir!" The intendant bows his head. "Aren't you a vision in scarlet?"

"I believe they call that color oxblood." Antoinette saunters in, her presence felt before she enters the room.

"Bonsoir, Madame Leroux." I force a smile. "Thank you for inviting me to your lovely home."

"You did not give me much of a choice," She whispers under her breath and quickly recovers with a gracious smile.

She refers to my announcement in front of the Bishop last week that Madame Leroux would throw a lovely dinner party in honor of the successful Filles du Roi program. He offered Antoinette the front pew at church each Sunday, a highly coveted spot in Quebec's still-forming social circles.

The Bishop stands on the outskirt of the greetings, eyeing the scene with trepidation. "Monseigneur, it's lovely to see you." I bow my head.

His face is long with deep-set eyes and heavy lids. His round cap fits tightly on his elongated head, with tufts of light gray curls bouncing out from the back. Rumor has it that the Bishop built the sovereign council with a firm conviction that New France would be a pious, quiet community of farmers. After years quarreling, the Sovereign Council restructured, bringing in those more focused on money than the church.

"Bonsoir, Madame." Bastien rubs his dark, greasy mustache. "Bonsoir, everyone!" He snaps his fingers toward the kitchen. Poor Catherine scampers out with a silver tray of hors d'oeuvres and French wine, shoulders raised to her ears.

She rushes to the door to welcome Elisabeth.

Antoinette looks down her nose at her. Through our time together, she has mostly ignored Elisabeth, but tonight her distaste for having a husbandless peasant take up a seat at her precious table is evident. Behind Elisabeth, Louise and Andre enter arm in arm. He glances at me, and I must control the flutter in my stomach when his eyes meet mine. James wraps his arm around my back, his fingers tightening around my waist.

Everyone says their polite greetings, the intendant oblivious to the undercurrents of tension. The candles and fireplaces light the evening with warm flickering hues of saffron and gold. He boasts the successes of New France in a prolonged soliloquy while the rest of us stand in a circle, eyeing each other.

The Bishop's dark eyes tell of a complicated man. He sneers at Bastien and Antoinette. He sees their sins as if they're presented on Catherine's silver tray, gluttony and greed. The intendant fights for his own power, his tray glittering with the promise of betrayal to the Bishop. Can he see that my silver platter presents with the suggestion of heresy and lies?

Our group watches the Lerouxs, eager to remind them that here in New France, nobility does not guarantee power.

"And that is how we grow our colony under the direction of the King." The intendant concludes his speech.

Elisabeth gestures to the kitchen. We excuse ourselves, much to the horrified look of Antoinette.

"Oh, girls, I'm so happy to see you!" Catherine wraps her arms around us.

"Catherine, we need to speak with you."

"What about?"

"I can't imagine you're happy here." I rest my hand on her shoulder.

"I'm fine." Her eyes are hollow.

"No, you aren't."

"Antoinette needs me. She has no one she can trust. Certainly not that disgusting husband of hers."

"What do you know?" I ask.

She looks behind us, at the door to the dining room. "The Colonel is awful. He goes to the cabaret most nights. He's been seen stumbling out of places in the mornings with other women."

"What? Does Antoinette know?"

"Yes. She doesn't want to touch him, so she ignores his indiscretions. I can't blame her. I think she's really sad and lonely. That's why I stay. She's more fragile than anyone realizes."

"How would you like to get rid of Bastien?" I ask.

"That would be wonderful. For everyone."

"Then find us information. Something that can prove his disloyalty. He's been stealing from the King. We need proof."

"I don't know. What about Antoinette? Girls, I know she's been awful, but we can't leave her. She needs us."

"Antoinette made her choices. You can't live life for her anymore," Elizabeth says.

"I know." She looks down at her chapped hands. "She'll never let me leave."

I give her hand a squeeze. "You let me worry about that."

We slip out from the kitchen. James places his arm around my waist, his smile directed at Andre.

"Please, everyone, take your seats," Antoinette says. We sit at the grand oak table, its exquisite detailing oiled to a bright shine.

Bastien sits at one end, the intendant at the other. The Bishop leads us in a prayer, which he intentionally draws out.

Catherine serves an elaborate spread that must have taken her days to prepare. No maize or squash here. Antoinette prefers the food we knew in France. Imported cheese and wine, fresh cuts of caribou and moose cooked in lard. I suspect eating local vegetables is too basic and close to the Native world for her liking.

"Tell me, girls, how are you adjusting to life in the colony?" the intendant says.

"Very well, Monsieur," Louise says as she turns to smile at Andre.

"Wonderful." He smiles as he surveys the table. "And how have you found the process of traveling from your homeland to begin life here in New France?"

"The trip was difficult, Monsieur." Antoinette sighs.

"Yes, the sea journey can be quite trying."

James interjects, "It's most remarkable that these young girls have supported our men as they have."

"Yes, the King is very proud. These women have done a great service to their country," the intendant says.

Antoinette fluffs her curls. "Shouldn't we send for more women of station? More colonial elite?"

"There is plenty of aristocracy in France. This country is about change. Starting something new and different," Andre says. He looks at me, and I swallow a gasp when his eyes meet mine.

"Go on," the intendant says.

"They brought the best of France with them, in my opinion. Strong, resilient, and courageous. They will strengthen any marriage they commit to and raise equally fearless children. They do it with the determination only struggle can bring. They are the face of New France."

My skin flushes hot under my uncomfortable dress.

The intendant beams with pride. "Quite right, Monsieur Boucher, quite right."

Antoinette and Bastien sip their wine between sighs.

"Our Catherine is a Fille du Roi." My voice catches Antoinette's attention, her eyes widening in disbelief.

"Why are you working as a servant, then? Do you not wish to marry?" the Bishop asks. Catherine looks around the table, stuttering to find her words.

"What a wonderful friend she's been to Madame Leroux, helping her settle into her new life," I say.

Bastien lets go of his fork, its pewter hitting the gold-rimmed plate. "We require a house servant. We can't possibly give her up now. There are so few capable girls here."

"I'm sure you can find another suitable replacement," the intendant says.

"I have just the candidate. Experienced in royal homes and stately Mansions of Rouen." My heart races with the memory. That giant house. That miserable family. Poor Jeanne and Clement.

"I couldn't possibly let Catherine go!" Antoinette says.

"We must not hold back this young girl from carrying out her mission to God and King. She was sent to marry. And marry she shall." The Bishop waves his hand through the air in a final sweep.

"It is decided then." The intendant raises his glass to request more wine. "Young Catherine shall end her employment in the Leroux home. Madame Beaumont, send me the information of your servant. I will have her on the next ship from Dieppe. We can't have our program disrupting the officer's lives. We will cover her passage."

Antoinette's eyes tighten, steady on me as she rests her hand on top of Bastien's.

The Bishop takes the opportunity to demand action on another matter close to his heart. "Have we made much progress on illegal alcohol sales to the Native communities?"

"Monseigneur, not this again." The intendant rolls his eyes.

"This is not something to be dismissed!" He slams his fist on the table, bringing all of us to attention.

"Surely you recognize the need for commerce and a strong economy." Bastien's voice is cool and calm. "If we take away alcohol, it could destroy our presence as a strong leader. It would weaken us."

Antoinette flutters her eyelashes and adds, "If they don't trade with us, they will find the nearest civilized people to supply it for them. The British."

The intendant takes a pause and furrows his brow. "I'm afraid this is a complicated issue that does not have one correct answer."

"The correct answer is given to us by God in a request for a peaceful society. There is no higher call than the one of piety." Monseigneur's voice lowers into a deep hush. He knows how to pull a room's attention.

"We've seen firsthand the damage inebriants inflict on the Native communities. It's devastating and needs our attention," James says.

"If they are unable to tolerate alcohol, it is not our concern. Let the clan Chiefs handle it. We are here to grow our power in the region, something the King supports!" Bastien says.

"The threat from the Iroquois continues to grow, and they are encouraging the alcohol trade to weaken us," Andre says.

"Our alliance is to the Crown." Antoinette glances at Andre, her temper building. "Our King, who was chosen by God to lead us, has determined that we must grow our colony. The British are gaining numbers. We must exceed their power, so they don't invade New France. My father's connections demand people to trade with."

The intendant reflects. "For now, we enforce the laws and let the rest go."

She smirks back at me as her hand again finds Bastien's.

"And what of you, child?" He looks at Elisabeth. "You're a quiet one."

"Yes, Monsieur." She eyes the table.

"Have you been meeting the eligible men that wish to marry? Any thoughts?"

She leans forward. "I'm taking my time, Monsieur."

Bastien leans back in his creaking chair. "Don't take too much time, you'll be spoiled goods."

"We want the Filles du Roi to take their time," the intendant says. "Make the right choice for them. They've made a great sacrifice for our country, and we vow to support them in their choices." He turns to Elisabeth, "How is it coming along?"

"I'm hesitant to enter into a marriage contract before I know the man."

"Very wise. It's important to feel confident in your choice. We want the women of France to know this is not a place to fear. It is somewhere they can thrive."

"We must be careful of giving women too much power," Bastien says as he sips his wine. "They don't understand the pressures of running a society. They need our guidance."

Antoinette smiles but underneath I can see her anger brew.

"Mademoiselle, your thoughts?" The intendant looks back at Elisabeth. She looks at me as I nod to her in encouragement.

"We are asked to hand over our lives and our bodies to men we don't know and a life we don't yet understand. Most of us can't read or write, increasing our fear of signing marriage contracts. We're eager to begin families but fear the long winters and farm work. We must make clothes and wash them with soap we make from our land. We will raise babies that might die in the harsh seasons. And we will do this through the threat of Iroquois attacks and without neighbors or a community. Women hold the future of our colony in their hands, and fear of their power can only hold us back. We need protection to allow us to populate New France."

"That is a wonderfully honest statement," the Bishop says. "Might we improve the laws to protect them?" He glares at the intendant.

"How can we do that?" the intendant says.

"The women need the authority to cancel marriage contracts or the promise of one when a man reveals himself to be less than honorable," I say. "They need protected against retaliation."

"I agree. We shall meet with the Sovereign Council and ask that Sister Marguerite assist us in writing new laws to protect the Filles du Roi. It is, after all, what the King would want."

He raises his glass to toast the table, dedicating it to New France, and the women who make the colony possible.

As Catherine clears the table, we gather by the fire to say our goodbyes. The Bishop asks us to take him back to the seminary, shooting a frustrated glance at the intendant. Louise hugs me, then smiles at her husband, who politely returns her affection.

"Bonne nuit." Andre kisses my cheek. Then the other. He whispers to me, his lips caressing my skin, "You don't need that dress. You are beautiful just as you are." He pulls back and looks deep into my eyes. The room disappears and for a moment, I chose Andre. He is my husband. He holds me and undresses me. His kisses warm my neck. Then, in a blink, that moment is gone. He escorts his pregnant wife to their sleigh.

I assist Catherine to the door with us, her bags in hand. Antoinette and Bastien will not protest with the Bishop present.

"Thank you for a lovely evening." I pull back as Bastien leans in to kiss my cheek.

"Catherine will return to the convent. I'm sure you can make do without her for a few months. See you at mass," the Bishop says.

I catch a glimpse of myself in the ivory framed mirror on the wall. Gone is the terrified girl who bites her lip. Now I see what Naira saw.

Situated tightly in our horse-drawn sleigh, the Bishop says, "Thank you for inviting me tonight. I'm happy to know we share convictions in fighting the alcohol trade. The sovereign council has stripped my power, but I still fight."

"I'm happy to help," James says, pulling beaver fur over us. "I'll find a way to stop Monsieur Leroux."

Catherine reaches in her bag and hands a key to the Bishop. "This is the key to their storage of illegal alcohol and guns. It's on the premises of the cabaret. "And here is a letter from the Iroquois, signed by a Mohawk Chief, detailing their plans to trade guns for land rights once they defeat the Hurons and Algonquins."

The timid girl transforms in front of our eyes. It wasn't James or the intendent that found a way to deal with Bastien, it was the Filles du Roi. Antoinette must be cleaning her dishes in her extravagant gown, plotting her revenge on the girls she dismissed as useless and forgettable.

Back at our home, James unpins my hair, letting the waves of chestnut brown flow down my back.

"See," he says between kisses. "I told you not to worry. I would find a way."

I let him undress me as I close my eyes to feel the memory of Andre's kiss. He lays me down gently on our bed. I let him believe that this night was his doing.

As James kisses my stomach, I wrap my leg around him, arching my back when I think of Andre's rough skin, his deep eyes.

I roll James to his back, letting his body relax into the soft fur on the bed. His eyes widen, and he smiles, grabbing my hips. There's a heat between my legs, an ache. I move to what feels right. My mind wanders everywhere it needs to go. I grab at his skin, seeing Andre in my mind and move my hips, feeling Andre's fingers caress my breasts. I feel what freedom can do for a girl who will no longer stay silent.

A DARK NIGHT

The days are short as winter has now taken hold. James doesn't want me to walk to and from the convent anymore. "The snow is unpredictable," he tells me.

"It is not a long walk. I'll be fine."

"Isabelle, I'm growing tired of your resistance." He ties his cravat without a glance at me.

"My need to leave the house? That is resistance?"

A frustrated breath whistles through his nose. "I have been patient with you. But you are not a child anymore. Stop making poor choices."

"What kind of poor choices?"

He turns to me, straightening his jacket. "We are important members of Quebec. I'm trying to make us a life while you run around like a child in the dark. What would others think?"

"I don't care what others think."

"And that is your problem." He swipes his cane from the corner and stabs it into the wood floor. "You are not the wife I need right now."

Something in me jolts awake, like I've been sleeping. "What wife is that?"

"The kind that smiles when I come home. The kind that sits next to me at church and sings in Latin because it is the right thing to do. Not the kind who leaves me alone to do heaven knows what out in the forest like a wild animal."

"You're still mad at me about that day in church? When did church begin to matter so much to you?"

"I have become what I was meant to be. It was foolish to fight my father all those years. He was right. We live up to our responsibilities and everything else is betrayal."

Through the window I see that the snow blankets the treetops and piles on the ground. A layer of glorious bright white with no green leaves in sight. No sunshine to grow towards, only the earth to hold me down.

"There was a time you admired my bravery. You understood my needs," I say.

He looks to the ground, unable to meet my eyes. "Your childish needs no longer need fed. Grow up, Isabelle."

He leaves. Slams the door and I'm alone in the quiet, empty house. I lower to the chair and stare at the fire. A gnawing fear bites at me and I bury my face in my hands. My legs jump and twitch, my limbs ready to take flight like a swallow off a cliff. I reach for the goblet of wine. My hands tremble as I pour it. The shaking retreats with a few sips, the goblet and this fire my only friends.

This is not my life. This is my mother's life.

I let the cold whip of the wind carry me toward danger. The unpredictable snow falls with the sun earlier than I expected. Rushing through the forest, my hand continually checks my knife. A peaceful haze floats above the earth, calling me to breathe it in. It pulls me back to the misty nights of La Rochelle. I'm once again the girl in the forest. Free.

The still beauty of the snowy evening is light and clear. The stars splashed across the sky in a dazzling display against the blue night. A break in the snowfall opens a flood of moonlight over a coat of white across the earth. A path is visible where the sleds and horses' hooves have packed down the snow.

Naira is with me in these woods, surrounding me with her snowy presence, guiding me somehow. My pace slows to breathe in the harsh, biting air that stings my chest. The snow absorbs the sounds of the forest, accentuating the wind that dances through the trees.

In the distance, illuminated by the bright moon that shines its silvery light, footsteps press into the snow. Cleared away from the main path, but still present up a small hill. The light pulls me there. Naira places her hand on my shoulder, guiding me closer. Something is out there, whispering for me to find it.

My feet follow each step, losing sight of the path that leads back home. I trust the whispers, as they feel familiar and pull at my heart. Tall fur boots protect my legs as they stomp through deep snow, featherlight and airy. Deep in the woods, a barn. Warm light fills the inside with a fire. Voices hum. At the wall, my hands cover a sliver of warm yellow light that spills through an opening between two boards. People stand in a circle, singing softly, holding candles. The hymn. The Psalms of David, quietly sung in French. The Latin of Catholic worship is far away on this winter's night, leaving me in the quiet of a secret Protestant worship.

My past has returned. A Protestant sermon, hidden from the eyes of my Catholic town.

My head spins. I grow breathless, closing my eyes to hear the voices, pretending that among them are my mother, Etienne, Henri. Tears stream down my face, my forehead against the rough wood, my hands feeling the vibration from the voices whispering on the other side. I sing along with them, letting the tears wash away all I've been holding inside.

My arm pulses. My fingers run along the skin of my forearm. On this clear black night in New France, my faith returns.

Suddenly, footsteps of crunching snow.

"Isabelle?" Andre steps out from behind the barn.

My chest heaves, and the world around me fades away. I look at him, then the barn with the voices, then back at Andre, and I know. I know everything I need to. I lift the bottom of my skirt and trudge through the knee-deep snow toward him. Quicker. Stronger. My knees lift high, the crackle of snow crystals under my boots. Near him, I drop my skirt and reach my arms for him, knocking him back to the piles of snow.

I bury my face in his chest and cry. He doesn't speak, but wraps his arms around me, pulling me closer. I cry for my mother and father and grandmother and sisters. All the families killed for practicing their faith. My selfishness burns a hole in my heart. My weakness has been masquerading as strength. I finally see it. Freedom was mine all along.

Sorrow flows out of me, unapologetic and raw. The sting in my throat makes it hard to breathe, my fingers tighten around Andre's shirt.

His breath flutters on my cheek, our chests rise and fall together. My hands wrap around his rough neck and into the base of his thick hair. He removes my hood, and feels my auburn curls, examining them in his palm as if they are jewels. My breath whistles in my ears. My heart surges.

He leans into me, touching his lips to mine, pulling my body toward his. My skin becomes one with the air around it, feeling as if I could disappear into the lightness of the moment. His lips move against mine, our hands grabbing each other's hair and necks.

The intensity coursing through me feels as if I might burst into flames, his touch cooling the fire enough to keep me smoldering. As his tongue dances with mine, I'm shattered into a thousand glorious pieces, letting in light between all of them. The softness of his hair falls around my fingers.

"You're a Huguenot?" I whisper.

He pauses. "Yes."

Our eyes hold each other. Nothing at this moment feels wrong. It all feels right. His embrace, the faith of my childhood, the snowy night guiding me home.

His hand reaches for my face, pulling me into his lips again. I melt into his touch. My arms wrap around his shoulders. His lips on my neck send chills through me. My heart soars into a black night full of danger.

My hands rub Andre's rough cheeks, my fingers touching his lips. "I don't want to think about the lives that await us at home. I want to feel this. You."

He leans his forehead to mine and exhales. "I don't know what to do next. I only know that wanting you will forever be a part of me."

All tightness dissipates from my body. The gripping stomach, the tightened fists I've held since I left La Rochelle. They float away on snowflakes and the warmth of Andre's eyes. All I feel is a warm, thumping heart.

He kisses me again. Hungry. Open. His fingers run up the back of my neck. I press my chest against him because nothing on this earth feels like being close to him. It's pure freedom.

"I want you, Andre. I always have."

He brushes the hair out of my eye, grazing his fingertips along my brow. His lips run along my jaw and land on my earlobe.

The voices in the barn fade to silence, the songs disappear into a silent hush.

"How did you know it was me out here?" I ask between breaths.

"I didn't. I stand watch during our services. I glimpsed a shadow outside. You were the last person I imagined finding."

"Did you know about my life in La Rochelle?"

"Louise told me," he says as he kisses my neck and chest. "I wasn't surprised. I think I've seen it in you this whole time."

"Is this why you left France?"

"They killed my family. I had nothing left," he says.

"And yet, you still practice. You didn't let fear change you." My fingers lace between his, woven like braided bread.

"I still hide my beliefs. But New France has its eyes on the Iroquois. They don't even think to look for us. Here I am free." He helps me stand. His arm wraps around my waist, tightening his grip against my skirt.

"What does Louise think about you being a Protestant?"

"She doesn't know."

"You live a life of secrets, Andre."

"Don't we all?"

The back of his fingers run along my cheek. "You have a new life now. You're a Catholic. A Daughter of the King. A soldier's wife."

"My life was never my choice to make. I married out of obligation. I converted to save myself. I'm no more Catholic than you are."

"But you are no longer a Huguenot."

"In my heart, I'll always be one."

We hold each other in silence, the footsteps trailing off into the night, the warm glow of the amber light fades to black.

Andre walks me inside the home set away from the barn. Shocked and fearful faces greet me. The families stop, frozen like ice when they glimpse an intruder.

Andre removes his hat. "This is Isabelle. She's a friend." They look at each other, not a word spoken between them. "It's not safe for me to take her out until you've returned to your homes. Surely you would not have her freeze in the night?"

A tall man with light skin and pale gray eyes steps forward. "Why have you brought her here?"

"I didn't," Andre says. "She happened to stumble across the barn."

"What do you want, Madame?" he asks.

"I don't want anything, Monsieur. Just a warm place until my friend can escort me home."

A woman whispers to the man with the gray eyes. He turns to me. "You are married to a soldier, I hear? My wife has seen you in town."

"Yes."

"Andre, take her away. We don't need any trouble," the man says.

I step forward. "Please, Monsieur, I do not wish you any harm."

"You're not wanted here." He turns to place his arms around his family, his back to me.

The distance between me and them. The Bibles that are surely hidden in this room. In their skirts. The life of secrets and faith. "Monsieur, I enjoyed your singing. The sounds of the beautiful voices dancing in the night." I clear my throat. "It's the sound of my childhood."

He looks over his shoulder, hesitantly.

"My mother and I were exiled from La Rochelle. Left with nothing. She died on the journey to Rouen. I converted because I was alone, and weak, and tired of fighting. I cannot ask for her forgiveness, but I may ask for yours." My nose stings and my lip trembles. "I'm sorry to give up on our people."

Andre reaches his hand for mine.

The woman places her hand on her husband's shoulder, gently pushing past him. "We've all made sacrifices," she tells me. "What matters is who you are in the truth of a quiet night."

"I think I've finally found my way to that truth." Tears rush to my eyes and spill over to my cheeks.

She embraces me, and I close my eyes to prevent the earth from opening up and swallowing me whole. My face twists into a deep cry, her embrace soothing the part of me I have long abandoned.

Here I am, deep in the woods, having followed the voices that welcome me home. We bow our heads as the man whispers a soothing prayer. Andre holds my hand, connecting me to a world beyond myself. My family is here with me, as is Etienne, Henri, and every person I have lost. They fill the room with love, telling me that although I have left them, they have never left me.

The weakness in my knees is gone, leaving a sharp mind and clear eyes. I sit with the woman who prayed with me. "My name is Isabelle."

"Nice to meet you, Isabelle. Welcome home."

"You've seen me in town?" I ask.

"Yes. I sell ebony to the town's merchants."

"You don't live in secret? Out here in the woods?"

"Things are different here. If they presume us to be one of them, they don't question us. But this is what our families have done for generations. In Canada, they've built an entire community of Catholics. They couldn't dream that hidden in the trees are the Protestants they tried to extinguish back in France."

Andre watches me from across the room, smiling. "How do you manage to live two lives?" I ask.

"Well, that is something we know all too well, isn't it?"

"I had hoped that one day I could live just one."

"And maybe you will. Just make certain it's the right one, or you will feel more helpless than ever," she says.

"You mentioned ebony. How do you find that?"

"We have the same artisan connections from France, as well as the West Indies," she says.

"Your connections, are they in Quebec City?"

"Some. Mostly north in Acadia and in the British controlled colony south of us."

I wave Andre over to us.

"I'm glad to see you getting acquainted," he says.

"How would you like to sell more than just ornamental wood?" I ask.

"I don't understand," she says.

"We need to disrupt the shipping control between La Rochelle and Quebec. There's a dangerous couple who's conspiring to start a war with the Iroquois."

"We have no interest in making enemies," she says.

"Of course, Madame. But are you not under threat from the Iroquois?"

"Of course, we are. We're armed constantly. We've lost loved ones to their attacks."

"They are a threat to us all." Andre lifts his shirt to reveal the scar of a whip mark from his time with the Mohawk.

I rest my hand on his arm and squeeze.

"You could help us by helping yourselves," I tell her.

She looks at Andre, intrigued. "I'm listening."

· · ·

Andre carries me away from the barn on his horse, a loaf of bread they wrapped for me in my lap. Andre's arms around me, I never want this horse to stop galloping. Its hooves clap against the snow-covered ground, the brilliant stars twinkling above me. Andre's chest against my back.

"Thank you for introducing me to them."

"It was a magical evening, Madame."

He pulls back on the reigns. The horse stops, his hooves clop in place on the powdered ground. The soft sprinkle of snow falls from hemlock boughs like sugar.

"What are we doing?"

His hand wraps around my belly, his arm pulls me close to his chest. His lips land softly on the curve of my neck and I lean my head back to feel the sparks inside my body.

"I want to hold you again. While it's just you and me. Before I must return you home."

My shoulder drops without a thought, my body twists and my hand reaches for his neck. I kiss him with the brightness of yellow birch trees and sunshine. My fingers burrow into his hair and I grab a fistful of thick golden locks to pull him closer. His lips feel like the flesh of a ripe peach.

"What do we do now?" I say, my mouth dusting his.

"We'll find a way."

Approaching our house, Andre whispers in my ear, "Isabelle, I'm here. I will always be here."

The horse comes to a stop as James appears on the porch with an angry frown.

"Isabelle, I was terrified something happened to you." He limps down the stairs. Andre helps lower me to the ground. James hugs me, our gazes lift to Andre.

"She's fine, just a little lost in the woods," Andre says.

James reaches out to shake Andre's hand. "Thank you for returning her to me." He sighs. "Foolish girl."

Andre tips his hat. "Good night."

He trots off and James leads me into the house. I look out the window, trying to catch a glimpse of Andre, but he has already gone.

"I instructed you to stay out of the snow," he says.

"I refuse to live in fear, alone in this house."

"I am your husband, Isabelle. Do as I say."

The life I could have rests at my fingertips. In the forest, flying on horseback. "I long to be in nature. You know this."

"What were you thinking?" He throws a metal cup to the ground.

"I did nothing wrong."

"We've come so far and still you make questionable choices. It's as if you wish to be that childish girl again. Risking your life and believing in something that ruined you and stole your family."

"What something is that?"

"You know exactly what. You left that life. Now leave that wild girl behind too." He rubs his hip, limping to grab his cane.

"My faith did not steal anything. The Catholics did that."

He steps up to me, jaw tightened. "You are one of us now, Isabelle."

"You fell in love with that wild girl. Now you want to hold me in your hands and squeeze me until I have no air left to breathe."

"I'm trying to protect you." He grabs my arm.

"How is this protection?" I throw my arm from his hand. "You don't treat me like a wife. You treat me like a child."

"And you are not the same, either." His brow tightens. "You don't look at me the way you used to. You look at me like I'm a stranger."

I have no words. He's right.

He rubs his chin, coughs. Looks at his cane and breathes out, slowly. He turns from me and marches upstairs without a glance back.

The wind whistles in between the cracks around the doorway, seeped in through slivers of darkness. James's boots thump unevenly above me, one foot dragged behind the other.

My fingers tap the side of a goblet of wine. The bread Marie gave me rests on the table, and I long to feel the welcome embrace of the evening. As I slice into it, the knife hits something hard.

My fingers wipe away the crumbs, a sheet of vellum tucked inside like a gift. Gently unfolding the calfskin, my heart begins to race. A Geneva Bible, edges charred and wet from baking. I bring it to the light of the fire, the size and weight send me back to my childhood. Secrets again in my palms, behind hushed prayers and furtive glances, under the watch of a loyal Catholic.

It is how we traveled from house to house in France. We baked the Bible in bread, hid it in our hair, our clothes.

This is how you live a secret life.

The front of the book has a large, stitched H in gold thread. I fold back my sleeve, the mark that defined me and stole my hopeful childhood. The letter H means something new to me. It means home.

TAMING THE DEVIL SPIDER

The last few weeks have been a swirl of secrets and lies. The plan initiated in the barn that night happens in secret outside our town. When James kisses me, my body aches for Andre. When my hands run over his scars, the guilt rises in me like a tide.

"Colonel Leroux assigned me to the Iroquois territory to the west." James throws his hat to the table.

"When?"

"I leave tomorrow. He convinced our superior after attacks on local farms."

"How can they send you to battle when you're still injured?"

"Colonel Leroux is not concerned about my injuries," he says.

"How long must you be gone?"

"If it's up to Bastien, forever." He paces the room. "I'm not going. I will not leave you alone."

"Do we have a choice?"

"I'll find a way. If the King only knew what he was doing, that would be the end of him. Then I could take my rightful place in charge. Just as my father dreamed for me."

"What about your dreams? Do you aspire for power?" The question rolls around me, turning my stomach queasy. Power and greed are what I fled from.

"All men wish to be powerful, dear. The King will find out soon enough."

"The Bishop must have notified him."

"Yes. What with the weather and difficulty sailing, it might take months to reach him. And the intendant seems powerless against the governor. Corruption everywhere."

He pulls me into his chest, his heart beating rapidly against my ear. "I am not going to leave you. I must convince the Lieutenant that I'm needed here."

"I'll be fine, James."

"If your behavior lately is any indication, you, my dear, cannot be trusted."

My face still against his chest, my breath deepens, and my teeth bite hard against each other. The anger builds inside me until… the thumping of horse hooves.

James peers out the window. He mutters, "Andre." James opens the door, holding me behind him.

"We need to go to the cabaret. Now," Andre says.

I push James's arm away. "Why?"

"Madame and Monsieur Leroux. They're captured by the Mohawk."

"Let the Mohawk take them. They'll get what they deserve," James says. His arm locks into place in the doorway to block me.

"Bastien gave the order to march on the Iroquois tribes tomorrow. You will be there, yes?"

"How did you know?" James says.

"What happens if Bastien dies?" Andre says.

"We still march. He convinced the governor."

"It's a setup. The Iroquois know you're coming. Bastien gave specific orders to eliminate you, and everyone in your regiment."

"And he's the only one that can give the order to retreat," James says. "Stay here." He says with his hand to my face. The two men gallop off into the forest.

Once they leave, I mount my horse to carry on behind them. The end of day hovers, the sun drifting toward the horizon. Leaning forward, my face in the wind, the horse flies over a coat of fresh snow. The trees crack, releasing a dusting of fresh white crystals that shine in the light.

The crowd that normally spends the night drinking and laughing, huddles together in the snow, watching the cabaret, helpless against the Mohawks standing guard in front of the building.

The Mohawk sit still on their horses, their faces lit up with bright red grease. Their hair is gone, save for a patch that stands tall and sharp. Deerskin drapes their shoulders. Red bands line their upper arms. They stand watch with muskets in their hands pointed in every direction as the rest of them remove guns and knives and barrels of liquor. The governor watches, his cabaret taken over by his enemies.

Climbing down from my horse, my feet crush the icy snow. They inch slowly toward Andre and James.

"Isabelle, I instructed you to stay home!" James's voice is a heightened whisper.

"I'm here now."

We step forward to see through the windows. Bastien and Antoinette are tied to the posts inside, mouths gagged, their eyes darting all directions.

"How do we get them out?" I say.

"There's nothing we can do. Let the Mohawk take their goods," James says.

"Andre, how did this happen?" I whisper to him.

"It's the only way the Iroquois would agree. They needed assurance they could trust them."

James turns to me. "You had something to do with this? You lied to me? And disobeyed me?"

Andre lifts his hand to James. "I've been working as a coureur de bois."

"A forest runner?" I ask.

"I'm an illegal fur trader. I cross the line outside Montreal and secretly trade with the Natives west of the legal French territory. I have connections who carried the message west. It's those connections that made this happen. Not Isabelle. It's also how I discovered Bastien's plan to have your regiment killed."

"We're the only skilled soldiers. Without us, the colony would be left to volunteers and unskilled fighters," James says.

The Mohawk howl in high-pitched calls as their horses prance in circles. James wraps his arms around me, pulling me from Andre. The Mohawk scream in Iroquoian, their guns raised. The men gather the last of the barrels from the cabaret and load them into a wagon.

"We delivered word that Bastien kept the high-quality goods for himself, leaving the lower quality for them," Andre says. "So they came here, threw everyone out, and took what they feel they're owed."

One of the Mohawk pulls back an arrow. His tuft of hair grows long to a braid, with feathers jutting out from his head. He releases it, narrowly missing a woman in the crowd. The people scatter, and more arrows screech through the air. We run toward the trees, ducking to the ground as the arrows soar above us.

"What are they doing?" I yell.

"They don't know who they can trust," Andre says as we run. "They want to show what happens if you cross them."

Near the cover of trees, an arrow whirs past my ear and lands in a pine trunk. James throws me to the ground, flat on my belly.

I bury my head, lost in the snow as James throws his arms over me. A sea of arrows spirals through the sky, raining down on us like hail. I peek my eyes from under James's arm to see one slice through a woman's back, another pierces a man's shoulder. Gasps and cries fill the air as people collapse all around us, blood trickling onto the pristine white snow.

A man rushes toward his wife, only to meet the sharp end of a spiraling animal bone boring into his eye. I throw my face back into the snow. The screams continue, shots and arrows flying into the night.

James shakes me out of frozen panic. "Run, Isabelle. Go!" An arrow sticks straight out of his leg, the back of his breeches torn, blood seeping into the fabric. His face twists in pain as he yanks it out of his flesh.

Andre drags me from him, back toward our horses.

"Get her out of here!" James yells as he collapses.

I push off Andre with all my strength, sending him to the ground. James stares at me, furious. Behind him, something shoots into the air like lightning. It glows red and orange and arcs through the trees in a graceful dance. We all look up at the glowing ball in the black sky. It ends in a crash through the roof of the cabaret, landing at the bar behind Bastien and Antoinette. Smoke billows up through the hole in the roof. Another flash through the sky, and another sets the wall ablaze.

One man positioned his horse in front of the door, musket in hand, giving orders to the others. The smoke floats through the sky, meeting the falling snow. In it, a face. The shadow of Naira. I ball my fists and close my eyes, slowing my breath. *Everything I need is already in me.*

The flames grow, the wood pops and hisses. James screams, "Isabelle, don't! Just let them die. We will find another way."

"Andre, help me!" Lifting my skirt, I leap over James, swiping the knife from his holster, too swift for his hand to catch my leg as he swipes for me. My feet shoot across the earth, snow packed down by trampled feet and streams of blood. Through the trees, the clearing nears.

My dress catches on a tree branch, ripping my sleeve from shoulder to wrist. A line of blood streams down my arm from the torn flesh. The cold air snaps against the exposed skin. I run, eyes focused on the man on the horse. The man who I'll need to face to save Antoinette.

Behind him, the walls grow in fiery red. Antoinette inside, screaming through her loosened handkerchief in her mouth. The air smells of wet ash, the night turned gray with smoke. I run straight for the man, screaming as my feet pound the ground. In front of him, my boots plant in the snow, arm raised to the sky, blade in hand.

He stops still and the horse rears up. I don't blink. I don't move. My arm raises higher, blood dripping to my shoulder. I widen my stance and firm my feet into the earth. My stomach tightens, fear falling beside me like embers. The light behind him glows in fiery dots where the Mohawk hold their gaslit arrows. His long braid whips like a horse's tail, the red bear grease shining from under his eyes.

"I could kill you," he says.

"Yes." I stand unmoving, fist to the sky.

He circles me, my eyes steady on the men lined up on their horses, their fiery arrows aimed at me. He stops the horse in front of me and holds his torch to better see my face. He lifts the fire as his eyes scan up my bloody arm and stop at the scarred wrist that now pulses with heat. My arms widen, my chest open, and I welcome their arrows.

"You wish to save them?" He gestures to the cabaret.

"Only one of them. The girl didn't wrong you."

He bows his head, gestures his hand toward the burning house. The glow of the fiery night flickers around us.

A window shatters from the heat. Their faces glow against the fire climbing around them. "Isabelle! Help!" Antoinette screams.

Andre pushes me back, knocks down the door with his shoulder and covers his face with a cloth.

I slip in behind, slicing through the ropes that bind Antoinette, sawing frantically. Her feet are free, but she bucks her arms, continuing to scream and cough. I slice as quickly as my hands will allow. The cloud of smoke pulls the air from our lungs, making us cough and my head grow weak. Andre moves toward us, but a falling beam blocks his path. He runs to the outside, crashing a window at the side of the cabaret.

A final slice frees her hands. A thick coat of hot smoke and confusion paralyzes me. I see nothing. Antoinette grabs my hand, drags me to the window. I lift her to Andre, who pulls her out like a child's doll, where the snow turns the fiery edges of her dress to smoke. I barely escape the flames as I jump through the window to the snow below. The harsh cold air stabs at my chest. Rapid breaths, coughs. Seizing chest.

Andre pulls me up. We stumble back as the house begins to crumble. Dead bodies and bloody snow everywhere. Antoinette's pale face dusted with ash, her sapphire eyes rimmed swollen and red. She wears a humbled expression I have not seen since the morning after Madeleine's death. We turn to watch Bastien take his punishment, the Mohawk around the house to ensure his body catches the flames.

The remnants of this horrid night come to rest around us. Flutters of snowflakes land on our blackened skirts. Antoinette reaches her hand to mine. The house crumbles to bits of charred wood and ash. Her hand squeezes mine, reminding me what a complicated beast this life always turns out to be.

.   .   .

James's injuries aren't severe. The brandy helps dull his pain. "I'm glad it's all over," he says.

"Me too, James."

"Isabelle. I know you lied to me." His eyes grow heavy from the liquor. "You had something to do with that. And I know you have a past with Andre. I see it when you look at him."

"Rest now." I lay the blanket over him.

"You are mine, Isabelle, and I demand that you respect me." His eyes close, on the brink of slumber. "Your past is gone. You're no longer the wild girl who does as she pleases."

I glance at the floorboard that secretly hides my Bible. *What I am, what I have always been, is wild.*

"You must confess your sins," he mumbles.

My hand rests on his forehead. "Get some sleep now, James."

He's as handsome as ever. The copper freckles dot his nose and cheeks, filled in with time. Back in La Rochelle, sneaking away to meet him in the forest, this face made me dream and hope. I was so young, and he seemed so strong. The danger of him drew me in, he needed to tame my restlessness. One wanted fire, the other wished to put out the flame.

Downstairs I spot Antoinette through the window. She stands in front of the house, holding the reins of her horse. I wrap myself in fur and open the door.

"Hello, Antoinette, you look well."

"I've recovered nicely. My lungs are healthy now. My nerves finally settled," she says.

"It was an awful night."

"Bastien lied to me. My power is nothing if I can't trust the man by my side."

"You trusted him?"

"I trusted that we wanted the same things. I looked the other way when he would stumble drunk out of the cabaret with a woman on his arm." She looks down, tightens her fur against her body. "I offered him power, money. But he couldn't contain his greed. Offered up our own soldiers to feed his hunger. I didn't know about that until the Mohawk captured me. Tied me up and threatened to kill me for my husband's betrayal."

"He's gone now, Antoinette. And you will be fine."

"Isabelle," she says as I walk toward the door. "I know Andre did it."

I turn back to her, the boards creaking under my shoes.

"He runs illegal fur trades. And I know that my husband ordered his capture. If anyone had cause for disrupting our trade, it would be him."

"You will have to bring that up with Andre."

"And I know that you risked your life and your marriage to be close to him." Her head tilts and her eyebrows raise.

"You know nothing, Antoinette. Now, I must get back to my husband."

"For a simple girl from nothing, you certainly have learned to find your teeth," she says. "Well done."

"My life has given me no other option."

"Why didn't you have me arrested? I know Catherine gave you the key, proof of our secret," she says.

"Why did you do it in the first place?"

"Do what? Build our empire? I was merely carrying out my father's wishes."

"That is why I didn't turn you in. I pray that someday you have the strength to stand up to your father. You don't need his power. Not here."

"He needs mine because I'm here," she says.

"Under it all, maybe you and I aren't so different," I say. "Fighting our past carries us into dangerous situations."

"You've found your dark side, Isabelle. Perhaps you are like me."

"You were right. Hope is more dangerous than fear. Hope has us believe we will not break, when all fear ever does is protect those that want us broken." I straighten my dress and breathe in the sharp cold air.

"Power creates beasts," she says.

I sneak out a smile. "And weakness topples giants."

We tuck our hands in the pockets of our dresses and look up to the flutter of snowfall. We breathe in the silence of our new land. Our new selves.

HOMECOMING

Winter has softened its hold and spring floats through the air. The first ship of the season arrives today. Elisabeth joins me at the docks. It's been a long six months. I haven't seen Andre since the night at the cabaret. The woman from the Huguenot home found me and delivered a message that they sent Andre south. An important trip that couldn't wait. James's leg took months to heal, a result of his already damaged body. I have stayed to help him recover. He prays every night. Asks God to send us a child.

Louise frequently voices her frustration that her husband left her alone. She stayed at the convent until her baby girl was born.

Me? I pray in secret and long for Andre while my husband kisses me. I had hoped that with Andre gone, my desire for him would lessen, but it's only grown stronger. This is what it means to love a wild heart. Unpredictable heartache. I've grown to understand James's deep sadness. How it feels to want something you cannot control.

I wear the clothes of a Catholic wife, waiting for the snow to retreat to allow me out of my suffocating life. The hopes of fall faded with the winter. Once again, I live with hidden Bibles and bitten tongues.

Elisabeth's arm linked through mine, she tells me of her marriage and her new home.

"He's very good to me." She smiles.

"I'm so glad you're happy."

"It's something I have searched my whole life for, a feeling of being wanted. I don't mind the demands of farm life. We work from the moment our eyes open to when we collapse in exhaustion on the bed in the evening, but we do it together. I finally have a real home."

My arm wrapped around her, we watch the sea, its surface shivering in the wind. We accept the long cold winters of Quebec City and the threat of Mohawks because this is our land. We've found a place. A home.

The massive ship appears in the distance, bringing memories of our arrival one year ago. It bobs and leans side to side, weary from the long months at sea.

The giant ship docks and men scurry around, preparing to unload passengers and much-needed cargo. Jeanne appears, our servant from the Dupre house in Rouen. She is pale and disheveled from the journey but finds a smile at the sight of me. She speeds up her walk, rushing to embrace me in motherly pride.

"Isabelle, what a delightful sight. It warms my heart to see how you've thrived since leaving Rouen."

"Thank you, Jeanne. I'm so glad you're here."

"I was shocked to hear that the King of France wishes for my assistance in the colony. When I saw your name in the recommendation, I knew I had to come. So, what am I doing here, Madame?"

"I want you to meet someone." I lead her to Elisabeth. "Jeanne, this is Elisabeth. Your daughter."

Their vanilla faces shine in the morning light. The rush and activity of the crowd grows distant, the silence between us heavy.

Jeanne gasps, trying to speak, but no words come out.

One day on the St. Jean-Baptiste, as we were dressing for bed, Elisabeth's raven hair flowed down her back against her creamy white skin. There was a mark on her arm. She saw me looking and said, "It's a strange little thing, I know."

"It's a purple heart," I said.

"Yes, it's always been there. I like to think it's the remnants of the family that I never knew. That they sent me on my way with a reminder that I was not alone," she said with a forced smile.

Jeanne places her hand on Elisabeth's face, fingers trembling as her daughter's tears fall softly onto them. "Is it really you?" Jeanne asks, voice stumbling through tears.

"I don't understand," Elisabeth says.

"Your mark. Your purple heart. Jeanne described it to me as well as your dark hair, and the family in Paris."

"I never wanted to say goodbye to you." Jeanne's hand covers her mouth. "We had no money, no food. I don't deserve to be standing here with you. I'm so sorry." She turns, weeping into her hands.

Elisabeth stares, emotionless. Worry washes over me. Have I made a horrible mistake, bringing up the pain that has been in slumber all these years?

She steps forward, takes a moment to exhale, and reaches out to hold Jeanne's hand. "I spent a lifetime without you, and it has brought me nothing but emptiness and pain. I'm not sure how to open my heart, but I would like to try."

Jeanne turns to her, eyes red. "You look like me."

Elisabeth smiles, nods.

Jeanne wipes her eyes and turns to me. "Is this why you brought me here?"

I nod, yes. "If I had the chance to bring my mother back, I would fight for her."

They embrace, crying into each other's shoulders. My eyes fill with tears, watching the joyous reunion of two lost souls. Separated by poverty. Joined together in a new world.

"Isabelle, you're sending her to work as Antoinette's lady's maid?"

"No. If Antoinette gives you any trouble, you send her to me. Now, go on. You two need time to catch up. I'll join you later for a celebration."

They smile and walk off, but Elisabeth runs back to throw her arms around me in a hug. She pulls back, holding my arms in a firm grasp. "You've always been bright and warm like the sun, despite the dark places you've seen. You're a magnificent creature, Isabelle. I'm proud to call you my friend."

She walks away with her mother, a family beginning anew. The sudden chill of wind whips through me. I turn to see Antoinette. She greets someone, a cold fearful look on her face. It's her father.

Antoinette holds her gaze to mine as she saunters off. My head held high, I swallow the worry that tumbles around inside me. The man who controls La Rochelle shipping. The man who exiled us and stole our home now stands at the foot of Quebec City.

As I catch my breath, my worry fades. Dozens of the King's Daughters stumble off the boat with that unmistakable look of fear and hope. They keep coming, probably one hundred of them. A sea of young women plucked from their dire, hopeless lives in the countryside of France. The women I helped save. There will be hundreds more.

I see in them the girl I was and the woman I've become. I was born a Huguenot. I lost my sisters, my mother, my home, yet I push forward. Every child killed, every mother that died with them in body or spirit, every father devastated when he could not feed his family, they all stand with me. Those that came and went before my time are a part of me. I do not begin and end, I am merely a continuing saga in the practice of persistence and the power of believing.

. . .

Through the forest dripping with melted snow, my feet trudge through the mud and ice toward home, knowing James awaits my return. A galloping horse approaches, and I step to the side to allow them to pass. The horse stops, and feet hit the sloshy ground. My heart beats into my throat. I turn slowly.

Andre.

He smiles widely, his arms open.

My breaths deepen. I'm unable to move my feet. Tears rush to my eyes. "Andre, you're back."

He runs to me. His arm scoops me into his chest, spinning me around until my back pushes against a tamarack trunk. The force pulls out a gasp of thrill. He leans close, nearly kissing me. Our lips close enough to exchange breaths. Chills crawl up and down my neck the way only his touch can create. His fingers caress my face like smoke rising from a fire.

I grab the back of his hair in my grip and pull him back from me. Our lips are still barely touching.

"What is wrong?" he asks. "Have you not missed me?"

"I ached for you." I don't want to let go. I want to feel lost in him. Now more than ever.

"So kiss me."

"Louise. The baby." My hands slide from his hair, down his shoulders.

"We both have responsibilities." He steps back from me.

"I care for James, but I would leave him right now if I knew I could be with you. But it's more complicated than that."

"Everything is complicated." He reaches for me but stops and lowers his hand.

"You're a husband," I say. "And a father." My stomach begins to ache.

"But I don't love her."

"What does that matter?"

"I want to be with you," he says.

"Being together would ruin everyone's lives." My fingers claw into the rough bark of the tree trunk.

He scans my face, his eyes reddened and lip trembling. "Is it too late for us?"

I slip away from him, hands on my knees to lighten my breath. "I don't know how to live with James, and I don't know how to live without you."

"We are permitted to break marriage contracts," he says.

"You don't break your relationship as a father."

"No, I would never do that." He reaches for my hand. "But I cannot stay married to a woman I don't love when the one I do stands right before me."

I catch my breath. The warm sun softens the snap of cold on my face. "You'll take care of Louise. And the baby."

"Of course," he says.

"I've been living a life of secret prayer. Secret love." I shake my head. "I'll stay at the abbey. Until things settle. And then, maybe…"

"And then, maybe." He rests his hand on my cheek, a warm smile across his face.

I rest my hand on his, pressing them both to my cheek. "What now?"

"I have something to show you," he says.

He lifts me to his horse, wraps his arms around me and buries his face in my neck. I look to the sky, feeling his touch with the burn of desire. We run through the forest, the sun beginning to soften the icicles that drip from tree branches.

The horse gallops to his house where Louise's muddy shoes sit by the front door. The fabric of curtains peeking through the window of her home. "Is she here?"

"No. She's at the convent still. She's angry with me for leaving." He helps me down and leads me to the front door. "I have something from home for you."

"Home?"

Andre opens the door. Inside is a young man. He has wild black hair and a bright red cravat, a devilish smile shining. "Henri?"

"Isabelle. My old friend."

Tears instantly fall from my eyes, and I run to him, throwing my arms around his slight frame. "Oh, Henri, is it really you?" I lay my cheek on his shoulder and cry, his arm wrapped around my back. We hold each other and weep. There are no words. We only cry and embrace each other in the memories of another lifetime.

I wipe my tears and touch his face. "I thought you died."

"I nearly did," he says. "But I'm here now."

Andre pours wine for us as we warm near the fire. Henri tells me that he traveled to Nantes, to board a ship there. "They caught me without proof of passage and threw me in jail. They sentenced me to the galleys."

"Oh, Henri."

"They kept me in prison for weeks, waiting for the next ship to sail. Without food, I drank from the rain that trickled in from the cracks in the walls. I lay there, feeling my ribs sharp under my skin and remembering my father. I deserved to die. I welcomed it. When they chained my neck to the oar, I felt nothing."

I reach for his hand, a softness in him I had not seen in the wild boy from my childhood.

"My hands blistered and bled, rowing for hours and endless hours," he says. "I pushed through days and weeks of searing pain and aching limbs. The skin on my backside worn raw from the pressure of the wood bench. We ate, slept, and rowed in the same spot amid our filth. When the man next to me died, they threw him overboard without a thought. They replaced him with another Huguenot, a man from Nantes sentenced for stealing bread from a Catholic house."

Andre fills my goblet.

Henri carries on. "He still had fight left in him. I rowed through weeks of darkness, wishing for death. We arrived in Acadia, bringing weapons for the settlers there. One night, sleeping in a pile of other prisoners, we heard a strained howl. The guard suffered an attack. He just collapsed. No one was around, so we stole his clothes, his musket and sword, and broke into the wild forest. Months later, we found ourselves in a Dutch colony south of here, called New Amsterdam. They're all Protestants, Isabelle. We kissed the ground when we found them."

"I left Quebec so abruptly because of this lost group," Andre says. "Many Huguenots escaped custody and were lost in the forest. They needed someone to guide them south to safety. I found three of them. I led them to New

Amsterdam. There, I met a young man from La Rochelle who once knew a wild young Protestant named Isabelle."

I'm unable to speak, thinking about all the places we could have ended up. Here we sit, in Andre's house. Three heretics in a catholic-ruled colony.

"You came to see me?" I ask.

"Yes." He glances at Andre. "And there's something else."

"I know that look in your eyes. You want me to do something dangerous."

"Not dangerous, exactly," Henri says.

"What is it?"

"The English have taken over our town. They've renamed it New York City. There are thousands of Protestants, Isabelle."

"What do you need me for?"

"Things in France are getting worse. Our people are being tortured and killed. The Sun King won't stop until we're all dead or converted. People are fleeing, but the laws have tightened, making it impossible to find a way out."

I swallow against a dry throat that tightens when I try to speak.

"We've started a secret organization, one that helps Protestants out of France. We bring them to New York, or any other colony in the British lands. We've been successful, but we need information about the King. His plans."

I shake my head. "I don't know about the King's plans."

"You will," Henri says. "You married James, yes? A Lieutenant now, I hear."

I look to Andre whose face is solemn, it reveals nothing.

"A group of men from the Royal Counsel will be arriving in Quebec next month to make plans for increased trade. Their goods from La Rochelle are all made from Huguenot hands. Pottery, Silk. Clocks. Violins. They will have plans. Ideas. We need you to find information."

"We?"

"Andre has agreed to travel. To help our people escape in secret. Will you play your part?"

"I must stay married to a man I do not love in exchange for secrets. More lies."

"Just for a few months," Henri says. "Do it for the children who still live in fear." He raises his pant leg to reveal his scar. His burned H. "Think of all you could do."

"A Huguenot rebellion." The fire warms me. Softens my tension as I breathe out any doubt.

Andre's deep, dark eyes overflow with resolve. With fight.

"How many can we save?"

"Thousands," Henri says.

James prepares an attack on the Iroquois while I set my rebel spirit on fire in this house.

Andre reaches for my hand. "We can do this together."

My hand tightens around his.

"One more thing," Andre says with a hint of a smile. "Naira has sent word to the Huron. She released a prisoner with a message to bring to her tribe. She's alive, collecting information from the Mohawk. She's living the same brave life you are about to embark on."

"A life of secrets and lies to protect the ones we love," I say.

Andre leads me by the hand. He slides a bench from the wall to the fireplace and gestures for me to stand on it. I step up and look at him, confused.

"The one next to the wall," he says.

One brick isn't like the others. The mortar has cracked, the black light peeking out from around it. A flush of heat rises in my limbs. I claw at the brick and pull. I place it on the mantel and reach my hands into the cold dark space inside. The Bible fills my hands and heart with everything I need to know. Andre places his hands around my waist and lowers me to the ground. We gather in front of the fire, our secret prayer circle come back to life behind the eyes of our Catholic town.

I pull back my sleeve. "This is why I will fight."

All I thought I lost was with me all along. It is not in church that I've found my faith, but in the fight for truth.

Henri and Andre stand before me, our hands on our Geneva Bible, my gaze fixed to theirs. I nod to them with a smile.

We ready our plan for rebellion. And it starts with me.

THE END

BEHIND THE NOVEL

I discovered the story of the Filles du Roi while researching my husband's French-Canadian ancestry. I discovered that he, and my daughters, are descended from at least three dozen of these amazing women. I became engrossed with their stories of bravery and survival, and their contribution to North American history.

Isabelle Colette is a fictionalized character, but her story is very much grounded in historical truth. The persecution of the Huguenots is a sad but important part of European history. Hundreds of thousands fled Europe, unwilling to compromise their religious beliefs. Their escape played a role in not only the French Revolution, but also in the formation of many American towns.

Most French Canadians can trace their ancestors to one or more of these eight hundred Filles du Roi, these young girls who fled their homeland and braved a new world.

Many thanks to Black Rose Writing for giving Daughter of the King a home, and myself a chance to bring Isabelle's story to the world. Thank you to my critique group, Brigette, Lisa, and Naomi, who helped me through many edits and versions to bring Isabelle to life. And lastly, writing books would not be possible without the support of my husband, Mike. He always encourages my love for storytelling and reaching for my dreams.

ABOUT THE AUTHOR

Born in California wine country, Kerry Chaput began writing shortly after earning her Doctorate degree. Her love of storytelling began with a food blog and developed over the years to writing historical fiction novels. Raised by a teacher of US history, she has always been fascinated by tales from our past and is forever intrigued by the untold stories of brave women. She lives in beautiful Bend, Oregon with her husband, two daughters and two rescue pups. She can often be found on hiking trails or in coffee shops.

To learn more, connect with her at
www.kerrywrites.com
or
Twitter @ChaputKerry.

NOTE FROM THE AUTHOR

Word-of-mouth is crucial for any author to succeed. If you enjoyed *Daughter of the King*, please leave a review online—anywhere you are able. Even if it's just a sentence or two. It would make all the difference and would be very much appreciated.

Thanks!
Kerry Chaput

We hope you enjoyed reading this title from:

BLACK ROSE
writing™

www.blackrosewriting.com

Subscribe to our mailing list – *The Rosevine* – and receive
FREE books, daily deals, and stay current with news about
upcoming releases and our hottest authors.
Scan the QR code below to sign up.

Already a subscriber? Please accept a sincere thank you for
being a fan of Black Rose Writing authors.

View other Black Rose Writing titles at
www.blackrosewriting.com/books and use promo code
PRINT to receive a **20% discount** when purchasing.

Made in United States
Orlando, FL
05 August 2022

20583256R00148